AMAZONS

they came astride gray horses dappled with sun
and their hair flew behind them
pointing back to the village
where the babies grew, they sang and i was alive
to hear them. i was hungry.
my hair hung heavy on my back.
if i spoke at all, i whispered
or else dug letters in the deep earth. their song
touched me on my face, breasts,
slid down my spine. i had never heard such
music. the village, i knew, would be
uncluttered. they would feed me.
when i found the way.

MELANIE KAYE

AMAZONS!

Edited, with an introduction by

Jessica Amanda Salmonson

DAW BOOKS, INC.

DONALD A. WOLLHEIM, PUBLISHER

1633 Broadway

New York, N.Y.   10019

Acknowledgments: Melanie Kaye, "Amazons." © 1978
by Melanie Kaye, from *Conditions 2*. Reprinted by
arrangement with the author. Verse by Emily Jane
Brontë © 1928 by the Columbia University Press.

FIRST PRINTING, DECEMBER 1979

1 2 3 4 5 6 7 8 9

DAW TRADEMARK REGISTERED
U.S. PAT. OFF. MARCA
REGISTRADA. HECHO EN U.S.A.

PRINTED IN U.S.A.

CONTENTS

Introduction: *Our Amazon Heritage*   7
Jessica Amanda Salmonson

The Dreamstone, C. J. Cherryh   16

Wolves of Nakesht, Janrae Frank   31

Woman of the White Waste, T. J. Morgan   51

The Death of Augusta by Emily Brontë,
    edited by Joanna Russ   61

Morrien's Bitch, Janet Fox   67

Agbewe's Sword, Charles R. Saunders   84

Jane Saint's Travails (Part One), Josephine Saxton   107

The Sorrows of Witches, Margaret St. Clair   117

Falcon Blood, Andre Norton   126

The Rape Patrol, Michele Belling   143

Bones for Dulath, Megan Lindholm   153

Northern Chess, Tanith Lee   171

The Woman Who Loved The Moon,
    Elizabeth A. Lynn   188

Additional Reading compiled with Susan Wood   204

DEDICATION:

to a musician, maenad and companion
whose name means
"many shrines of the moon goddess,"
Diane Policelli

AMAZONS!

Introduction:

OUR AMAZON HERITAGE

Jessica Amanda Salmonson

"I will not resign myself to the lot of women, who bow their heads and become concubines," said Thieu Thi Trinh in the year 248 AD. She said, "I wish to ride the tempest, tame the waves, kill the sharks. I want to drive the enemy away to save our people." By the age of twenty-one Thieu Thi Trinh had led thirty battles and liberated Vietnam, for six months, from Chinese tyranny.

Restless as the moon, in every human epoch the female of our species has soldiered and adventured, to great sorrow, and great reward. An officer in a Minnesota regiment, Mary Dennis at six-foot-one was one of several women who we know fought in the front lines of the American Civil War. Kit Cavanaugh was not the only woman to become a dragoon, fighting with the British Army and taking wounds, at first disguised as a man but later fighting openly as a woman. She survived to a natural death and received a military burial. Many white observers noted with dismay the presence of women braves among various Native American peoples. In 1900 and 1901, Yaa Asontewa, an African chief, led her Ashanti followers into war. Queen Christina of Sweden cut off her hair, wore pants, abdicated the throne, and became a notorious adventurer throughout Europe in the sixteen hundreds. In Thirteenth Century Japan, the warrior aristocracy produced several women samurai. Among these was Tomoe. According to the Kamakura, she was match for "god or devil" and in one long battle, "when all the others had been slain, among the last seven rode Tomoe." The histories of every nation, culture and society reveal, however re-

luctantly, countless amazon figures. The difficulty in writing
this introduction has not been in finding historic as opposed
to mythic amazons, but in choosing so few representatives
among so many.

I would like to take the reader on a brief world tour of our
amazon heritage:

In the Sixteenth Century, Francisco de Orellana explored
South America. He reported being set upon by a women's
army on the Marañon River, later called the River Amazon.
Although amazons were never again described from the
Amazon River Basin, tribal legends recount uniformly, an
earlier era of women's domination. The modern anthropol-
ogists Yolanda and Robert Murphy found that even today
Brazilian tribal women live apart from men "in convivial sis-
terhood." Their authority exceeds that of men in all practical
matters.

A veritable Robin Hood of Latin America was Doña Cat-
alina de Erauso. At a young age she ran off from a Spanish
convent, asking bitterly of her family, "Why have you made
me manly and strong like my brothers, only to compel me,
now that I am fifteen, to do nothing but mumble a lot of in-
terminable prayers?" Earning her way to Central America in
the early sixteen hundreds, she became a soldier of fortune of
great swordskill and reknown throughout Mexico, Peru and
Chile. When she returned briefly to Europe, clad as a cavalier
("filling the hearts of girls with love, of their gallants with
terror," by one account) Pope Urban VIII granted her
special permission to wear men's garb and King Philip
awarded her a pension for defending the Spanish territory
and flag. She remains today an important folk hero of the
Latino romantic age.

Sir Walter Raleigh described amazons of Guiana, who met
with men only on the ritualistic occasion of fertility celebra-
tion. Sons born among the amazons were sent to the men's
tribes for rearing. At all other times the sexes kept to their
own society. Better documented are the amazon forces of Da-
homey in West Africa, described by Sir Richard Burton and
others with the vilest terminology, revealing their personal
dismay more than the specific nature of the soldiery. The
commonly upheld French-devised explanation for this aspect
of African culture (and one justification for conquest) was
that these women served a brutal king who forced them into
warfare. However, many African tribes had separate women's

governments which whites rarely knew about. Being matrilinear, even kings legitimized their rule through women's lineage. Male chiefs were responsible to the queen mother of the women's "secret societies" with little or no direct influence over women or their armies.

A specific African amazon was Madame Yoko: diplomat, organizer, agriculturalist, warrior—and ruler of fourteen tribes constituting the Kpa Mende Confederacy of the eighteen hundreds, largest chiefdom of Sierre Leone. Far from being an historic anomaly, she is fairly representative. In her day fully fifteen percent of all tribes around Sierre Leone were ruled by women. To this day, despite the imposition of white values, nine percent of the tribes have women chiefs. Although their histories have been obscured, deleted or mangled by the white man's pen and interpretation, many of the greatest warchiefs of Africa, as well as the peacemakers, were women.

The Trung sisters, with thirty-six women generals, led eighty thousand troops against the Chinese in 40 AD, freeing Vietnam for the first time in a thousand years. Women warriors of today are said to be descendants of the Trungs. Of the major insurrections against China to follow half were led by women. Were the amount of information currently available regarding Vietnam provided as well for other nations of the Orient, we might expect similar revelations to surface.

White invaders cast a jaundiced eye upon the great number of women warriors among the Native American Indians. One of the few approving accounts comes to us from Edwin T. Denig who in 1855 wrote the biography of a woman chief among the Crows: "Long before she ventured on the warpath she could rival any of the young men in all their amusements and occupations, was a capital shot with the rifle, and would spend most of her time in killing deer and bighorn, which she butchered and carried home on her back when hunting on foot." In a battle confrontation, "Several Blackfeet came to meet her, rejoicing in the occasion of securing an easy prize. When within pistol shot, she called on them to stop, but they paid no attention. One of the enemies fired at her and the rest charged. She immediately shot down one with her gun, and shot arrows into two more without receiving a wound. The remaining two then rode back to the main body, who came at full speed to murder the woman. They fired showers of balls and pursued her as near to the fort as they could.

But she escaped unharmed and entered the gates amid the shouts and praises of the whites and her own people." When councils were held, this woman ranked third in the band of 160 lodges. She had a long career of hunting and warring until, by treachery alone, her traditional enemy the Blackfeet murdered her during her attempt to secure peace between Blackfoot and Crow.

Native American attitudes soon bent to the pressures of the narrow and rigid white conquerors. What was a commonplace account for early Spanish, French and English expiorers became less ordinary in the classical "old west" era. All the same, the sex-role-rigid whites were not devoid of amazons of their own:

Muleskinner, stage driver, range rider, gambler, sharpshooter, midwife, railroad woman—the life of Calamity Jane was not as unusual for a woman as some would prefer to think. Partly because she shared her fame with an equally extraordinary man (Wild Bill Hickok) and partly because, unlike others of her breed, she was literate and could write part of her own story, we have more knowledge of Martha Jane Cannary Hickok than of most Old West amazons.

A gentle healer and samaritan on the one hand, who cured the sick and "couldn't eat a mouthful if I saw some poor little brat hungry," Calamity would yet shoot off the hat of any man who couldn't watch his manners. In 1880 she wrote in a diary for her daughter, Jane junior, of an adventure with Wild Bill: "Everyone blamed the Indians but they were white men who did the killing and murdering and robbed the boys of gold dust. Your father dared me to drive the stage that trip after the killing. I did and found it was myself in one hell of a fix, Janey. The outlaws were back of me. It was getting dark and I knew something had to be done, so I jumped off the driver's seat on the nearest horse then on my saddle horse which was tied to the side and joined up in the dark with the outlaws. Your father was bringing up the rear but I couldn't see it in the darkness but after they got the coach stopped and found no passengers but heaps of gold they got careless. Your father and I got the whole bunch. There were eight of them and of course they had to be shot for they wouldn't give up."

All of these extraordinary women may provide a tantalizing glimpse of the potential roles and positions of women in lost or forgotten ages. On every inhabitable continent and isle, myths of a totally matriarchal heritage as well as of legendary amazons are pervasive. A major example: the ancient verse *Aethiopis* tells how the amazon queen Penthesilia temporarily liberated Troy. The aid of Penthesilia's amazon nation may well have been elicited by Hecuba, Queen of Troy, whom contrary to homeric and euripedian retellings long after the historic defeat, was the powerful ruler of Troy. Achilles' retaking of the city marked the demise of the last stronghold of goddess monotheism which had been extant among the Mediterranean nations since Mesopotamian settlement. It may also have marked the downfall of the last great societies which women governed and defended.

From a scholarly basis, we can show only that the jural and social systems of many early peoples were matrifocal, matrilocal and matrilinear and that the position and power of women under these societies was greater than it is today. Evidence from studies of present-day aboriginal peoples reveals that, before white intervention, Melville Island Tiwis, the Australian Pitjandjara, certain Eskimo peoples, the G/wi and !Kung of Kalahari, Congo pygmies, and the peaceful people of the Philippine rain forests have been egalitarian, or sometimes at least partially woman-dominant. This contradicts the previous and discreditable theories of women's inherent, biologically linked inferior social status and physical ability. It is tempting to extrapolate from these modern anthropological and available archeological evidences, an age of sophisticated worldwide matriarchal civilization. Indeed the hypothesis cannot be credibly challenged except by reasoning which, unless selectively applied, refutes all other prevailing theories as well.

The mythological evidence is vast and helpful, but it is dangerous to interpret "myth" as "history" (just as it is dangerous to interpret "history" as "fact"—we can scarcely believe the daily press on current events in the memory of us all, much less the biased chronicles of times which bear no witness). It must be allowed that mythology reflects a common experience handed down from antiquity, revised with every century or civilization, combining that antique experience with contemporary rationales and justifications for successive generations' realities. We can only speculate what the common experience may have been, which produced the universal myth of women's previous rule—and in the fantasy story especially this speculation can be imaginative and entertaining, as well as, very possibly, as close to truth as any scientific hypothesis. We can at least dismiss all detractors who continue, sometimes hysterically, to reason that women were never mighty. Amazons have lived and fought from the Neolithic to the streets of Chicago, Belfast, and Peking.

Historic and prehistoric anthropology and social archeology are one part fact to nine parts imagination. Our "knowledge" of entire civilizations is often extrapolated from a single spare clue via circuitous routes of highly subjective assumptions. If the resultant conclusions sit well with all preconceived notions (usually ethno- and androcentric), they are incorporated into the traditional texts as true, irrespective of the nine parts fantasy. If the results are shocking and sit uneasily with traditional views, lay persons and academicians alike will hasten to discredit the one part fact by indicating the nine part invention. Such has been the case with those who provide evidence of women's power and rule in earlier (and sometimes recent) periods. What we may say, however, with total assurance is this: given the variegation in prehistoric and early societies as dictated by ecological considerations, a *diversity* of social and cultural institutions is absolutely certain. This includes, of course, women's domination and/or equal status, or any combination intellectually conceivable.

In this vein and of special note are a Eurasian people, possibly the first to war astride horses, known to us as Sarmations. The women of this race gained a reputation for strength and education, and are the earliest proven source of amazon legends. The most plausible etymology of the word "amazon" is that it is derived from the Circassion expression "maza" or "moon." There is every likelihood that a cult of women who practiced warfare, equestrianism, and moon worship separated from the bulk of Sarmation society to live on the eastern and southern shores of the Black Sea and the Caucasus. The Scythians, traditional enemies of the Sarmations, called these women "Oiorpata" or "mankillers." The best evidence suggests an area of specific amazon dominion to be a port in northern Anatolia, now in the investigatory hands of archeologists.

But it would be misleading to give this cult society credit for the entire amazon archetype, for legends suggest an amazon "race" of far earlier origin. The moon cultists themselves likely had a heritage reaching into their own antiquity, epochs of which we know nothing. There are indications of uniform gynecocratic rule up to and beyond the first millennium BC, in Syra, Crete, Greece, Lybia, Asia Minor and Thrace. The image and reality of the amazon has been with us since time immemorial, and specific women heroes appear in every unrevised epic. Boudicca led a rebellion in the year 60 against Romans occupying England. Jeanne d'Arc, though wielding banner in lieu of sword, led French soldiers against the English, and drew the battle plans. Aethelflaed resisted Danish invaders from 910 to 915, restoring Wales' crumbled defenses. Harriet Tubman operated an "underground railroad" to remove her enslaved people from Confederate America, and served as a soldier in the northern Union Army. Many of Russia's combatants in the Second World War were women, including Major Tamara Aleksandrovna who commanded an airborn regiment on more than 4,000 sorties and 125 combats. "One-Eye" Hawkins, a patch on one eye, escaped to New Providence after being sold as a bond servant by her husband. She became a pirate in the days of Blackbeard, Captain Kidd, Mary Reed, Anne Bonney, and similar folk heroes. Major-General Li Chen was a leader in Mao Tse Tung's campaigns. She stayed with the 6,000 mile Long Walk. She engaged in battle even during pregnancy.

Not all amazons were warlike, of course; some were merely adventurous. Imbibing mystic learning in many oriental countries, Alexandria David-Neel, a Knight in the French Legion of Honor, was the first European woman to visit the far, forbidden city of Lhasa in Tibet. Hungarian Florence Baker returned to civilization after presumed lost, to report the discovery of the once mythic "Source of the Nile." The list is simply endless. The amazon archetype is, then, both ancient and modern, psychological and real—born of an uninterrupted history of fighting women and adventurers. The majority of their names have been lost to antiquity, or in recent instances, to the tendency of modern chroniclers to overlook or trivialize the continuing warrior-strength of women.

Fiction is part of the mythological fabric of culture-history which shapes and defines our perceptions of "reality." Occasionally, folklore may reflect the past more accurately than historic documentation, as the former is born of the experience of the common people while the latter is the "official" and preferred version of whoever is in power. Fantasy as a literature, more than any other form of storytelling, is mytho-

logical in scope—and if we are the product of our myths, the
ways we change our myths today will change the kinds of
people we become tomorrow. Without inflating the importance of a single book, it is yet possible that *Amazons!* is a
positive contribution to the culture-history of our world in
transition—a world regaining the knowledge that women are
strong.

The stories herein are provided for entertainment value
first and foremost. But the very act of women taking up
sword and shield, to a society like our own which is ruled
predominantly by men, is an act of revolution, whether performed in fact or in art. In this context, *Amazons!* is far
from escapist literature. It is inescapably subversive!

Women have not played many interesting or important
roles in heroic fantasy as defined by its authors of the few
decades past. Foregoing simple credibility, writers (curiously,
mostly men) have commonly relegated women to a series of
contradictory images of demonic rage and angelic passivity:
virtuous ethereal lady, or frigid hen; noble prostitute, or
vicious whore; beauty/princess, hag/witch; languid sex symbol, or the domatrix of the more masochistic side of male
imaginings; the feline child protector who fights only from
maternal instinct, or the Medean baby killer; evil sorceress (if
powerful), or helpless prize (if meek); incompetent burden,
or, at best, the spunky "girl" who guards her man's back by
day and warms his bed by night.

This, of course, applies only to stories which feature
women in any context at all. A truly "good ol' boys" adventure preferably contains no bothersome wenches at all—
merely a lewd reference or two in order to confirm the
protagonist's and his friends' fundamental normalcy. By far
the largest role women play in heroic fantasy or "sword and
sorcery" is not in the text of the authors, but in illustrations
rendered by artists of intriguing if limited ability. They habit-
ually depict women of peculiar thigh and mammary proportions. Even the rare "amazon" from this school of art stands
ready to trip on her tresses; and she is always holding forth
swollen breasts as though cognizant of the fact that the bold
barbarian really only want to suckle his momma.

One popular definition of heroic fantasy has been that it
takes place in worlds where "magic works, the heroes are
mighty, the women beautiful." In less romantic terms, it has
been escape fantasy for the least mature aspects of the male

ego: escape into worlds where simpletons are rewarded for unprovoked violence and undisguised misogyny. Even diehard aficinados of the genre are wont to say, "It's bloody awful, but it's *fun*." But for readers (men or women) who cannot revel in warped attitudes toward women, it isn't even fun.

It has been pointed out that, by and large, women in the heroic fantasy of the recent past have been either helpless, evil, absent, drawn funny, or at most inferior companions who, when the going gets tough, can bat a foe with short-sword instead of purse. It could be argued that the male heroes are granted little more humanity, with body proportions dictated by a thyroid problem, an overabundance of testosterone assuring death at seventeen from hardened arteries, and simple-minded fist-and-sword responses to every situation. However, this is by no means the case with complex heroes devised by the likes of Moorcock or Leiber. And even the most blundering dunderheads, while being short of human, are at least depicted as savagely noble, powerful, and on some obscure level "good" and self-motivated—attributes regularly denied women. The message is a fearful contribution to the culture-myth: men are heroic, if only in a roguish fashion; women are not.

No literary arena is of necessity so steeped in prejudice or so rooted in its own repetition and inexperience, and fortunately the exceptions are becoming more common. Many of us are fond of heroic fantasy *not* "in spite" of its lacking merit, but because the unrestrained magic and adventure provide a limitless *potential* that has yet to be sufficiently plumbed. The influx of genuinely amazonian heroes into the genre can only benefit heroic fantasy. Simple credibility can no longer be circumvented. Characterization, internal logic, and coherent plot may actually become the staples of the form, once authors begin to *think* of their worlds in terms of soundly conceived alternative cultures, sex roles, social mores, codes, ethics, the position and power of women as well as mythic places where magic is the technology and heroism the forte. This may be the giant step which removes the genre from its stagnant, unimaginative mimicry and pulp era influences, returning it to its nobler heritage of ancient mythology, intelligent extrapolation, and good storytelling.

With that grand promise, I give you *Amazons!*

THE DREAMSTONE

C. J. Cherryh

An anthologist has many rewards: seeing a book concept take shape while nurturing it to deadline, sharing an experience with well-established and new authors alike, encouraging stories that might otherwise not be written at all, strengthening bonds of friendship and discovering new friends and talents (as I automatically feel compassion toward anyone whose writing enriches me). Many of these rewards are embodied in C. J. Cherryh's contribution: my first contact with an author I'd admired a long while, the creation of a tale that might well not have existed but for this collection, discovering in my hands a lead story that epitomizes my own gut feeling of what fantasy can present in terms of feminine images contrary to those pummelled into us by most of what we read.

Valerie Eads of Fighting Woman News, *a women's martial arts magazine, has drawn comparisons between certain of C. J. Cherryh's characters and the realities of actual samurai. Indeed there is a realism to each Cherryh story which makes it easy to believe the people from* Gate of Ivrel, Hunter of Worlds, Well of Shiuan, Fires of Azeroth *and other of her fine novels actually live, breath and battle somewhere in this infinite universe.*

"Dreamstone" is a departure from her usual work in that it is High Fantasy rather than s-f. Every tale in Amazons! *ruins the safe stereotypes of woman's passivity—but C. J. Cherryh goes one step further, shattering also the cute portrayals of dainty winged fairies as the primary inhabitants of Eld. The afternoon that "Dreamstone" arrived from Oklahoma City, I sat on the post office steps reading it, soon oblivious to the cars and pedestrians and bustle of Seattle. Beguiled by the terror and adventure, I was honestly unable to look up until*

*the final page. When I finally awoke—the city more a
dream than the weirdwoods of the story—I did so shaking, and in tears, for the impact of this story's splendor
and emotion.*

*The author promises this to be the first in a series of
High Fantasy adventures. The fortune is ours.*

Of all possible paths to travel up out of Caerdale, that
through the deep forest was the least used by Men. Brigands,
outlaws, fugitives who fled mindless from shadows . . . men
with dull, dead eyes and hearts which could not truly see the
wood, souls so attainted already with the world that they
could sense no greater evil nor greater good than their
own—*they* walked that path; and if by broad morning, so
that they had cleared the black heart of Ealdwood by night-
fall, then they might perchance make it safe away into the
new forest eastward in the hills, there to live and prey on the
game and on each other.

But a runner by night, and that one young and wild-eyed
and bearing neither sword nor bow, but only a dagger and a
gleeman's harp, this was a rare venturer in Ealdwood, and all
the deeper shadows chuckled and whispered in startlement.

Eld-born Arafel saw him, and she saw little in this latter
age of earth, wrapped as she was in a passage of time different than the suns and moons which blink Men so startling-
swift from birth to dying. She heard the bright notes of the
harp which jangled on his shoulders, which companied his
flight and betrayed him to all with ears to hear, in this world
and the other. She saw his flight and walked into the way to
meet him, out of the soft green light of her moon and into
the colder white of his; and evils which had grown quite bold
in the Ealdwood of latter earth suddenly felt the warm
breath of spring and drew aside, slinking into dark places
where neither moon cast light.

"Boy," she whispered. He startled like a wounded deer,
hesitated, searching out the voice. She stepped full into his
light and felt the dank wind of Ealdwood on her face. He
seemed more solid then, ragged and torn by thorns in his
headlong course, although his garments had been of fine linen
and the harp at his shoulders had a broidered case.

She had taken little with her out of otherwhere, and yet
did take—it was all in the eye which saw. She leaned against
the rotting trunk of a dying tree and folded her arms un-
threateningly, no hand to the blade she wore, propped one
foot against a projecting root and smiled. He looked on her
with no less apprehension for that, seeing, perhaps, a ragged
vagabond of a woman in outlaws' habit—or perhaps seeing
more, for he did not look to be as blind as some. His hand
touched a talisman at his breast and she, smiling still, touched
that which hung at her own throat, which had power to answer his.

"Now where would you be going," she asked, "so reck-
lessly through the Ealdwood? To some misdeed? Some mis-
chief?"

"Misfortune," he said, breathless. He yet stared at her as if
he thought her no more than moonbeams, and she grinned at
that. Then suddenly and far away came a baying of hounds;
he would have fled at once, and sprang to do so.

"Stay!" she cried, and stepped into his path a second time,
curious what other venturers would come, and on the heels of
such as he. "I do doubt they'll come this far. What name do
you give, who come disturbing the peace of Eald?"

He was wary, surely knowing the power of names; and
perhaps he would not have given his true one and perhaps he
would not have stayed at all, but that she fixed him sternly
with her eyes and he stammered out: "Fionn."

"Fionn." It was apt, for fair he was, tangled hair and first
down of beard. She spoke it softly, like a charm. "Fionn.
Come walk with me. I'd see this intrusion before others do.
Come, come, have no dread of me; I've no harm in mind."

He did come, carefully, and much loath, heeded and
walked after her, held by nothing but her wish. She took the
Ealdwood's own slow time, not walking the quicker ways, for
there was the taint of iron about him, and she could not take
him there.

The thicket which degenerated from the dark heart of the
Eald was an unlovely place . . . for the Ealdwood had once
been better than it was, and there was yet a ruined fairness
there; but these young trees had never been other than what
they were. They twisted and tangled their roots among the
bones of the crumbling hills, making deceiving and thorny
barriers. Unlikely it was that Men could see the ways she
found; but she was amazed by the changes the years had

wrought—saw the slow work of root and branch and ice and sun, labored hard-breathing and scratched with thorns, but gloried in it, alive to the world. She turned from time to time when she sensed faltering behind her: he caught that look of hers and came on, pallid and fearful, past clinging thickets and over stones, as if he had lost all will or hope of doing otherwise.

The baying of hounds echoed out of Caerdale, from the deep valley at the very bounds of the forest. She sat down on a rock atop that last slope, where was prospect of all the great vale of the Caerbourne, a dark tree-filled void beneath the moon. A towered heap of stones had risen far across the vale on the hill called Caer Wiell, and it was the work of men: so much did the years do with the world.

The boy dropped down by the stone, the harp upon his shoulders echoing; his head sank on his folded arms and he wiped the sweat and the tangled hair from his brow. The baying, still a moment, began again, and he lifted frightened eyes.

Now he would run, having come as far as he would; fear shattered the spell. She stayed him yet again, a hand on his smooth arm.

"Here's the limit of *my* wood," she said. "And in it, hounds hunt that you could not shake from your heels, no. You'd do well to stay here by me, indeed you would. Is it yours, that harp?"

He nodded.

"Will play for me?" she asked, which she had desired from the beginning; and the desire of it burned far more vividly than did curiosity about men and dogs: but one would serve the other. He looked at her as though he thought her mad; and yet took the harp from his shoulders and from its case. Dark wood starred and banded with gold, it sounded when he took it into his arms: he held it so, like something protected, and lifted a pale, resentful face.

And bowed his head again and played as she had bidden him, soft touches at the strings that quickly grew bolder, that waked echoes out of the depths of Caerdale and set the hounds to baying madly. The music drowned the voices, filled the air, filled her heart, and she felt now no faltering or tremor of his hands. She listened, and almost forgot which moon shone down on them, for it had been so long, so very

long since the last song had been heard in Ealdwood, and
that sung soft and elsewhere.

He surely sensed a glamor on him, that the wind blew
warmer and the trees sighed with listening. The fear went
from his eyes, and though sweat stood on his brow like
jewels, it was clear, brave music that he made—suddenly,
with a bright ripple of the strings, a defiant song, strange to
her ears.

Discord crept in, the hounds' fell voices, taking the music
and warping it out of tune. She rose as that sound drew near.
The song ceased, and there was the rush and clatter of horses
in the thicket below.

Fionn sprang up, the harp laid aside. He snatched at the
small dagger at his belt, and she flinched at that, the bitter
taint of iron. "No," she wished him, and he did not draw.

Then hounds and riders were on them, a flood of hounds
black and slavering and two great horses, bearing men with
the smell of iron about them, men glittering terribly in the
moonlight. The hounds surged up baying and bugling and as
suddenly fell back again, making wide their circle, whining
and with lifting of hackles. The riders whipped them, but
their horses shied and screamed under the spurs and neither
could be driven further.

She stood, one foot braced against the rock, and regarded
men and beasts with cold curiosity, for she found them
strange, harder and wilder than Men she had known; and
strange too was the device on them, that was a wolf's grinning head. She did not recall it—nor care for the manner of
them.

Another rider clattered up the shale, shouted and whipped
his unwilling horse farther than the others, and at his heels
came men with bows. His arm lifted, gestured; the bows
arched, at the harper and at her.

"Hold," she said.

The arm did not fall; it slowly lowered. He glared at her,
and she stepped lightly up onto the rock so she need not look
up so far, to him on his tall horse. The beast shied under him
and he spurred it and curbed it cruelly; but he gave no order
to his men, as if the cowering hounds and trembling horses
finally made him see.

"Away from here," he shouted down at her, a voice to
make the earth quake. "Away! or I daresay you need a lesson

taught you too." And he drew his great sword and held it toward her, curbing the protesting horse.

"Me, lessons?" She set her hand on the harper's arm. "Is it on his account you set foot here and raise this noise?"

"My harper," the lord said, "and a thief. Witch, step aside. Fire and iron are answer enough for you."

In truth, she had no liking for the sword that threatened or for the iron-headed arrows which could speed at his lightest word. She kept her hand on Fionn's arm nonetheless, for she saw well how he would fare with them. "But he's mine, lord-of-men. I should say that the harper's no joy to you, or you'd not come chasing him from your land. And great joy he is to me, for long and long it is since I've met so pleasant a companion in Ealdwood. Gather the harp, lad, and walk away now; let me talk with this rash man."

"Stay!" the lord shouted; but Fionn snatched the harp into his arms and edged away.

An arrow hissed; the boy flung himself aside with a terrible clangor of the harp, and lost it on the slope and scrambled back for it, his undoing, for now there were more arrows ready, and these better-purposed.

"Do not," she said.

"What's mine is mine." The lord held his horse still, his sword outstretched before his archers, bating the signal; his face was congested with rage and fear. "Harp and harper are mine. And you'll rue it if you think any words of yours weigh with me. I'll have him and you for your impudence."

It seemed wisest then to walk away, and she did so—turned back the next instant, at distance, at Fionn's side, and only half under his moon. "I ask your name, lord-of-men, if you aren't fearful of my curse."

Thus she mocked him, to make him afraid before his men. "Evald," he said back, no hesitating, with contempt for her. "And yours, witch?"

"Call me what you like, lord. And take warning, that these woods are not for human hunting and your harper is not yours any more. Go away and be grateful. Men have Caerdale. If it does not please you, shape it until it does. The Ealdwood's not for trespass."

He gnawed at his mustaches and gripped his sword the tighter, but about him the drawn bows had begun to sag and the arrows to aim at the dirt. Fear was in the men's eyes, and the two riders who had come first hung back, free men and less constrained than the archers.

"You have what's mine," he insisted.

"And so I do. Go on, Fionn. Do go, quietly."

"You've what's *mine*," the valley lord shouted. "Are you thief then as well as witch? You owe me a price for it."

She drew in a sharp breath and yet did not waver in or out of the shadow. "Then do not name too high, lord-of-men. I may hear you, if that will quit us."

His eyes roved harshly about her, full of hate and yet of wariness as well. She felt cold at that look, especially where it centered, above her heart, and her hand stole to that moon-green stone that hung at her throat.

"The stone will be enough," he said. *"That."*

She drew it off, and held it yet, insubstantial as she, dangling on its chain, for she had the measure of them and it was small. "Go, Fionn," she bade him; and when he lingered yet: "Go!" she shouted. At last he ran, fled, raced away like a mad thing, holding the harp to him.

And when the woods all about were still again, hushed but for the shifting and stamp of the horses and the complaint of the hounds, she let fall the stone. "Be paid," she said, and walked away.

She heard the hooves and turned, felt the insubstantial sword like a stab of ice into her heart. She recoiled elsewhere, bowed with the pain of it that took her breath away. But in time she could stand again, and had taken from the iron no lasting hurt: yet it had been close, and the feel of cold lingered even in the warm winds.

And the boy—she went striding through the shades and shadows in greatest anxiety until she found him, where he huddled hurt and lost within the deepest wood.

"Are you well?" she asked lightly, dropping to her heels beside him. For a moment she feared he might be hurt more than scratches, so tightly he was bowed over the harp; but he lifted his face to her. "You shall stay while you wish," she said, hoping that he would choose to stay long. "You shall harp for me." And when he yet looked fear at her: "You'd not like the new forest. They've no ear for harpers there."

"What is your name, lady?"

"What do you see of me?"

He looked swiftly at the ground, so that she reckoned he

could not say the truth without offending her. And she laughed at that.

"Then call me Thistle," she said. "I answer sometimes to that, and it's a name as rough as I. But you'll stay. You'll play for me."

"Yes." He hugged the harp close. "But I'll not go with you. I've no wish to find the years passed in a night and all the world gone old."

"Ah. You know me. But what harm, that years should pass? What care of them or this age? It seems hardly kind to you."

"I am a man," he said, "and it's *my* age."

It was so; she could not force him. One entered otherwhere only by wishing it. He did not; and there was about him and in his heart still the taint of iron.

She settled in the moonlight, and watched beside him; he slept, for all his caution, and waked at last by sunrise, looking about him anxiously lest the trees have grown, and seeming bewildered that she was still there by day. She laughed, knowing her own look by daylight, that was indeed rough as the weed she had named herself, much-tanned and calloused and her clothes in want of patching. She sat plaiting her hair in a single silver braid and smiling sidelong at him, who kept giving her sidelong glances too.

All the earth grew warm. The sun did come here, unclouded on this day. He offered her food, such meager share as he had; she would have none of it, not fond of man-taint, or the flesh of poor forest creatures. She gave him instead of her own, the gift of trees and bees and whatsoever things felt no hurt at sharing.

"It's good," he said, and she smiled at that.

He played for her then, idly and softly, and slept again, for bright day in Ealdwood counseled sleep, when the sun burned warmth through the tangled branches and the air hung still, nothing breathing, least of all the wind. She drowsed too, for the first time since many a tree had grown, for the touch of the mortal sun did that kindness, a benison she had all but forgotten.

But as she slept she dreamed, of a close place of cold stone. In that dark hall she had a man's body, heavy and reeking of wine and ugly memories, such a dark fierceness she would gladly have fled if she might.

Her hand sought the moonstone on its chain and found it

at his throat; she offered better dreams and more kindly, and he made bitter mock of them, hating all that he did not comprehend. Then she would have made the hand put the stone off that foul neck; but she had no power to compel, and *he* would not. He possessed what he owned, so fiercely and with such jealousy it cramped the muscles and stifled the breath.

And he hated what he did not have and could not have, that most of all; and the center of it was his harper.

She tried still to reason within this strange, closed mind. It was impossible. The heart was almost without love, and what little it had ever been given it folded in upon itself lest what it possessed escape.

"Why?" she asked that night, when the moon shed light on the Ealdwood and the land was quiet, no ill thing near them, no cloud above them. "Why does he seek you?" Though her dreams had told her, she wanted his answer.

Fionn shrugged, his young eyes for a moment aged; and he gathered against him his harp. "This," he said.

"You said it was yours. He called you thief. What did you steal?"

"It is mine." He touched the strings and brought forth melody. "It hung in his hall so long he thought it his, and the strings were cut and dead." He rippled out a somber note. "It was my father's and his father's before him."

"And in Evald's keeping?"

The fair head bowed over the harp and his hands coaxed sound from it, answerless.

"I've given a price," she said, "to keep him from it and you. Will you not give back an answer?"

The sound burst into softness. "It was my father's. Evald hanged him. Would hang me."

"For what cause?"

Fionn shrugged, and never ceased to play. "For truth. For truth he sang. So Evald hanged him, and hung the harp on his wall for mock of him. I came. I gave him songs he liked. But at winter's end I came down to the hall at night, and mended the old harp, gave it voice and a song he remembered. For that he hunts me."

Then softly he sang, of humankind and wolves, and that song was bitter. She shuddered to hear it, and bade him cease, for mind to mind with her in troubled dreams Evald heard and tossed, and waked starting in sweat.

"Sing more kindly," she said. Fionn did so, while the moon

climbed above the trees, and she recalled elder-day songs which the world had not heard in long years, sang them sweetly. Fionn listened and caught up the words in his strings, until the tears ran down his face for joy.

There could be no harm in Ealdwood that hour: the spirits of latter earth that skulked and strove and haunted men fled elsewhere, finding nothing that they knew; and the old shadows slipped away trembling, for they remembered. But now and again the song faltered, for there came a touch of ill and smallness into her heart, a cold piercing as the iron, with thoughts of hate, which she had never held so close.

Then she laughed, breaking the spell, and put it from her, bent herself to teach the harper songs which she herself had almost forgotten, conscious the while that elsewhere, down in Caerbourne vale, on Caer Wiell, a man's body tossed in sweaty dreams which seemed constantly to mock him, with sound of eldritch harping that stirred echoes and sleeping ghosts.

With the dawn she and Fionn rose and walked a time, and shared food, and drank at a cold, clear spring she knew, until the sun's hot eye fell upon them and cast its numbing spell on all the Ealdwood.

Then Fionn slept; but she fought the sleep which came to her, for dreams were in it, her dreams while *he* should wake; nor would they stay at bay, not when her eyes grew heavy and the air thick with urging sleep. The dreams came more and more strongly. The man's strong legs bestrode a great brute horse, and hands plied whip and feet the spurs more than she would, hurting it cruelly. There was noise of hounds and hunt, a coursing of woods and hedges and the bright spurt of blood on dappled hide: he sought blood to wipe out blood, for the harping rang yet in his mind, and she shuddered at the killing her hands did, and at the fear that gathered thickly about him, reflected in his comrades' eyes.

It was better that night, when the waking was hers and her harper's, and sweet songs banished fear; but even yet she grieved for remembering, and at times the cold came on her, so that her hand would steal to her throat where the moon-green stone was not. Her eyes brimmed suddenly with tears: Fionn saw and tried to sing her merry songs instead. They failed, and the music died.

"Teach me another song," he begged of her. "No harper ever had such songs. And will *you* not play for *me*?"

"I have no art," she said, for the last harper of her folk had gone long ago: it was not all truth, for once she had known, but there was no more music in her hands, none since the last had gone and she had willed to stay, loving this place too well in spite of men. "Play," she asked of Fionn, and tried to smile, though the iron closed about her heart and the man raged at the nightmare, waking in sweat, ghost-ridden.

It was that human song Fionn played in his despair, of the man who would be a wolf and the wolf who was no man; while the lord Evald did not sleep again, but sat shivering and wrapped in furs before his hearth, his hand clenched in hate upon the stone which he possessed and would not, though it killed him, let go.

But she sang a song of elder earth, and the harper took up the tune, which sang of earth and shores and water, a journey, the great last journey, at men's coming and the dimming of the world. Fionn wept while he played, and she smiled sadly and at last fell silent, for her heart was gray and cold.

The sun returned at last, but she had no will to eat or rest, only to sit grieving, for she could not find peace. Gladly now she would have fled the shadow-shifting way back into otherwhere, to her own moon and softer sun, and persuaded the harper with her; but there was a portion of her heart in pawn, and she could not even go herself: she was too heavily bound. She fell to mourning bitterly, and pressed her hand often where the stone should rest. He hunted again, did Evald of Caer Wiell. Sleepless, maddened by dreams, he whipped his folk out of the hold as he did his hounds, out to the margin of the Ealdwood, to harry the creatures of woodsedge, having guessed well the source of the harping. He brought fire and axes, vowing to take the old trees one by one until all was dead and bare.

The wood muttered with whisperings and angers; a wall of cloud rolled down from the north on Ealdwood and all deep Caerdale, dimming the sun; a wind sighed in the face of the men, so that no torch was set to wood; but axes rang, that day and the next. The clouds gathered thicker and the winds blew colder, making Ealdwood dim again and dank. She yet managed to smile by night, to hear the harper's songs. But every stroke of the axes made her shudder, and the iron about her heart tightened day by day. The wound in the

Ealdwood grew, and he was coming: she knew it well, and there remained at last no song at all, by day or night.

She sat now with her head bowed beneath the clouded moon, and Fionn was powerless to cheer her. He regarded her in deep despair, and touched her hand for comfort. She said no word to that, but gathered her cloak about her and offered to the harper to walk a time, while vile things stirred and muttered in the shadow, whispering malice to the winds, so that often Fionn started and stared and kept close beside her.

Her strength faded, first that she could not keep the voices away, and then that she could not keep from listening; and at last she sank upon his arm, eased to the cold ground and leaned her head against the bark of a gnarled tree.

"What ails?" he asked, and pried at her clenched and empty fingers, opened the fist which hovered near her throat as if seeking there the answer. "What ails you?"

She shrugged and smiled and shuddered, for the axes had begun again, and she felt the iron like a wound, a great cry going through the wood as it had gone for days; but he was deaf to it, being what he was. "Make a song for me," she asked.

"I have no heart for it."

"Nor have I," she said. A sweat stood on her face, and he wiped at it with his gentle hand and tried to ease her pain.

And again he caught and unclenched the hand which rested, empty, at her throat. "The stone," he said. "Is it *that* you miss?"

She shrugged, and turned her head, for the axes then seemed loud. He looked too—glanced back deaf and puzzled. " 'Tis time," she said. "You must be on your way this morning, when there's sun enough. The new forest will hide you after all."

"And leave you? Is that your meaning?"

She smiled, touched his anxious face. "I am paid enough."

"How paid? What did you pay? *What* was it you gave away?"

"Dreams," she said. "Only that. And all of that." Her hands shook terribly, and a blackness came on her heart too miserable to bear: it was hate, and aimed at him and at herself, and all that lived; and it was harder and harder to fend away. "Evil has it. He would do you hurt, and I would dream that too. Harper, it's time to go."

"Why would you give such a thing?" Great tears started from his eyes. "Was it worth such a cost, my harping?"

"Why, well worth it," she said, with such a laugh as she had left to laugh, that shattered all the evil for a moment and left her clean. "I have sung."

He snatched up the harp and ran, breaking branches and tearing flesh in his headlong haste, but not, she realized in horror, not the way he ought—but back again, to Caerdale.

She cried out her dismay and seized at branches to pull herself to her feet; she could in no wise follow. Her limbs which had been quick to run beneath this moon or the other were leaden, and her breath came hard. Brambles caught and held with all but mindful malice, and dark things which had never had power in her presence whispered loudly now, of murder.

And elsewhere the wolf-lord with his men drove at the forest, great ringing blows, the poison of iron. The heavy ironclad body which she sometime wore seemed hers again, and the moonstone was prisoned within that iron, near a heart that beat with hate.

She tried the more to haste, and could not. She looked helplessly through Evald's narrow eyes and saw—saw the young harper break through the thickets near them. Weapons lifted, bows and axes. Hounds bayed and lunged at leashes.

Fionn came, nothing hesitating, bringing the harp, and himself. "A trade," she heard him say. "The stone for the harp."

There was such hate in Evald's heart, and such fear it was hard to breathe. She felt a pain to the depth of her as Evald's coarse fingers pawed at the stone. She felt his fear, felt his loathing of it. Nothing would he truly let go. But this—this he abhorred, and was fierce in his joy to lose it.

"Come," the lord Evald said, and held the stone, dangling and spinning before him, so that for that moment the hate was far and cold.

Another hand took it then, and very gentle it was, and very full of love. She felt the sudden draught of strength and desperation—sprang up then, to run, to save.

But pain stabbed through her heart, and such an ebbing out of love and grief that she cried aloud, and stumbled, blind, dead in that part of her.

She did not cease to run; and she ran now that shadow-way, for the heaviness was gone. Across meadows, under that other moon she sped, and gathered up all that she had left behind, burst out again in the blink of an eye and elsewhere.

Horses shied and dogs barked; for now she did not care to be what suited men's eyes: bright as the moon she broke among them, and in her hand was a sharp blade, to meet with iron.

Harp and harper lay together, sword-riven. She saw the underlings start away and cared nothing for them; but Evald she sought. He cursed at her, drove spurs into his horse and rode at her, sword yet drawn, shivering the winds with a horrid slash of iron. The horse screamed and shied; he cursed and reined the beast, and drove it for her again. But this time the blow was hers, a scratch that made him shriek with rage.

She fled at once. He pursued. It was his nature that he must; and she might have fled otherwhere, but she would not. She darted and dodged ahead of the great horse, and it broke the brush and thorns and panted after, hard-ridden.

Shadows gathered, stirring and urgent on this side and on that, who gibbered and rejoiced for the way that they were tending, to the woods' blackest heart, for some of them had been Men; and some had known the wolf's justice, and had come to what they were for his sake. They reached, but durst not touch him, for she would not have it so. Over all, the trees bowed and groaned in the winds and the leaves went flying, thunder above and thunder of hooves below, scattering the shadows.

But suddenly she whirled about and flung back her cloak: the horse shied up and fell, cast Evald sprawling among the wet leaves. The shaken beast scrambled up and evaded his hands and his threats, thundered away on the moist earth, splashing across some hidden stream; and the shadows chuckled. She stepped full back again from otherwhere, and Evald saw her clear, moonbright and silver. He cursed, shifted that great black sword from hand to hand, for right hand bore a scratch that now must trouble him. He shrieked with hate and slashed.

She laughed and stepped into otherwhere and back again, and fled yet farther, until he stumbled with exhaustion and sobbed and fell, forgetting now his anger, for the whispers came loud.

"Up," she bade him, mocking, and stepped again to here. Thunder rolled upon the wind, and the sound of horses and hounds came at distance. A joyful malice came into his eyes when he heard it; his face grinned in the lightnings. But she laughed too, and his mirth died as the sound came on them, under them, over them, in earth and heavens.

He cursed then and swung the blade, lunged and slashed again, and she flinched from the almost-kiss of iron. Again he whirled it, pressing close; the lightning cracked—he shrieked a curse, and, silver-spitted—died.

She did not weep or laugh now; she had known him too well for either. She looked up instead at the clouds, gray wrack scudding before the storm, where other hunters coursed the winds and wild cries wailed—heard hounds baying after something fugitive and wild. She lifted then her fragile sword, salute to lord Death, who had governance over Men, a Huntsman too; and many the old comrades the wolf would find following in his train.

Then the sorrow came on her, and she walked the otherwhere path to the beginning and the end of her course, where harp and harper lay. There was no mending here. The light was gone from his eyes and the wood was shattered.

But in his fingers lay another thing, which gleamed like the summer moon amid his hand.

Clean it was from his keeping, and loved. She gathered it to her. The silver chain went again about her neck and the stone rested where it ought. She bent last and kissed him to his long sleep, fading then to otherwhere.

She dreamed at times then, waking or sleeping; for when she held close the stone and thought of him she heard a fair, far music, for a part of his heart was there too, a gift of himself.

She sang sometimes, hearing it, wherever she walked.

That gift, she gave to him.

WOLVES OF NAKESHT

Janrae Frank

Throughout history there have been women who, to escape the restrictions so many societies impose, coped by learning to live in the guise of men. Some may have believed themselves truly men and, thereby, became so. Others likely retained a strong woman-identity and knew themselves to be, like a chameleon, merely clever and, after a fashion, free.

Janrae Frank explores the life, interrelationships, contradictions, well-being and growth of a woman who lives as a man in a land that would not otherwise tolerate her strength. Cimquar the lion-hawk, or Tomyris the amazon: parent, priestess, soldier. Rarely has a character of this complexity been developed in the sword-and-sorcery adventure mode.

The author is a Texan, a martial artist, a tough bantam-weight who has taken on opponents twice her size, sometimes in emergency situations—and won. She views herself as a Shy Lion. She is working on two novels set in the Sharone amazon empire.

Oil-fed torches mounted on walls or atop street posts broke the dark streets into patterns of bright orange and deep shadow. Few people traveled the streets of Aekara at that late hour, and none walked boldly—save two plainsmen, one scarcely more than a youth, the other, his lean, weather-worn mentor. A slender girl waltzed between them, watching the swirling folds of her mid-calf skirt turn orange and red, then black as they passed from light to shadow and back. The elder warrior wore a lion's black-maned pelt as a jerkin.

31

She slew the beast with a dagger, so the Euzadi called her the lion-hawk, Chimquar. All believed Chimquar a man.

The ringing clash of steel on steel ended the quiet. The handful of people abroad halted to mark the direction of the sounds. Their errands would not bear close inspection and a fight meant first brigands, then guardsmen. Chimquar and her wards suddenly became the only people on the streets for many blocks around the clash.

Chimquar paused, listening to the sound of fighting coming from the direction in which they traveled.

"Do we go on?" Hazier asked.

Chimquar nodded, her hand resting on the hilt of her Sharan longsword. Her wards dropped back a short way as she had taught them. Makajia produced a long dagger from beneath her skirts.

A Sharan war cry carried down the street. "Aroana! Goddess defender!" Chimquar halted. It had been several years since she heard that cry on any lips save her own. For the first time she hesitated to answer it. She planned to join her sister, ending her long exile. Anaria, alone, would understand her concealment in men's raiment, first of her race in the far lands of men. The others would not, and Chimquar would once more be the scarcely tolerated outcast in their midst. Chimquar longed increasingly to see her homeland.

"Aroana! Aroana!" The cries came again, insistent, desperate. The Sharans had no allies, no aid. Chimquar drew her sword, thrusting aside her concerns. They would have aid.

Chimquar saw three women at bay near an alley, encircled by swordsmen. The Sharans had taken toll of their attackers, their swords gleamed red in the torchlight. Yet they could not hold much longer against so many. One woman fell as Chimquar reached them. The remaining pair moved to stand over their fallen comrade. A man lunged in; one Sharan shifted slightly, avoiding his thrust and opening a long gash in his side.

"Aroana!" Chimquar shouted, entering the fray. The first man to turn died. Momentary confusion ensued among the men at the unexpected attack by Chimquar and Hazier. Makajia darted about, wielding her dagger to great effect. Three men fell in the first minutes of surprise. Chimquar's sword whirled in a circular motion, parried the attack of two foes, then slashed out, felling one. She eluded a thrust and lunged in under the man's guard; the dagger in her left hand catching the returning move of his sword and she sent her own blade home. Chimquar moved on another man. She had neither time nor light enough to mark the nature of her foes, yet she recognized the moving patterns of their attack. She fought Euzadis—renegades.

Hazier stepped back, giving ground. His shoulder struck a wall and his backward step came short. A sword arched at his head. He ducked forward, lashing out with his own weapon. The man sprang back, another rushed in. Hazier moved sidewise, his foot struck something and he fell backwards, frantically blocking the rain of blows from his opponents with his sword and dagger. Makajia darted out of the shadows where she had hidden, knowing herself overmatched by the warriors. Her dagger flashed. One man no longer endangered her brother.

"Renegade!"

The second man turned to see the tall man with the lion mane about his shoulders. His surviving companions were already in full flight. "Chimquar," he snarled, then fled.

Chimquar let him go. She stood nearest the fallen Sharan whose companions now stood off in the wake of their fleeing foes. Chimquar knelt, cradling the Sharan's head and shoulders, and glanced briefly at the returning pair. Makajia tore a strip of cloth from the bottom of her white blouse and pressed it to the wound in the woman's ribs. The woman gazed up at Chimquar, astonished to behold a plainsman. Pain deepened the lines in the Sharan's weathered face, her breath came in ragged pulls. She and her companions all were the Sharan queen's livery and Chimquar marveled that they had come so far into these lands. The double-axe embroidered above the unicorn blazon marked the woman as Hautaren, temple-warrior, one of the elite from which knights, captains, and generals rose. Chimquar had been Hautaren, hence her greeting came automatically, "*Kalur Aroana bai ew, Hautaren,*" she murmured.

"*Kalur Aroana widare ew, Euzadi,*" the woman returned hoarsely. Her eyes clenched shut as a wave of pain took her. When it eased, she gazed again at the nomad. "Tamlys Lodarian." She forced the words out, indicating herself. The Sharans dropped to their knees beside her. Chimquar sat back, allowing them to bend nearer. One warrior clasped Tamlys' hand mutely.

"Meadusea." Tamlys named her first, then the younger one: "Katalla Maelistya."

Hazier joined his mentor. The lingering excitement of the battle and the nearness of members of his mentor's legendary race gave Hazier's face an expression disrespectful of the dying Tamlys. Katalla favored him with a savage, withering stare. Hazier dropped his eyes quickly. Chimquar caught the exchange of glances and their portent of trouble.

"The farther east . . . we go,"—Tamlys struggled with her words—"the fewer allies we find."

"Chimquar is ever the Sharan's ally."

"So." Tamlys sighed. "We have found you."

"No words," Meadusea said, concerned. "Rest, Tamlys."

"My time nears." Tamlys' voice steadied as though she found strength with acceptance. "I must speak. Jalaia Torrundar's daughter said. . . ." Her voice dwindled off into silence. Then she spoke again, "She said: 'seek Chimquar.' "

Chimquar tensed, wondering how much they knew of her. Her left hand closed on the leather pouch at her side and the lump of the crest ring it held. Ending her self-imposed exile meant facing the nobles and Hautaren that had made her outcast. If these women knew that Chimquar and Tomyris Danae were one, what would they do? But the Thunder God's daughter would never have betrayed her. Chimquar looked up. Katalla and Meadusea stared at her as if awaiting some response she had not given.

"Jalaia said you would aid us." Meadusea's soft, grave voice took the strands of the tale from Tamlys. "A storm separated us from our company. We could find neither them nor the object of our quest." She was older than Chimquar and no less proud. Chimquar saw the brief passage of doubt and confusion mingling with the sorrow in Meadusea's face. The Hautaren had never before encountered hostility as unreasoning as in the eastern Lands of Men. Chimquar averted her eyes. Meadusea's distress provoked memories best left alone. "Hazier." Chimquar spoke Euzadi. "Pile some bodies across the alley. They will return that way."

Katalla's hand went to her sword, her black eyes narrowed. Hazier moved to his tasks and Katalla watched.

Tamlys opened her eyes and clasped Chimquar's hand. "A plainsman . . . I did not believe. But you will aid them. You will!" Tamlys eyes searched the nomad's face, seeming to reach her soul (as some Hautaren could) and Chimquar tasted the full, bitter cup she had brewed in her youth. Chimquar beheld a great strength and gentle wisdom in equal measure in those searching eyes, provoking memories of her shield-sister, Shaila Odaren, who had not survived the Witch Wars. She felt alone, walled out by her own choices. "I will aid them as far as it is in my power, Tamlys," she murmured. "I swear it! By the Powers of Earth, I swear it!"

"Jalaia spoke true," Tamlys whispered and died.

Meadusea slipped her arms under her shield-sister's body, took her from Chimquar and rose. "Those men will return."

"Yes." Chimquar scanned the street as she spoke. "How far are your horses?"

"Four blocks," Meadusea replied, calm despite the tears running down her cheeks.

"Makajia will take you to our meeting place. Go quickly."

"What about you?"

"Hazier and I will distract them. You get clear of the city." Chimquar gestured and Makajia moved to Meadusea's side.

"Meadusea!" Katalla cried angrily. "You listen to him? What more harm do we need?"

"Jalaia trusts him," Meadusea turned away, walking beside Makajia. The Euzadi girl's step had lost its gaiety.

Katalla faced Chimquar, her expression an open challenge. The brooding power in Chimquar's eyes forced Katalla to drop her gaze. The Sharan woman cursed under her breath.

The sound of footsteps mingled with shouts. "Chimquar," Hazier warned, "they come."

Katalla raised her eyes to Chimquar's again, held them a moment, then she set off after Meadusea and Makajia.

Chimquar removed a torch from a wall, scanning the bodies. Katalla needed to learn the lessons of those lands, as Askani, the old Euzadi seer, had taught Chimquar. *Anger casts a spear without gauging the distance.* A half-smile crossed Chimquar's lips, remembering the hunched, arthritic, old man that had taught her the Euzadi ways, making possible her concealment.

"Chimquar?" Hazier stood beside the bodies piled across the mouth of the alley. The shouts and footsteps neared.

Chimquar glanced up and down the street, wondering how much more shouting it would take to draw guards. She could not wait for them. "Torch the pile, Hazier," she said, quietly.

The youth wrestled a torch from its wall-mount, and emptied the unguent contents of its hollow base upon the bodies, touching the burning end to their lacquered, leather armor. The flames licked up, greater and eager, filling the air with stench. Men in the alley howled in rage and frustration, turning back to find another path. Chimquar ignored them. Some bodies still scattered in the street wore Euzadi headbands of worked leather, the tribal marks obliterated with blood and black paint: Renegades, followers of Bakran, Chimquar's bitterest foe. Asking after her, the Sharans had drawn Bakran's attentions. A cold rage kindled within her. Cautiously, she walked down the west end of the street. "Bakran! Bakran, do you hear me?"

"I hear you!" a man's deep voice answered east of her.

Chimquar's keen ears heard the movement of his men. At the end of the first block she thrust her torch into the south opening of the cross street. It was a dead end. "Bakran?"

"Speak on, Chimquar." He sounded pleased. "I have you this time."

Nay, Bakran. You do not have me. She spied an iron gate in the middle of the next block. A narrow balcony jutted from the stone mansion half a spear's length above and beyond the gate. Lit windows shone around it. She walked slower with Hazier at her heels. She heard men moving at either end of the street. "Hazier, that gate, the balcony, then the roofs. Confuse the Sharan's trail when you find it."

He hesitated and she shoved him. "Go!" He gained the gate. Chimquar ran behind him, gauging the distance of the closing warriors. One reached her and she hurled the torch in his face, climbed the gate and sprang at the balcony. Her hands caught the edge. She pulled herself up, swung one leg over, then the other. Chimquar stood silently before the closed glass doors. A soft harmony of lute and pipes came from within the room. Hazier waited on a sturdy vine-covered trellis beyond the balcony. Chimquar turned from Hazier to see a renegade climbing the gate. "Go on," she ordered the youth.

"Chimquar," he protested.

"Nay! Go on." Her voice rose slightly. "Go after your sister."

"You're going to get yourself slain." His words came bleak and drawn out.

Chimquar smiled at his concern. "I won't Hazier. Now, go!"

"Aroana defend you!" He swarmed up the trellis.

A thud, and the scrape of a scabbard on stone, turned Chimquar. The man had gained the balcony. She sprang before he could get both legs over, seizing his sword arm and jerkin with a twist that hurled him through the fragile glass doors. The tinkling clash of falling shards of glass preceded the woman's scream. Men's shouts followed immediately. Chimquar bounded across the balcony and went up the trellis to the roof. A man emerged onto the balcony, sword in hand, glanced about and reentered the manor house. The garden below filled with light as men and servants poured out bearing weapons and torches. Chimquar crouched in the shadows of a chimney, watching until the confusion died down, then she crossed the roof and sprang onto the next. She made her way from roof to roof, leaping the narrow streets until she reached the stable.

Chimquar dropped silently from the roof behind the stableman, startling him. He eyed her doubtfully. She threw a handful of coins at his feet. He stooped to retrieve them and she slipped into the stable after her horse.

She rode quietly to the west gate. The guardsman there, accustomed to the strange comings and goings of the nomads, let her out a narrow, postern gate. The morning sun rose on her right hand as she turned her little plains-bred mare north.

Makajia heard the peace bells jingling and sprang to her feet. "Chimquar!" she cried joyously, then paused to ascertain the direction and raced off. Her skirts swirled around her legs, scarcely hampering her stride. "Chimquar!"

A slow, shy smile tickled the corners of Hazier's mouth. He glanced at Meadusea, who sat across from him, then leaned and picked up a silver bracelet set with turquoise stones which Makajia had dropped. The girl had been polishing and adding the last touches to her handiwork.

"You are fond of your mentor," Meadusea said.

Hazier watched Makajia running. He could barely see Chimquar. "When I was a child, I ran to him like that."

"Little flower," Katalla said sarcastically. She stood beneath the cottonwoods lining the streambank, pulling a cream-colored shirt over her mail. She flicked her wet braids out and laced the cuffs tight. Then she picked up her brown tunic, stalking to Hazier and Meadusea.

"I did not understand Chekaya's words," Hazier said, shaking his head.

"You insist on that name." Meadusea grinned wryly.

"Chekaya," Hazier struggled silently with his Engla. "A swift cat—dog-footed. Chekaya Tamures; powerful Chekaya."

"You can quit calling me that," Katalla said with asperity. Hazier dropped his eyes, his mouth twisting petulantly.

"What goes here?" Chimquar drew rein near Hazier. Makajia slipped off behind Chimquar and took the reins close to its head like a squire for a knight. Meadusea had seen squires, pages, stablehands, and nomad boys hold or take a horse for warriors and nobles, but never before a non-Sharan girl.

Meadusea rose with Hazier. The youth clasped Chimquar's arms in brief greeting. Chimquar turned to Meadusea. "*Kalur Aroana bai ew, Meadusea.*" Chimquar's soft accent mingled Sharan and Euzadi.

"*Kalur Aroana widare ew, Chimquar.*"

Katalla stood mute and hostile behind Meadusea. Chimquar reminded herself of her promise to Tamlys, refusing to be provoked, yet denying Katalla a proper greeting. The younger Sharan was slender, promising more speed then strength.

Meadusea had shorn off her umber braids as a sign of her sorrow, tying a suede band around her head. She was the same height as Chimquar, large-boned and powerful where Chimquar was lean and long-muscled.

Chimquar ran her thumb and forefinger down her seamed, sun-battered face. A score of years on the Great Plains had burned her darker than the Sharans, aged her face to match her years in a way that the long-lived Sharans did not. "You buried Tamlys?" she asked tersely. She walked past them, heading for the stream. Hazier walked beside her.

"We did." Katalla stalked after the Euzadis.

Makajia led Chimquar's horse beneath the trees, tethering it with her own.

"You're not a friendly one, are you?" Meadusea said, her words milder than true annoyance.

"I'm no village gossip!"

"I didn't suggest it," Meadusea said smoothly.

"We should return to Shaurone," Katalla broke in. "Tamlys is dead. Leave this quest to Anaria!" She halted, facing off in front of Meadusea.

"Go if you wish, Katalla. I will not."

Chimquar knelt by the stream, bringing up a drink in her cupped hands. Her insides rolled. They were looking for her.

"Tomyris is as dead as Tamlys!" Katalla sounded exasperated.

Three rough-edged words forced themselves from Chimquar. "Tomyris Danae is alive."

"I knew it!" Meadusea exclaimed. "I knew it!"

"Where is she?" Katalla demanded drily, coming to stand above Chimquar.

"She doesn't want to be found." Chimquar stood, walking away.

"At least we could carry some word to her sister," Meadusea suggested.

"I am taking you to Anaria."

"Plainsman!" Katalla snarled. "I don't like you—and I don't trust you. Meadusea's making a bloody fool of herself." Katalla's hand went suggestively to her sword.

"You'll be the bloody fool," Chimquar warned softly.

"No man is my equal!" Katalla flung back.

Chimquar stared silently at Katalla, struggling to rein in the temper she had spent years learning to control—it was still like a green broken horse. "Believe what you will. Time is short. Those men already track us, and Anaria is three days north." *I'm keeping my promise, Tamlys.*

"So close—" Meadusea breathed.

Chimquar turned toward the horses. How much more hostile would Katalla be if she knew Chimquar was Sharan? Chimquar felt her choices slipping out of her hands. Katalla would count it betrayal. So would most of her people. It might be best to send some word to Anaria with Meadusea, then put as many leagues as possible between herself and her homeland.

"Chimquar." Hazier still walked beside her. "My mount pulled up lame."

"Free it," Chimquar said, obeying Euzadi custom. She halted, looking back at Meadusea. "You have Tamlys' horse?"

Meadusea nodded.

"I want it."

The three tall, deep-chested destriers lifted their heads at the warriors' approach. Round shields hung from their light cavalry saddles and twin javelins hung at the right sides. A wry, satisfied smile came on Chimquar's lips. *Even a fool must see these hybrids are the finest steeds on this continent!* She remembered the lush green of the northern valleys where her people bred mares to unicorn stallions. Her memory conjured images of the small crofts and the temple where she and Anaria had spent many summers, learning the ways of the Hautaren there. Chimquar's smile deepened. It would be so good to see those valleys once more. Then abruptly she wrenched herself from those thoughts; she would never see those valleys again—not now.

Chimquar headed for a sorrel stallion, flaxen-maned, tethered apart from the others. "That one?"

"Yes," Meadusea answered. "Adoni."

The stallion put his ears back as Chimquar approached. She whispered to him in Sharan. His ears pricked up and he quivered. Chimquar ran her hand over him, speaking low to conceal her fluent use of the Sharan tongue. She loosed him and Adoni let her mount. She exulted at the smooth, easy power of the stallion as she swung him around. Her hand dropped to Tamlys' shield and she lifted it from the saddle, slipping her arm through the straps. It still felt right. She sent the stallion into a canter, then a full gallop, reined in and turned back.

Meadusea and Katalla came alongside. "You may have all of Tamlys' things," Meadusea said, "save her sword."

"Payment for his trouble?" Katalla said, sneering.

Meadusea gave the younger woman a severe glance, started to speak and Chimquar interrupted. "I didn't ask for anything save the horse—which I have need of. I don't ask for her sword." Chimquar idly rubbed the hilt of her sword. The gesture drew the Sharans' eyes.

"A longsword." Meadusea was clearly surprised. "I've not seen a plainsman with one."

"I'm not Euzadi born." Chimquar left them.

Hazier discarded his own saddle and shifted his saddlebags to Chimquar's mare. He looked up as his mentor joined him. "I'm ready," he said.

"Me, too!" Makajia tossed her head haughtily and swung into the saddle of her black filly.

Chimquar moved across the plains, Hazier and Makajia behind her, the Sharans last.

A large herd of long-horned bison and antelope moved away from the riders passing them down wind. A sleek, black-flecked shape stalked the edges of the herd, singling out a young antelope that had wandered too far from its fellows. It sprang suddenly. The antelope fled, bounding and turning. The hunting cat moved with it, never missing a turn, anticipating its prey's each move.

"There!" Hazier pointed. "Chekaya!"

Katalla saw the swift cat bring down its prey. "I no longer mind the name." Her voice was soft and without its usual harshness. "There is a sudden, swift beauty to the beast."

A long, low howl slid across the plains. It was answered from the east and west. Chekaya abandoned her fresh kill. The herds broke into a panicked run, which quickly became a stampede. The howling rose again, louder, higher pitched with an almost human wail rising with it. The very air seemed chilled. The horses danced nervously as Chimquar and her companions drew rein. Chimquar's eyes raked the land, knowing that true wolves could not panic Chekaya, knowing the strange sound she heard. Hazier's lips parted in a word of dismay that went unspoken. Then the sorrel stallion, Adoni, struck the earth with his cloven forehooves, threatening to rear.

"Nakesht," Chimquar hissed. Then two outriders topped a distant rise. "And Bakran!" She pressed her knees to the stallion and galloped north. The open, bereft of a Euzadi wagon-ring was no place to battle the man-wolves of the Nakesht. The unlikely alliance of Bakran and the Nakesht puzzled Chimquar.

The Sharans unsheathed their swords, galloping at Chimquar's heels. The difference between their steeds and the plainsbred horses showed at once. Makajia's small size and light weight compensated for the difference between her filly and the Sharans', but her brother fell farther and farther behind. Chimquar looked back at Makajia's shout, and saw a Nakesht wolf plunge out of the tall grasses. She gestured sharply for the Sharans to go on, and swung back with one of the javelins to hand.

Hazier slowed. "Nay!" Chimquar shouted, and Hazier clapped his heels to the mare's sides. His mentor charged the wolf. The javelin left her hand in a smooth throw. The wolf stumbled and fell. Chimquar circled back, watching for more wolves. She felt the stallion tense to rear. A wolf erupted out

of the grass before her. Adoni lashed out with his forelegs.
Then a hard weight struck Chimquar. She struck blindly at
the bulk of the snarling wolf carrying her from the saddle.
They struck the earth together. It snapped for her throat, its
teeth closing on the heavy thickness of the lion's mane around
her neck. Chimquar wrenched its jaws apart, threw herself
and the wolf sidewise, twisting its head as her weight came
down on the beast. Bone snapped. She released it. A man lay
dead with a wide, golden slave collar around his neck.

Wolves harried her stallion. Chimquar's dagger appeared in
her hand as she got to her feet. A tearing pain ripped her left
arm. The sudden weight of the wolf threw her off balance.
She slashed at it. Her dagger glanced off the wide collar,
sinking into its shoulder. She twisted the blade, jerking it free.
Yowling, the wolf turned to rend the hand that held the
blade. Chimquar's dagger plunged and ripped. The wolf no
longer moved. She shifted the dagger to her left hand, fighting the pain in that limb. Chimquar drew her sword and
stood, facing the wolves. They circled her warily while others
bayed the stallion; she and Adoni had taken toll of them.
One charged. She stepped aside, her Sharan longsword raked
its ribs. A growl made her whirl, she swept her sword in a
low arc. The second wolf dodged. Then the first one, ribs
bleeding came about with its companion. Chimquar impaled
one, kicked the other in the head, and freed her sword before
a third attacked. A javelin impaled the fourth.

"Aroana!" Meadusea came. She and her bucking mount
fought in fierce unison, centaur-like. Her bright blade slew
and none of the wolves breached her guard. She drew them
from the stallion, and Adoni broke for his new mistress.
Chimquar caught the saddle and swung up. Meadusea saw
her and turned, racing after their fleeing companions. The
wolves regrouped to pursue when a high, eerie wail rose behind them. They melted into the grass, returning to their master.

Katalla rode rear guard to the youth and his sister—a sign
to Chimquar that her prejudices did not usurp her Hautaren
honor.

Chimquar fumbled with the saddle bags to free them, then
dragged them across her lap, feeling inside for cloth to bind
her arm. Her hand closed upon a horn, then the cloth.

"You're hurt." Meadusea dropped back to ride beside her.

"I've taken worse," Chimquar replied brusquely, working one-handed.

"Rein in. I'll help."

"Nay." Chimquar shrugged off her concern and finished. She reached into the saddlebag, bringing out Tamlys' horn. The Sharans should have mounted guards on the outer perimeters of their encampment. She fingered the horn. Its call would carry a good distance on the open plains.

"They will be back?" Katalla asked as Meadusea and Chimquar reached her.

"Yes." Chimquar gazed at the northern horizon, her eyes hard and distant. "Their master with them—and Bakran." A Euzadi curse rolled off her tongue. Hazier glanced back. Makajia's color deepened. Neither offered to interpret for the Sharans.

"Bakran?" A curious expression crossed Meadusea's broad strong-boned face.

Chimquar started to answer when Katalla interrupted savagely. "You know them?"

"I know them." Chimquar's words emerged taut. Her knees pressed the stallion's sides. She moved past Katalla and Hazier. "Let the horses breathe."

"You know them?" Katalla came alongside Chimquar.

"Bakran is my enemy," she answered harshly. "That is a tale I do not wish to tell." *Bakran has burned too many villages—slain too many people. . . .* A fair-skinned face came to mind. Chimquar fought remembering, her face twisting.

"That isn't enough."

"Don't push me!" Dark, violent power blazed in Chimquar's eyes.

Katalla dropped her eyes, unable to meet that power, but she had recognized its nature. "You're part Sharan! A half-breed!"

"I said, I am not Euzadi born." Chimquar's voice softened strangely. "Now drop back beside Makajia."

Katalla frowned, but obeyed.

Chimquar felt tense and uneasy. If Katalla thought further she would realize there were no Sharan or half-Sharan men Chimquar's age. Only a flourishing slave trade had kept large numbers of men in Shaurone during the time when the Waejontori curse prevented the birth of sons to Sharan women. The numerous men in the household of Chimquar's mother had not been Sharan. Chimquar hoped Katalla would not recall all aspects of the curse which had ended several years before her birth.

Chimquar counted on the hours it would take the Nakesht to recover his precious collars. Night would come, bringing the full moon, Tala Who Loves Earth: the full light of She Who Holds Back Darkness would deter the Nakesht from battle as the distant, disinterested sun did not.

She kept her companions moving all night, alternating the pace to spare the horses. Chimquar held herself apart, avoiding Katalla's questions and provocations. They diminished the distance to Anaria's camp enough to halt at dawn.

"Makajia," Chimquar called, dismounting. She led her stallion farther from her companions.

The girl came, leading her black filly. She held her head high, but her dark eyes were dull with weariness.

Chimquar caressed Makajia's head. "You've not ridden so long and hard before." Makajia smiled shyly. Chimquar still wondered how the girl could be so bold and wild one moment, and so shy and quiet the next. Chimquar bent to look her in the eye. She had tried not to make the girl an outsider among the Euzadi as she had Hazier. Chimquar knew she had caused Hazier's life to be more difficult than it should have been. He was her pride, but Makajia was her jewel. The warrior straightened, swinging Makajia up. She giggled, threw her arms around Chimquar's neck and pressed a kiss on her cheek. Chimquar held her briefly, fiercely as though to press all the love of many years into that embrace, then set her down and stood back. She took the horn from the saddle bag and slipped the strap over Makajia's head. "I have something for you to do, little one."

"I can do anything!" Makajia asserted proudly.

Chimquar pulled off the saddle and pack from the stallion. "It's half a day's ride to the ruins, Makajia. We can hold off the Nakesht and Bakran there." Chimquar took her crest ring from her pouch, pressing it into the girl's hands. "You know where I have said Anaria's camp is?" Makajia nodded. "Give that to her. Blow Sharan calls all the way, Makajia. They will come to you." Chimquar lifted the girl onto the stallion's bare back. Every ounce of extra weight gone, Adoni could probably outrun the wind spirits. She put the reins in Makajia's hands. "Adoni! Davan, Adoni! Volasyar!" Chimquar cried in Sharan. The stallion leaped away, running like dark flame before a gale. One person whom Chimquar loved would survive her—at least. Chimquar smiled slowly. She picked up the saddlebags and threw them across Makajia's filly.

"What have you done?" Katalla demanded, rage coloring her voice. "Are you mad?"

"She will reach Anaria." Chimquar was grim.

"She bears no arms!"

"She's no warrior!" Chimquar growled back, looking up from the saddle. "But nothing can catch her."

"They'll tear her to pieces! You know the ways! Why didn't you teach her the ways!"

"What goes here?" Meadusea joined them, watching the fading figure of Makajia. It was already too late to overtake the girl.

"The half-breed has sent the girl to Anaria—weaponless! Those creatures will tear her apart!" Katalla's face was a dark mask of rage.

"Half-breed?" Meadusea pulled that out, staring curiously at Chimquar. "You mean Sharan, Katalla?"

"Yes!" the woman snapped.

Chimquar stood still under Meadusea's scrutiny. "Sharan sword, words, and some ways. There are no Sharan men your age."

"None?" Katalla gasped, eyes wide, then loathing twisted her features. "Goddess Damned, skin-changing wolf-bitch!"

A tremor of rage ran through Chimquar. The back of her fist bloodied Katalla's mouth the same instant her left foot snapped into the young Sharan's stomach. Katalla landed in the dirt, sobbing for breath. She rolled on hr side, drawing her dagger. Meadusea placed her foot firmly on Katalla's arm. A glance passed between them and Katalla sheathed the blade. Chimquar left, leading the filly apart.

"What is your name?" Meadusea asked gently, following her.

Chimquar glanced up sharply. "That's none of your concern."

"It is hard in these Lands."

"You think it is hard now?" Chimquar murmured, her voice rough. "I was first in these Lands. First!"

"The way you reared the girl—"

"Is none of your concern!" Chimquar snarled. "On that stallion she is safe. She can out ride the Wind-Lady."

Meadusea shook her head. "I want to understand you. But
the way you have reared the girl to be so—"

"Don't say it!" Chimquar's voice rose in warning. "Should
I have made her an outcast in her own land? None knows
better than I what it means to be outcast. You don't want to
*under*stand—you want to excuse!" Chimquar mounted and
moved away. Hazier joined her, but kept his questions to
himself.

Mid-morning the wolves returned, pacing them, their cries
keeping the horses and riders tense. The Sharans held a javelin ready, shields rested on their left arms. Chimquar
searched the grasses with her eyes, her ears anticipating the
cries of the Nakesht Master and Bakran's men. Chimquar
mused grimly, *It is odd Bakran has not attacked. Some aspect
of his deal with the Nakesht must be holding him back. He
must want my head badly.*

The roofless hull of a stone house rose in the distance, the
south wall gone completely, the east side a sloping fragment.
Chimquar kicked the filly into a canter, then a full gallop.
Hazier sprang forward with her. Meadusea and Katalla came
a few strides behind. The sudden full flight triggered the ac-
tions of their pursuers. A high human wail sounded. The
wolves answered and came leaping at the heels of the racing
horses. Chimquar drew her sword. The wolves avoided her
blows, concentrating on her horse.

Six beasts splintered from the pack, out-stripping the horses
to gain the ground ahead of them and turn, teeth bared, to
halt the flight. Chimquar's filly plunged into the middle of
them. A wolf fixed its teeth in the filly's throat. Chimquar
leaned out to cut it away. The filly stumbled and fell, ham-
strung. Chimquar sprang free a moment before the beast
swarmed over the hapless horse, landed wrong and stumbled,
falling. She lost her grip on the sword and it lay a yard off.
She stretched her hand to reach it and a wolf landed on her.
Chimquar dug her right hand into the folds of skin around its
throat, twisting hard. Her left hand got the dagger from her
boot top and with it opened the beast's belly. It was a naked,
gutted man with golden collar she saw dead. Another wolf
charged. Chimquar flung herself out of its path, her hand
closing on her sword. She rolled over, the steel blade flashing
in the morning sun. The wolf dodged neatly and came back.
Chimquar gained her feet and impaled the lunging beast.

"Heads up!" Meadusea extended her empty sword hand to Chimquar. Chimquar took the hand and sprang up behind the warrior. Meadusea's gelding covered the last yards swiftly, jumping a small pile of tumbled stone to enter the ruined dwelling.

Chimquar leaped down, turning to face the wolves with steel. The cries of their master rose and once more the wolves held back. Then Hazier and Katalla reached the dubious fortress.

A line of horsemen drew up twenty spear-lengths from the ruins. One man sat at their head, his huge body muscled to grotesqueness. A bright, crimson scarf made a headband holding his black mane from his face. He rode out a few yards and shouted, "Chimquar! Surrender and the others go free."

"Lies, Bakran!" *I know you too well.* "You've already promised them to the Nakesht!"

A gaunt figure rose at Bakran's feet. His horse shied. Wolves gathered about their Master. Bakran's horse reared. He cursed, struggling with it, then brought it back to the Nakesht.

The Master raised one hand and dropped it. The wolves surged forward and their Master ran among them, crying them on. The renegades followed.

Meadusea and Katalla took the empty expanse where the south wall had stood. Chimquar dropped back along the east wall fragments. Some would come that way and, on foot, she would have a better chance there. Hazier wavered in the middle. Chimquar gestured sharply at the Sharans. The youth went to their side as the men struck.

The wolves circled the ruins with their master. Chimquar listened to the cries of the battle, scant spear-lengths from her as she watched the wolves. Her instincts were to aid her companions, yet she waited, knowing the Nakesht would come. She had to hold the rear when they came. An image of Makajia on the tall stallion, her neck pressed against his neck, his pale mane whipping around her narrow face came into Chimquar's mind. Then the first wolf came over the wall. She sprang before it, her sword impaling it in mid-leap. Another attacked as she kicked her blade free. Her dagger grazed its ribs and it turned, coming again. The day-old wound throbbed and hurt, slowing her dagger hand. Teeth closed on that arm, tearing the wound further. Chimquar

cried out in pain and anger, bringing her sword blade down
on the beast's back. It writhed, snapping in bloody circles on
the ground. Two more danced around her. Chimquar feinted
at one, then pivoted to meet the charge of its mate. The wolf
dodged too slowly and died. It was easy telling which wolves
were truly dead, for even in their death throes they had
turned to men. It was like fighting in an illusion or a dream,
slaying beasts but felling men, but Chimquar had no moment
to consider the eeriness of the battle.

Teeth raked her calf. Chimquar twisted, landing a sword
blow on the wolf's head. She whirled back, kicking and striking with sword and dagger. The battle became a blur, she
ceased to think, reacting by reflex. She moved and fought in
a sea of teeth that threatened to overwhelm her. Some wolves
got past her. Only the death of their master could stop them.

The hollow, whistling laughter of the Nakesht Master drew
Chimquar. She glimpsed him half a spear-length beyond the
wall watching. Anger and desperation became a hot, screaming rage within her. All the long bottled and controlled energies became a violent strength. She broke from the wolves,
vaulting a low piece of wall. "Aroana Goddess! Goddess!"

The Master's note changed. He retreated. His wolves drew
together, swarming over the warrior, clinging to her like ticks.
Chimquar cut them away, the force of her rage making her
oblivious to her wounds. The Nakesht retreated again, waving
his arms and crying in his strange, whistling tongue. Bakran
appeared, stepping into Chimquar's path.

"You're a dead man, Chimquar!" He said coldly.

"Man?" Chimquar paused, laughing crazily. "I'm woman!"

An incredulous expression entered Bakran's face.
Chimquar rushed him, her blade dancing swift and hard
about him. He dodged, gave ground. Chimquar moved after
him, breathing raggedly, her strength faltering. Bakran's
sword left a bloody furrow across her ribs. She brought her
longer weapon down biting into his arm. Bakran lost hand
and weapon. Chimquar left her sword standing in his stomach. She lurched toward the retreating Nakesht, her sword
arm pressed against her ribs. Her rage-born strength drained
away as her pain overtook her. She staggered, went to her
knees, then fell on her face. Her left hand lost the dagger as
she fell.

The core of her awareness fought the darkness lapping at

it. Clawed hands pulled at her, turning her over. The mate to her lost dagger slipped from its arm sheath into her hand. She thrust up into the face of the Nakesht Master. He fell dead across her.

Chimquar heard horns blowing and many Sharan voices shouting. She tried to get up, but her body would not answer her will, and she passed out.

A soft voice chanting her name and wet drops falling on her face touched Chimquar's drifting awareness, disturbing the warm, fuzzy haze enveloping the warrior. A sweet-sharp fragrance colored the air she inhaled, it cleared her head and she took a deep lungful of it. Heaven Flower so far from the Western Forests? She felt for Makajia. Her fingertips brushed the girl's tear-streaked face. Chimquar opened her eyes. The outlines of the Euzadi girl's narrow, creamed-coffee face slowly congealed.

"Chimquar!" Her chant broke off with a fresh, joyful sob. She buried her head against her guardian's chest. Chimquar stroked her head and shoulders, awkwardly, her limbs feeling stiff and weak. Chimquar murmured soft, meaningless words to Makajia, soothing, reassuring.

Light flowed in suddenly. Makajia sat up quickly. Chimquar levered herself up on her arm. Makajia snatched several pillows, shoving them to her back.

The slender figure standing in the tent's entrance lowered her lamp and limped in. She placed her lamp on a small table beside the dim candles, then moved to Chimquar and knelt.

Chimquar looked into the unchanged face of her younger sister, Anaria. After so many years among the lesser races, the imperceptibly slow aging of her long-lived race startled her.

Anaria raised a flask to her sister's lips and Chimquar drank. It filled her body with warmth, eased it, clearing the last cobwebs from her mind. *Pollonae.* "Anaria. . . ."

"Shh, Tomyris. Just listen to me." Her voice was soft, yet stern. "You and your children are coming home. I am not surprised to find you are Chimquar." Anaria waved aside Chimquar's attempt to speak. "Not all like that fact. But if you are not Hautaren enough to face them, you will be of no use to the High Priestess who sent us after you. Shaurone is growing, changing. Great deeds are in the offing." Her sternness dissolved into a child-like lostness. "Do I have to beg you again? Or will you listen this time?"

Chimquar remembered a very young girl crying, pleading, and cursing her on a moonlit wold. She could not repeat that night's decision. "I want to go home," she said, then smiled.

WOMAN OF THE WHITE WASTE

T. J. Morgan

T. J. Morgan lives in California but has an Oklahoma background. Introducing herself as one of the "weirdfolk granted a special dispensation to be Strange," she holds that, delusions of grandeur notwithstanding, she prefers "Don Williams and Merle Haggard to jazz, wears cockroach-stompers (that's cowboy boots), and ascribes to the belief that there is no finer piece of machinery on the road than a Peterbilt." She reads s-f and comic books and makes the world's finest cheese enchiladas.

Her fiction tends to the romantic, but here we have something of an exception—a tale she says forced itself to be written in all its present intensity, violence, emotion and heroism. I received many manuscript submissions dealing with the subject of rape, but felt that most of them missed the point of this anthology by the mere assumption that women have always, and will always, be confronted by this issue. It is not heartwinning to think women need be raped to metamorphose from victim to warrior. What is heartwarming is to know women will fight if we continue to be raped.

T. J. Morgan has brought us a heartwinning story.

There are those who say she was born in a rude stone hovel little different from any other dwelling of her village. There was nothing to make her birth remarkable.

51

> Others swear that her mother,
> caught far from shelter upon
> the White Waste, bore a child in
> the snow whose coming was watched
> over by six white she-bears.

She ran—a pale shadow against the stark white land. The screaming and the drunken curses faded behind. Then the only sounds were her own ragged breathing and the crunch of crusted snow beneath her bare feet. When at last she stopped, she was well beyond the village. Before her, spread out like a vast ermine blanket, the White Waste stared silently back. Its winter face was ages old and unchanging in all that time. Ellide blinked against the icy sheen. Tears froze in silver streaks down her pale, wind-flushed cheeks. The still, dry cold that had been little felt as she ran now, suddenly, bit deep.

The Yarl had struck at dusk. Four hundred bearded warriors little different outwardly from Ellide's own people. What followed was no more a true battle than fox fighting wolf. Inside a slender hour, those who opposed the invaders lay dead. Those who had not come forth—the women, the old, the very young, and some men who thought life a more precious commodity than pride—were pressed into whatever service suited their new masters.

Unbidden, that scene came back to her. Though the cold had frosted her hair to her head in brittle strands, and her skin was white with rime, her cheeks burned crimson warm. Like so many beast prodded together for inspection, she and a dozen or more other young women had huddled in the great hall, scrutinized with ill-concealed lust. Her group was picked over by the Yarl officers in their turn, until only Ellide remained, large gray eyes and white hair giving her the look of a frightened snow fox.

It was no new experience, being passed over. She was not sure whether she should be grateful, or distressed. She stood alone, shivering in her rough woolen tunic. The Yarl commander frowned. He was like the ones he led, little older, clearly no wiser; but an alien blood ran in his veins, marking him with a darkness of hair, a narrowness of eye, that was foreign even to the Yarl—and malignant. He watched her, silently, and she knew fear.

"It's a hell of a night and the men will have little enough to keep them roused. Give this one to them. By now I imagine they'll be too drunk to notice how ugly she is!"

Throaty laughter followed, was picked up and borne along by the others. Ellide was too stunned to hear.

She remembered pain. More pain than she thought it possible to endure. Odors: grimed men, sour wine, blood—her own and theirs. There were thirty of them; the Yarl's finest had lodged in the great hall, where they might be called on moment's notice. When the last of them had finished with her, had wandered off and collapsed too drunk to find his pallet, Ellide crawled into the darkness of a corner and retched.

It seemed an eternity ago that she had silently fled the village, unnoticed by the sentries who dismissed her furtive figure as a trick of the shadows. But the memory was enough to double her over in new paroxysms of sickness. When the dry heaving ceased and she had rubbed blinding, salty grit from her eyes, she became aware of the change wrought across the waste.

Beginning as a far off, indistinct cry, low and morose, the sound grew into a caterwauling cadence. Rushing across the ice fields, that terrible wind drove before it white flurries— and the first stinging bite of that glaring, shrieking gale cleared her mind of all else.

She turned to find the trees she had passed in her flight— but where there had been a forest of thick-limbed pines sagging under their burden of snow, now there was only swirling, sinuous white. Dull, dazed apathy gave way to panic. She took a handful of foot-biting steps in what felt the right direction. She faltered. Not thinking then, trying not to feel the cold that was killing her by creeping degrees, she ran, her breath a frozen vapor streaming behind.

How long or how far she ran, stumbling, falling, rising to run again, she didn't know. There was no reckoning time or distance within the embrace of the storm. She knew only that she was tired, so terribly tired; and where she had been cold before, unnatural warmth now pervaded her limbs and crept up around her breast. Her senses dulled until she could not be certain whether or not she still moved. Her brother had died in this way, lulled by the false peace the eternal cold granted as a final boon to those lost in the freezing waste. She remembered when they found him, his stiff frozen face layered over with a sheet of blue ice. He had died smiling, uncaring and unknowing.

As easy as it would be, Ellide did not want to die.

Without warning her knees buckled, toppling her into a thigh-deep drift of new snow. The warmth was something she could no longer ignore. She sat without moving, restful within the illusory secret silence of its comfort. Thinking was difficult, but she knew she was dying. Her lips formed silent words; she spoke the oldest prayer.

A woman's prayer, it was a final entreaty to the Spirit of the White Waste—She who had guarded the snowfields since before the time of the men and their gods. Though she died, Ellide no longer cared. There had been little in the village she loved before the raiders came. Now there was nothing. Those who were left caused her no regrets, for she had ever been set apart from them in one way or another. There was no man for her to mourn, no family for whom to shed tears—only a memory so painful, so bitter, that death seemed less a doom than a kindly release.

Abruptly she awoke. She did not want to open her eyes to face the blazing halls of the afterlife—but curiosity burned as strongly as fear. She blinked warily, gained her feet, and gazed around.

The storm still whipped the waste into frothy ethereal spires and mammoth, illusive mountains. But she was set apart, sheltered somehow even in its midst. She felt the wind as no more than a furry softness on her face and body. There was neither sensation of warmth, nor cold. Dull apprehension filled her somber eyes when she looked to where she expected to find her own frozen body, but the emotion gave way to stricken wonder when she saw only the compressed outline of where she had lain.

I'm alive, she thought, but a part of her rejected that as impossible. She blinked, strained to see past the walls of close-set ivory furling around her.

Something moved—something even whiter than the snow, and taller by heads than any man who had ever walked. A scream died in her throat as the shadow coalesced.

Rearing upright on two massive hind legs, the gossamer white of its fur rippling like a field of wind-blown wheat, a snow bear stood with its head lifted to the gale. If it was aware of her presence it gave no sign. Its dark nostrils flared and the black rimmed lips parted to reveal long ivory tusks. It snuffled softly. The slab of pink that was its tongue curled nearly double in a great yawn, as if the creature had been roused from long slumber. Then, as though remembering something, it turned and caught her in a cool, unblinking stare.

Those eyes were large, fearless. Within their purple-flecked brown depths coursed a wisdom as ancient and unfathomable as the icy green waters of the sea. Held by those eyes, Ellide could not move, could barely breath. Doubts raced like fleeing hares across the plains of her mind, but there was no place to hide, no haven where those searching eyes did not follow.

Suddenly and without knowing how she came by the knowledge, without understanding the why of it, she knew what was reared in silent majesty before her. Confused, she shook her head, made a move to back away, then crumpled to her knees in the snow, hands clasped and held before.

For as long as she could remember her people had spoken of this One, though faith in Her was fading with each generation, with each new god the men discovered and brought home from their travels. With little else to console her, Ellide had always clung to childhood beliefs with grim and stubborn tenacity, learning covertly the old prayers which others thought to be no more than odd, ancient ballads.

She did not know why this One had left Her great cave in the heart of the White Waste, but she was here. Intangible fingers probed her mind, touching her soul, her heart, in the passing. The sensation was as quickly gone. The bear-shape dropped to all fours, shaking its milk-white ruff so that sparkles of ice dazzled her eyes. Whether it disappeared then or simply backed out of sight into the storm she didn't know—but it was gone when her eyes had cleared. She was alone.

The winds died then as if a giant paw had swept the storm from the waste. For a long time snow scurried around in settling. A mile or so behind, she could see the dark line of the forest. Beyond these, a sky was streaked by curling wisps of gray smoke from village hearths. As ever, the snowfield was unchanged, but something caught her attention and drew her gaze to the ground.

A sword, whose blade might have been carved from living ice, with a hilt like milk-white first snow, threw back rays of

rainbow light. Beside this lay a mail tunic, aglisten with icicle
radiance as it caught the streamers of sunlight struggling
through the clouds. Both set her eyes to watering with their
brilliance, so that she stared askance, torn between fear-
tinged amazement and a hungry yearning to touch. She could
not explain that wanting—but when she reached out, let her
fingers curl around the sword hilt, a shock of warmth shot up
her arm. Confusion drew her solemn face into a troubled,
puzzled mask, and somewhere inside her a voice spoke from
a distant, dreaming cavern.

"The Cold Blade is yours, child-who-loves-me-and-remem-
bers. My gift to you."

Ellide shuddered, her fingers tracing a pattern down the
length of the weapon.

"To what end, Mother? I'm no fighter! I'm just a woman."

Soft and distant laughter answered her.

"*Just? Y*ou have much to learn, child, before you join me!
Rest easy, and do what you must. Do what you must."

"I cannot fight the Yarl!" she cried. "I am one person!
They are legion!"

"Are they more than the Snows-my-Sisters? Do you
remember my Promise?"

Ellide struggled to her feet, still holding the slender icicle
of a sword.

"Even if I could fight them, even if there were some magic
to be called forth as the old prayers say—why should I help
them! There is no great love between me and my 'people.'
Let the Yarl kill them all! I won't shed a tear." She took an
angry swipe at a snowbank, marveled briefly that she could
swing the blade at all.

"As you will, child. I cannot force your feet onto a path
not your choosing. But know this: there is a coldness within
your heart that will never leave you save when the last of the
Yarl has died. It will haunt you like an early-morning chill.
Your soul will not rest easy until it is done. Carry that burden not of your choosing—or free yourself. As you will."

She gripped the sword hilt until her knuckles very nearly
matched its whiteness. At last she nodded, drawing a long,
unsteady breath.

"I'll go back," she whispered—but, noticing anew her
bareness, made a sound of dismay. It was answered by the
same young-old laughter.

"Clothe yourself child. The cold will not always be at bay."

"In what?" she pleaded.

She found herself staring at a patch of snow without being able to focus on it clearly. It shimmered and faded, moving restlessly until she knelt, reached out, and felt not snow but fur beneath her fingers. Drawn away from the surrounding whiteness, it became a tunic—and in their turn she retrieved from the snows: white, hide-like breeches and furry white boots.

The voice was gone. She felt empty of the goddess' presence as she dressed in the pristine snow-garments. They felt to the touch like fox fur. She took up the ice-mail overcoat and started back to her village.

No one of those who occupied the great hall recognized the snow white apparition with the somber gray eyes who had shoved open the double oak doors and strode forth. This creature in fox fur and mail took the light from the massive hearth and shot it back in all directions, in every conceivable color. The vision commanded notice, but struck no chord of recollection in those wine-befuddled minds. To a man they would have laughed heartily had anyone suggested she was the same child they had violated, humiliated, and used up so completely.

Curiosity was not a strong Yarl trait, but those who saw her paused in their drinking, their "love-making," to stare in puzzlement. A harsh jeer greeted the drawing of the Cold Blade and the Yarl commander grinned back at his officers as he rose to go forward.

"Put that toy down, girl, before I take it from you!" He grunted wearily, amused but tired.

"You may take it," she said. "If you can." These words brought whooping laughter from the men. Ellide remained coldly composed.

Still chuckling to himself, he drew his heavy broadsword and with unexpected speed feinted in at her. If he expected her to drop the peculiar sword and flee he was disappointed. She met his strike with a parrying blow, batting aside the blue steel with something that was clearly not metal and looked so fragile it should have shattered with the impact. Instead, it rang like bells heard across the snow, and was whipped aside to flash forward again. Two layers of heavy leather parted beneath the tooth. Where it touched, a red weal formed on the Yarl commander's stomach. The wound turned frost-bitten white. Ellide stood back, silent and without compassion.

Something akin to anger replaced the Yarl's scorn, something that came shatteringly close to fear. He touched a gloved finger to the ice-rimmed wound and his tongue traced the dryness from his lips. Without a sound he attacked.

He fought as he would man to man, but the fox-lithe figure was never where he thought her to be. Always behind, or beside, she avoided his sword with sinuous, wraithlike ease—never missing an opportunity to jab him lightly in her passing. That she never struck a blow that would do any true harm unsettled him all the more. He noted with growing distress that wherever that slender blade scored him the flesh grew numb.

There was no more laughter within the hall. The drunken glaze had left the soldiers' eyes. They shoved their unwilling paramours off their laps, untangled themselves from legs, arms, mouths and strewn clothing to sit up and watch. They saw their commander swing again, saw the fox-white figure glide away. Saw the ice brand thrust up, settle between his lower ribs and jerk forward. It did not find his heart, nor had it been intended to.

She did not immediately withdraw the blade. The bearded warrior felt the cold begin its swift travel, numbing his limbs so that the great black-gray broadsword dropped from his frozen fingers. Cold fire burned his insides and he screamed, continued to scream until blue-white rime frosted him like a sheet of ice on water. Then he toppled forward on stiff legs, lips curled back in a silenced, frozen cry. Ellide pulled the blade free and turned to regard the others.

They were slack-jawed and sober, not yet certain whether they had seen truth or illusion. The dead man began to thaw, slowly, and blood oozed icily from the wound to spread across the flagstone floor. They surged up off couches and wooden benches, tossing beaten goblets away with the same indifference with which they had discarded the women. Swords were drawn from sheaths.

Ellide danced away, streaked down the shining stone steps, laughing over her shoulder as she fled the great hall to flit across the snow in the village plaza. They followed, shouting obscenities at the gossamer figure who loped easily out of reach, taunting them, beckoning with seductive gestures that inflamed them even in their bloodlust. From the hall, from the many places the Yarl had commandeered for their use, they followed, heeding the cries of their fellows to take up the chase.

So far ahead that their howling was but a murmur tossed to her by the wind, Ellide stopped where the pasture met the forest rim. As one touching a dearly loved friend she stroked the Cold Blade, pensive, then sheathed it at her hip. A cursory glance told her the men were still coming. She crouched in the snow, let the feathery drifts caress her. She began to sing—and if any from her village had been there to hear that whispered song, they might have known it for what it was. They might shrug and say it was only an old ballad that had been a prayer once, long, long ago—a prayer used to invoke the keeping of a timeless Promise from the Goddess of the White Waste.

Ellide sang the last words as the Yarl began the slow crossing of the nubby pasture. Her dreamy eyes opened wider. She waited patiently, silver moonlight casting her features in platinum. Around her, tiny winds began to stir, their minute breaths touching the immobile woman as she crouched. They darted away across the packed snow—and where they ran, small flurries of alabaster snowdust shot up, rode the currents, and followed.

In the center of that wide sheet of argent smoothness the Yarl paused. They could see snaky streamers of hurled snow rushing toward them, but could not judge whether or not it was more than what it appeared. It seemed nothing of consequence, so they pushed on, though unaccustomed to the cold and doubting the wisdom of the chase. And, like so many streams of breath, the snows fanned out, circled the men in a rapidly closing net of cold.

The Yarl realized their danger, though it took no form they were prepared to meet, or even understand. Steel slid from leathern sheaths, pointlessly: there was nothing before them capable of being killed. Nevertheless they lashed out at the intangible enemy, quickly finding steel ineffective against a foe that could not be cut nor made to bleed.

Ellide watched, fascinated even in her revulsion. Snakes of white clasped arms, legs, throats. The men fell. None of that lofty number left the pasture.

When they were finished there, the ghost snakes whisked off on the wind, down into the village itself.

Ellide rose, listened. The snow moved into the village,

seeking out those of the Yarl too drunk to have heard the cry
to battle. She heard the screaming freeze on the air, caught
like a fish in ice and preserved. When the village was silent
again she drew a deep, heaving breath and went down across
the pasture to the hall.

Light still blazed within the warmth of that silent building.
What it revealed was a tomb. Where once living men had
swaggered, cursed, spilled wine, caroused, sang . . . the dead
now ruled. They were ice-sculpture perfections, frosted and
splendid in death as they had never been in life.

Hesitant footsteps behind brought her around, reaching for
the Cold Blade. But only a handful of her own people stood
watching her with sad, curious eyes. Some, a very few,
thought they noticed a glimmer of resemblance between this
snow woman and one they had called "ugly Ellide," but most
were as puzzled as the Yarl had been.

These are my people, she thought, but no longer felt the
need to hide herself away from their eyes. The old dread of
humiliation was gone, and what remained was contempt. She
remembered what had been. She recalled every slight, each
hurting jeer—and walked past them, unspeaking, out into the
snow.

It was sharp and bright and silver clad, her land—and for
a long time she stood gazing up at the moon. The spray of
stars visible through the dissipating clouds were mute, poor
witnesses. She could not shake the feeling, the great emptiness within her that seemed a greater pain than the scorn
she had always known. It clung to her like a leaden cloak as
she walked, away from the hall, the light, away from all that
had once claimed her.

She left at dawn and only the mercurial clouds were
witness to her leaving.

THE DEATH OF AUGUSTA

Emily Brontë

Edited by Joanna Russ

This book owes a lot of its energy to Joanna Russ, who helped me find stories, resources, contributed ideas and sparked ideas of my own. Readers may not realize the months of thought and labor that go on behind the scenes to bring about a single anthology—it's not a simple matter of stapling a dozen manuscripts together. A lot of people contribute in a hundred fashions, but none so wholeheartedly as Joanna. It's not possible to extend enough thanks.

Among Joanna's previous works that would especially interest readers of amazon-related fantasy and s-f are: Picnic on Paradise, first published by Ace and reprinted along with other tales with the same woman hero in Alyx *by Gregg Press; the virtual classic of feminist science fiction,* The Female Man *from Bantam; Berkley Press'* The Two of Them; *and a wonderful children's fantasy (for children like us),* Kittatiny, A Tale of Magic *from Daughters, Inc. Despite being confined to bed at the time with an ailing back, unable to use a typewriter (which lack slows down a writer tremendously), Joanna yet made time to bring together, edit, and annotate a piece of Emily Brontë's less known work,* Gondal's Queen.

Constricted by the bonds of the Victorian world, the Brontës escaped into wonderful fantasy worlds with elaborate schema. Emily clung to her fantasies with the greater tenacity—but we needn't pity her that. Instead, it is for us, today, to build credence for those fantasies, to make them real. Emily Jane Brontë, too, is part of our amazon heritage.

Wuthering Heights was not the only novel Emily Brontë wrote.

As children, the Brontës invented imaginary countries: Charlotte and Branwell the country of Angria, set in Africa, Emily and Anne, four kingdoms which together made an island in the North Pacific: Gondal, cold, mountainous, rugged, full of lakes, forests, and rocky heath. While the most important character in Charlotte's Angria was the moody, Byronic Duke of Zamorna (ruiner of maidens and the author's erotic delight), the central figure of Emily's Gondal was a woman: Augusta Geraldine Almeda (sometimes called Rosina of Alcona), royal, passionately ambitious, strong, beautiful, and eventually Queen of Gondal.

Born in the Royal Palace of Alcona (one of the four kingdoms of Gondal) Augusta was early sent to the Southern College, or Palace of Instruction, a coeducational university for aristocratic youth. Here she began her adventures (one of which resulted in imprisonment) and her many love affairs—as well as her high-handed habit of exiling or imprisoning lovers of whom she grew tired. Joining her political and military strength with that of Prince Julius of Angora (the one real love of her life) the ambitious Augusta became with him—by conquest and treachery—co-ruler of all Gondal. But civil war ensued; Julius was killed and Augusta, waking from weeks of near-fatal illness, fled in disguise in the depth of winter. So extreme was her peril and so intense her drive for survival that she abandoned her infant daughter to death by exposure in the snow. Returning years later, she conquered Gondal and became its sole monarch. But soon after, wandering on the moors, attended only by Lord Lesley and Fair Surry—lovers absorbed in each other—her enemies found her.

Years before the Queen had exiled one of her lovers, Lord Alfred, together with his daughter, Angelica, a heart-starved little girl who had loved the Queen and never forgiven Augusta's cruelty to herself and her first lover, Amedeus, likewise banished. In the passage that follows, Angelica has returned secretly to Gondal, with her foster-brother Douglas, a fellow-member of a band of outlaws, and here, at the climax of the epic, she plots revenge:

Were they shepherds who sat all day
On that brown mountain-side?
But neither staff nor dog had they,
Nor woolly flock to guide.

They were clothed in savage attire;
Their looks were dark and long;
At each belt a weapon dire,
Like bandit-knife, was hung.

The two rehearse their bitterness, he "tortured by men and laws," and she, remembering her former love for Augusta:

"My soul dwelt with her day and night:
She was my all-suffing light,
My childhood's mate, my girlhood's guide
My only blessing, only pride."

She continues:

"Now hear me: in these regions wild
I saw to-day my enemy,
Unarmed, as helpless as a child
She slumbered on a sunny lea.
Two friends—no other guard had she,
And they were wandering on the braes
And chasing in regardless glee
The wild goat o'er his dangerous ways.
My hand was raised—my knife was bare;
With stealthy tread I stole along;
But a wild bird sprang from his hidden lair
And woke her with a sudden song.
Yet moved she not: she only raised
Her lids and on the bright sun gazed,
And uttered such a dreary sigh
I thought just then she should not die
Since living was such misery.
Now, Douglas, for our hunted band—
For future joy and former woe—
Assist me with thy heart and hand
To send to hell my mortal foe.
Her friends fall first, that she may drain
A deeper cup of bitterer pain.

> Yonder they stand and watch the waves
> Dash in among the echoing caves—
> Their farewell sight of earth and sea!
> Come, Douglas, rise and go with me."

Angelica and Douglas succeed in killing the lovers; they then turn to the Queen:

> They wait not long; the rustling heath
> Betrays their royal foe;
> With hurried steps and panting breath
> And cheek almost as white as death,
> Augusta sprang below—
>
> Yet marked she not where Douglas lay;
> She only saw the well—
> The tiny fountain, churning spray
> Within its mossy cell.
>
> "Oh, I have wrongs to pay," she cried,
> "Give life, give vigour now!"
> And stooping by the water's side,
> She drank its crystal flow.
>
> And brightly, with that draught, came back
> The glory of her matchless eye,
> As, glancing o'er the moorland track,
> She shook her head impatiently. . . .
>
> She turns—she meets the Murderer's gaze;
> Her own is scorched with sudden blaze—
> The blood streams down her brow;
> The blood streams through her coal-black hair—
> She strikes it off with little care;
> She scarcely feels it flow;
> For she has marked and known him too
> And his own heart's ensanguined dew
> Must slake her vengeance now!

And then? Possibly both die and Angelica flees; possibly Lord Eldred, Captain of the Queen's Guard, comes with his followers upon the Queen's body lying alone on the heath:

Long he gazed and held his breath,
Kneeling on the blood-stained heath;
Long he gazed those lids beneath
Looking into Death! . . .

But earth was bathed in other gore:
There were crimson drops across the moor;
And Lord Eldred, glancing round,
Saw those tokens on the ground:

"Bring him back!" he hoarsely said;
"Wounded is the traitor fled;
Vengeance may hold but minutes brief,
And you have all your lives of grief."

Left alone with the body, Lord Eldred remembers Augusta's tumultuous career:

"Wild morn," he thought, "and doubtful noon;
But yet it was a glorious sun,
Though comet-like its course was run.
That sun should never have been given
To burn and dazzle in the heaven,
Or night has quenched it all too soon!

"And art thou gone, with all thy pride;
Thou, so adored, so deified! . . .
But Gondal's foes shall not complain
That thy dear blood was poured in vain!"

Then—mystery. For the prose saga of Gondal is lost forever—thousands of words which Emily and Anne Brontë wrote and mention in their letters and journals. Only fragments remain. Emily Brontë continued to write Gondal poems until she died. If you take Fannie Ratchford's detective-story reconstruction, *Gondal's Queen*[1] in one hand and *The Complete Poems of Emily Brontë*[2] in the other and begin to read the poems in the order in which Ratchford

1. Fannie E. Ratchford, *Gondal's Queen, A Novel in Verse by Emily Jane Brontë*, University of Texas Press, Austin, 1955.
2. *The Complete Poems of Emily Jane Brontë*, ed. Clement Shorter, notes and bibliography by C. W. Hatfield. Hodder and Stoughton, Ltd., London, 1923.

reconstructs them, a shadowy glory begins to rise: Augusta Geraldine Almeda, kept sane in prison by the sight of a wreath of snow, the roofless and desolate chamber of Elbë Hall after the civil war, "Home of the departed, the long-departed dead," Zalona's white steeples glowing in the sun before its capture, the lake of Werna reflecting the mourning star on the cold winter morning of Augusta's birth "cold, clear, and blue," Mary Gleneden thinking of mariners returning from the South Pacific island of Ula (her "tropic prairies bright with flowers") to the "sleet and frozen gloom" of Gondal and yet knowing that as they approach their native land, they feel what we also come to feel about the grim northern Gondal:

> What flower in Ula's garden sweet
> Is worth one flake of snow?

MORRIEN'S BITCH

Janet Fox

*Weaving is an ancient, women's art, handed down by
the original Fates who spun the stories of every human
life into their tapestry of Time; when they snipped a
thread, a life ended. In a latter incarnation, they were
Sirens who wove the intestines of sailors into a rotting
mattress and their hair into a bedspread—the while la-
menting, and drawing more sailors to a doom for the
sake of promised love and old, sad stories.*

*Janet Fox is a spinner of yarns, a weaver of tales. I
was first exposed to her work in the small press, and in
newsstand magazines such as* Fantastic Tales. *Last year
she was chosen for Jerry Page's* Year's Best Horror *from*
DAW.

*Here Janet delivers a beautiful arras depicting a
woman who lives as a worm and weaves like a spider to
obtain all she desires through cleverness, wit, and superi-
ority. Its an uncommon story, and the author herself
says it scared her in the writing. I expect a wide range
of responses to this piece: some will be appalled, others
evilly delighted, and most simply captivated by Riska.
"Morrien's Bitch" is a unique hero if ever.*

The camp slept, each man rolled in his blanket like a
corpse as the fires burned down and banked themselves into
mounds of coals lit red from within. Riska crept among the
sleeping soldiers, crouching to diminish her silhouette. She
rummaged among one of the packs, her fingers deftly choosing what she wanted: two coins of a dull metal, a packet of
dried meat, a loaf of black bread, hard cheese—the kinds of

rations she had grown sick of in the past few months. There
was a hoarse shout as a passing sentry discovered her and
cried out, his alert tinged with a superstitious fear which delighted her. The men about her were stirring, sitting up,
reaching for swords and bows. She didn't panic. She shoul-
dered her swag-pouch and began to run. Though she was
soon pursued, she moved at a measured jogging pace. She
leaped from the lip of a dry riverbed, caught hold of stringy
underbrush to keep from falling all the way down. Where the
bank was steeply undercut, a tangle of brush hid an opening
like an animal's den. Into this she slid. One man saw the
brush spring back and tried to follow. He squirmed through
the opening and along a narrow burrow that ended in a wall
of root-grown earth. Puzzled, he backed out to confront the
laughter of his companions.

Not so deep in earth that she couldn't hear this laughter,
Riska paused, and smiled, her hand on the lever, then continued on down the slanting corridor now large enough for her
to walk upright. She came at last to a chamber and touched a
boss on the wall to flood the room with hazy blue light, illu-
minating the contents: a melange of richly ornate furniture
and art objects more like the collection of a pack rat than a
room for human habitation. She gnawed listlessly at the
bread and cheese, paying little attention to the wealth surrounding her.

"A ghost! My men in the field seeing ghosts?"

The aide looked properly chastened as Morrien paced the
length of the room, looking as if he'd like to drive his fist
through something solid, possibly the aide's face.

"It roams the camp, usually by night, though some claim
to have seen it skulking about early in the morning. It's nothing serious, not a threat, except that it damages morale. And
it takes things, sir."

Morrien thrust his face toward the sweating countenance
of the aide. "A ghost can't take things. What you have is a
garden variety thief."

The aide cleared his throat uncomfortably, started to say
something, then seemed to think better of it.

"What is it, man?" Morrien slapped his open palm gently
with his leather gauntlets.

"It's something they don't know how to fight. It disap-
pears."

"I'll send Dant, my Third. He'd like to make points while Kyren is off trying to squeeze some assistance out of the neighboring villages—not an errand likely to be successful, but one that's necessary for a dwindling army."

Riska became aware of the large, loud-voiced, red-faced Dant, though not by rank or name as she continued her raids on Morrien's camp. The more she saw Dant roaring and stamping his frustrated rage, the more often she scavenged through the camp, sometimes even when she had a surfeit of food piled in her home chamber. When pursued she disappeared into a burrow or crevice in the rocks, only to appear to others on the other side of the encampment.

One night she crept boldly toward Dant's tent. Stealthily she slipped inside, lulled by raucous snoring sounds. She knelt, not breathing, her thief-clever hands busy, then she sneaked out again, zigzagging to avoid patches of moonlight. As she slid toward cover she stopped long enough to give a sleeping soldier a sharp kick. His howl of pain aroused the camp and when Riska should have been running toward her exit, a shadowy cleft in the rocks, she crouched behind a tree, watching.

With a bellow Dant came pounding from his tent. Before he had fully emerged, the rope she had tied from his leg to the pole structure that supported the tent brought tent and man down together in a satisfying cursing, struggling mass. She fled for her escape hatch and slid to a stop when she saw that it was guarded. She wheeled and made a dash toward another opening she knew, but it was too far and all the camp was now alerted. She ran well, dodging and wheeling, but was caught at last, crushed down into the dirt under two or three heavy bodies. For the second time in her life she felt real fear and not just exhilaration.

Riska awoke to darkness, her limbs bent back awkwardly. As she ran her tongue across dry lips she felt the lower one split and swollen. Her captors must have been a little over-enthusiastic. Still, except for being tied, she felt strong enough to run if need be. She rubbed her head against the ground, trying to dislodge the blindfold, but made little progress. Then she lay listening, for footsteps and voices were coming.

"I had it put in my tent for the time being."

"It's human, not a spirit, believe me. Only a human would have the maliciousness to—"

Riska heard the other man laugh.

"You wouldn't find it so humorous, Kyren, if we discovered an Ultebren spy in our midst."

"Spies don't waste their time on schoolboy tricks."

Their voices were above her now and light made her eyes water as the blindfold was taken off. She recognized the red-faced Dant but not the man who was with him. He had tightly curled hair graduated in color from black to smoke to silver, and a small pointed beard. She didn't like the look of cold intelligence in his eyes.

"A spy, a spy for Amery of Ultebre! The crest, man, the crest." Riska wore a leather tabard with the crest of Ultebren royalty worked into it.

"Put him to torture. We'll have out his secrets."

Kyren's thin hand gripped her face and turned it into the lanternlight. "Ah no," he said. "Is that possible?" He jerked loose the ties on one side of the tabard and slid his hand inside. "Your spy is . . . a woman. No mistake."

Dant cursed without taking a breath for some moments.

"Where did you get the garment you wear?" Kyren demanded.

She looked down where his hand still moved lazily beneath the tabard. "Haven't you proved yet what you wanted to know?" She writhed a little as his fingers closed on a tender spot. Blinked back the pain. "I stole it. Up until four months ago I was a thief in Ultebre."

He leaned back, releasing her. "So you know a way into Ultebre's fortress, eh?"

"Then she's no real danger to us," said Dant. "We'll give her to the men. There aren't enough women here as it is and what there are resemble hags. This one is at least young, if lacking in beauty.

"And feminine graces," said Kyren. "But we haven't solved all the mysteries. When we searched the opening in the rock through which she meant to escape, we found a series of tunnels all of which led back to the entrance again. No one could escape by this, yet she has always escaped until now."

Riska struggled to sit up. "If you promise to release me, I'll show you the secret of the caverns."

Dant moved to untie her.

"No. I for one don't want to follow her into those uncertain darknesses by night. Perhaps tomorrow."

"You're afraid?" asked Dant so bluntly that Riska wondered how someone with such a loose mouth had lived long enough to rise so high. Kyren favored him with an arrogant look that he didn't half understand, though Riska understood fully and feared for him.

Morning found her totally numb in arms and legs from being bound so tightly all night. No chance to run now, but she thought eagerly of her caverns. Once in their winding darknesses, she was master and she would find a way to repay. . . . She was released and hauled to her feet—but without any feeling left in them, it was hard to stand. "I'll find a way to repay," she thought as she was cuffed and dragged to her feet again and thrust out of the tent. Dant was waiting outside and gave her a vicious look, evidently remembering that she had been the one to humiliate him.

"Do we have to go back to the caves?" she whined for his benefit. "I'm half dead with weariness, having spent most of the night showing all their secret ways, how to come and go like a ghost in the night."

"Kyren, that traitor. . . ."

"He was especially pleased that there is a hidden way into the heart of Ultebre itself so I pointed it out to him."

"He'll be off to Morrien with this news, branding me an incompetent."

"Not an incompetent, sir—fool, he said." Dant's yeasty face seemed to swell in a ferment of anger.

And at that moment Kyren appeared cool and unsuspecting. Innocent, of this at any rate.

Dant pulled his sword from its sheath with a sinister scraping sound. "Fool, is it? You dared to laugh at my misfortune this past night and you would say me ill with Morrien, *as you always have.*"

For a moment Kyren looked surprised and Riska held her breath, afraid that ophic intelligence would strike quickly to the real cause of the quarrel. But he was a fighting man, among other men, and with a sword drawn against him. He had no other choice.

The fight lasted longer than she thought it would. She began to see why Dant had gone so high. He was a headlong, dangerous fighter. However, the outcome was no different than she had expected. Kyren looked at the sprawled body

with an insolent gaze and called for a cloth to wipe his
sword. He cleaned it fastidiously, taking his time.

She shifted from foot to foot, testing. The guard still held
her by the arm, but rather loosely, his attention being grasp-
ed by the fight and now by the body of Dant. She sunk her
teeth into the soldier's hand. As he shouted, she twisted
away, but he had a better hold than she thought and she
came up hard, nearly falling.

Kyren now approached, shaking his head. She saw, with
some disquiet, that he had neglected to sheathe his sword.
"You betray yourself," he said, placing the edge hard against
her throat and pressing it, delicately. "Dant was a fool, but in
his way he was a good man and in that way, I respected him.
You thought him a tool, to be used and discarded. And you
didn't hesitate. Am I right?"

She nodded, feeling the swordedge break the skin. If she
lived, and he was fool enough to enter the caves—

He swung the weapon away, sheathed it. "You'd be dead
by now if you didn't have some secret knowledge of how to
enter Ultebre by stealth. Don't congratulate yourself. I'll have
all your knowledge by sunset, and if you're lucky, you'll have
your life. I can't promise any more than that, as you seem
somewhat stubborn."

"It isn't something I can tell. I'd have to show you. I'm
willing to go with my hands tied, blindfolded, if there's so
much to be frightened of."

"You almost convince me, but Morrien himself is on his
way; he'll be here by tomorrow. I prefer to wait for him. Tie
her tightly. If you or any other man on guard duty gets
lonely, remember that she's at your disposal."

"If this is important to you, and it seems to be, you'd do
better not to bait and anger me. I can be stubborn, and I
might manage to die without speaking.

"You take each small advantage and squeeze it dry, don't
you, advancing yourself with every turn. If I can believe my
ears now, the prisoner is setting the terms of her own captiv-
ity." She believed that he was as near to breaking out into
overt violence as he would ever come; so wisely, she fell
silent. She was pleased when she was taken to a tent and left
inside unbound. Nor must her guard have felt any loneliness
through the long afternoon.

Morrien was conducted to the prisoner's tent by an unchar-
acteristically shaken Kyren.

"This is just a girl," said Morrien. "After all you've told me, I expected an ogre, at least."

The prisoner looked up from where she sat on the ground. "Get up," shouted Kyren aiming a kick in her direction, which she avoided and rose lithely. She was not as tall as Morrien, but she was tall, long of limb and appearing to have a wiry strength unbecoming in a woman, to his way of thinking.

"I'm told you know of hidden ways into Ultebre's citadel. That you stole a garment from Amery's palace."

"I keep telling them so; and I keep offering to guide you, freely, yet all I get are threats of violence and torture." Though dark hair hung down raggedly over one eye and her mouth had a hard, sullen look to it, he could not believe all that Kyren said of her. She seemed helpless rather than ravening.

"Has she so offered?"

Kyren looked down, muttered, "Yes. But I don't trust her and you shouldn't either. I think of Dant."

"If the thing was done as you say, it was cleverly done. *I* could admire such cleverness."

The prisoner cast a triumphant glance at Kyren and warmed visibly to Morrien. He was a pleasant sight, his thick hair and beard the color of bronze, his face strongly beautiful, his heavy travel cloak adding to the width of his shoulders. "How do you come to know these warrens?"

"They're my home. My grandfather discovered their secrets and my father taught me all there is to be known of the cavernways. No one knows who built them; they were ancient in the time of my grandfather. We used them for our own purposes."

"Thievery."

"What could be more convenient? Routes of egress opening at all points in the city, out of sewers and drains, alleyways and cisterns; there are even many passageways opening inside buildings."

"Inside the palace of my cousin Amery and the dwelling of Jos'l his minister. I'd like to burst in on them at this moment as they gloat over expelling me from my rightful fiefdom. Amery acted as my friend while Jos'l subverted the army, bribing, and killing those who would not be bribed. When I escaped with what ragtag of an army I could keep about me, Amery captured Llana, my wife-to-be, tortured and killed her when he found her loyalty could not be bartered. I have a lot to *thank* those two for when we meet face to face, and perhaps now there's a chance we will."

"If you mean to kill Jos'l I'll be well satisfied. He's the one that signed the order—" her voice grew weak to inaudibility. By an effort she went on. "There were never enough women in the tunnels to satisfy the band of thieves my father had gathered, so the custom was to carry off women from Ultebre. But one managed to find her way back and a trap was laid. They caught all but me and a young apprentice thief who returned to his home in an outlying village. You know Jos'l's punishment for thievery."

"Impalement."

She bit her lip. "I watched from one of our secret egresses. I don't know why. I watched but there was nothing I could do." She shuddered and for all her efforts to control them, tears began sliding from her eyes. She turned away and wiped her face with the back of her hand as if she had done something shameful, then turned back to finish the story. "They guard many of the entrance ways now, though they can't penetrate deeply into them. Only I know all the turnings and a certain secret which I will show to your man, presently. I turned to the open country for survival, for I was alone and had no heart to return to the city."

"A sad story," said Kyren dryly, "if true. I'm willing to test the truth of this for you by various means of 'persuasion' which I know."

"I believe her," said Morrien, "and I don't think I'm overtrusting."

"If he doesn't believe it, let him accompany me into the caverns," said Riska.

Kyren hesitated. His cool intelligence said no, but pride struggled not to let himself admit that for some reason he feared to go with her. "Very well," he said grudgingly, "but I will take two of my best soldiers as well. And as you once agreed, you will be bound and blindfolded."

They entered a cleft in the rock. Blindfolded, Riska stumbled against a lichenous protrusion in the wall. Her cursing masked the low rumble of rock panels moving aside on metal tracks. "If you insist on my being blindfolded, at least see that I don't break my neck," she protested. They followed a narrow channel that had reportedly only circled back upon itself, yet this seemed straight enough. Cool air blew through the cavernways; it did not have the usual close dampness of a true cave. After a while Kyren noticed that the walls were smooth as if the builders no longer cared to camouflage the fact that these passageways seemed melted out of the rock.

"Who could have made these? Was there no clue?"

"My grandfather who discovered them said that the builders left nothing, except the result of their handiwork and the central core of the present city of Ultebre. Though sometimes I have searched these caverns for something they might have left behind."

"Perhaps as well they don't return, if they are as skilled in magic as this indicates."

They traveled for long hours through the tunnels. Kyren had no idea of where he might be when Riska cautioned him to quietness. The way led sharply upward. Riska must have done something, he wasn't sure what, because a door slid back in what looked like solid stone. Then they were climbing some winding stairs in what looked like a cellar half filled with rubble. A slot let through a spangle of outerworld light and Kyren set his eyes to it, unsure. Tall, fluted pillars held the roof up grandly and the walls rippled with lush tapestries, all worked in battle scenes in which the Ultebren crest was prominently displayed.

"The palace itself!" said Kyren, in his excitement forgetting himself and pulling her close. "Is there a way to enter?"

"Yes. I don't know whether or not it was discovered. We seldom used it because there were so many guards in the palace."

"If an army broke through here—and at other strategic spots in the city. Let's go back. Morrien must know."

At some point in the unrelieved darkness, Kyren saw Riska bound ahead, disappearing around a sharp turn in the tunnel. He shouted to his soldiers to pursue; but beyond the turn, the cavern seemed to take different direction than before, though Kyren couldn't be sure, having negotiated it but once. No sign of her ahead in the dimness, and now other openings were appearing to right and left.

A soldier dared say what Kyren would not. "We're lost."

"She waited. The she-vulture waited until she had me in her hands. I'll be your guide willingly, she said and must have laughed to herself in the saying." They wandered together in darkness. After a certain length of time it was no longer a seeking out of the right route but a shambling in blind despair. Trickles of water that seeped through the walls and down onto the floor quenched their thirst, but even the drive for survival withered against cool smooth stone, echoing silence and everlasting darkness. "She's buried us alive," said Kyren, as his thoughts circled endlessly in dreams of sound and light. "She simply walked off and left us here without a further thought, without any idea of mercy."

"She's but a semblance of a woman over the soul of a wolf-bitch," said a soldier ruefully as he scooped up tepid water from a runnel in the floor.

"I wonder what exquisite lie she'll tell Morrien."

"You think she'll go back there?"

"You should have seen her with Morrien. If ever bitch-wolf craved a master—"

"So much the worse for him if he's been chosen. But that changes nothing for us."

Images of the grave tormented Kyren as even his anger banked and all but went out. They huddled in a cul-de-sac in the rocks, their strength having given out. One of their number had fallen into delirium. Kyren wondered idly, "If one of us dies before the others—" A vision came to him of peeling a strip of flesh off a human thigh, of putting it to his lips. He groaned audibly and did not dare to put the obscene idea into words. But if one grew *very* hungry—the idea taunted him. He grew a little weaker from the mental conflict. His head drooped to his knees as if his skull were a heavy pod on a thin reed, drying toward autumn. The air that drifted through was cool, the silence complete.

He did not know how long she had been standing there. It didn't seem to matter, for he was too weak to try to kill her even if he could remember what he wanted to kill her for. She drew near; her hair and clothing held the smells of sunlight and vegetation; there was a slip of something green caught on her trousers. Like a baby she reached toward it.

She was helping him rise, then the others. "You were lost," she said persuasively, hypnotically into his ear as she guided him out of the blind tunnel. "I searched and searched. Then I reported it to Morrien. I returned after these many days to make a final search."

"He *believed* you?"

"Hard to say. No one was there to discount my story. I told him you abandoned me in the caverns, bound and blind-folded, once you decided you knew the way to Ultebre, but in your haste to return you took a wrong turning. Fortunately for me, a blindfold was an aid my father used to teach me the tunnels' windings. The story seemed likely enough, considering that you wanted to abandon me all along, isn't that right?"

His head swam. He could rage inwardly and swear to himself that Morrien would know the truth, but he could say nothing aloud, for he was in her hands, faint with hunger and paralyzed with fear that he would never see the light again.

"I'm not sure it matters what version of the story you tell him, for you will have to tell him that you have gone into the undefended heart of Ultebre. If he truly wants his revenge, then he, all of you, will have to stomach me as best you can."

Light and sound and the prosaic bustle of everyday life returned as they left the caverns, and Kyren began to doubt that she had done him a kindness in saving his life. They said that Kyren was like a man returned from the dead. They said also that after this time he was changed, that his nerve had been broken. In Kyren's absence Morrien had named Riska his Second, almost as a joke (the men said Morrien's bitch and laughed), but Kyren never disputed it. Though he hinted and said things by indirection, he never was able to tell Morrien to his face how he feared for him.

With Riska's guidance Morrien had several reconnaissance parties sent through to Ultebre. They found one entrance guarded but lackadaisically by a guard who seemed to consider his post a sinecure and spent most of his time napping or playing a game with painted strips of wood. The last patrol that returned brought a captive. "Our tunnel opened into the women's quarters," explained the leader. "We brought you a memento." He pushed forward a shivering girl dressed in a gauzy skirt and some strategically placed jewelry. "She says her name is Gisela. She's one of Amery's latest concubines, no doubt."

"I'm a dancer," said the girl sulkily. "The best in Ultebre."

"I warned them the trouble our band had when it started carrying off women," said Riska, but in his inspection of Gisela, Morrien ignored her completely. Kyren would have recognized and feared the expression on her face had he been there to see it.

"Dismissed," he said to the soldiers, looking at Riska to include her. They were in Morrien's chambers and Riska, as Second, occupied a room adjacent to them.

Gisela, once she had smoothed her rumpled skirt, seemed to make herself at home, obviously enjoying Morrien's gaze on her.

"Get rid of her," said Riska with a sound of disgust.

Morrien looked over at her, half-smiling as if amused by what he'd heard. Riska was always difficult to get along with but she'd never given him a direct order and he didn't look as if he wanted her to start now.

She met his look angrily, directly. "In this place you'll bed me and no other." Morrien looked at Gisela, her eyes bright and comprehending, and felt almost embarrassed at Riska's bluntness.

"I don't want *you*," he said, returning plain speech for bluntness, putting a wealth of disgust in that last word.

"Do you want Amery's life—and Jos'l's? And all their tribe? Do you want to see their blood run at your feet, their faces bloated in death?" She was dark of eyes and olive of skin but she could blaze with a dark radiance.

He made an abrupt gesture, sending Gisela scuttling from the room. Not that he was afraid of the outcome of this confrontation—not that at all—if Riska insisted on humiliating herself. . . .

"Behind my back they call me she-wolf and sewer-rat. I don't mind the names. In a way they're true—but you need me. Above ground your pitiful army would be defeated. In the caverns, with me to lead, you can appear anywhere you choose. If you tried to explore for yourself it could take half a lifetime and in the meantime Amery and Jos'l despoil Ultebre at their leisure."

He advanced on her until they were nearly eye to eye. "You'd command me to your bed with revenge as the price. Are you so . . . desperate as all that?"

"I'm only practical. I find you attractive and it seems unlikely that I'd have my way with you under normal circumstances, being thought savage in appearance—not that *I'm* not satisfied with how I look, you understand."

He felt his hold on his temper began to loosen. What kind of unnatural bitch was this—any other woman would have been dissolved in tears by now. Perhaps if she had, he might have been persuaded to give the comfort she sought, but not ordered, not under threats.

She watched his hand twitch toward a knife on a belt he wasn't wearing. "Killing me wouldn't solve anything. I'm very much afraid there's but one answer." She reclined on a dais covered in furs. She seemed to enjoy the anger that came and went across his face, as he struggled for control. She had great faith in his self control.

To continue their eye-to-eye confrontation, he had to bend down over the dais. "You might, in some ways I know, be 'persuaded' to lead us about the caverns." He put the balls of his thumbs gently on her eyelids. "One doesn't need eyes underground, for example."

She drew away slightly, then regained her composure. "You would find me stubborn, I'm afraid, and afterward a very confused guide. I might even leave you to wander the tunnels til you died."

Silence for some moments.

He threw himself down onto the dais beside her. "What are you trying to do? Do you want to bring me to my knees, carry me off, rape me? He lay on the dais, hands beneath his head, half-joking, half in a kind of confusion. "Here I am, helpless, in your hands. Go ahead. I'll be very interested to see how you accomplish it."

She could not suppress a laugh. She put her hand gently on his chest. "I don't say I wouldn't like to, if it were possible, but I believe we'd find it awkward. No, I'll abide by tradition in this."

He made a sudden movement, more menacing than anything else. "Very friendly, very gently," she cautioned. "Treat me as you intended to treat her. You can even pretend I'm Gisela, I don't mind."

He tried, closing his eyes as he kissed her when all his instincts were screaming for blood. He fantasized snapping her scrawny neck, doing other unprintable things. When the kiss was ended, she drew back, a mocking smile on her lips. "You're a disappointing lover. I release you. You're free to go to your little Gisela."

He blinked.

Had she changed her mind, finding this whole process too degrading, or was she playing the kinds of power games he found so amusing when she played them against other people. For some moments he was blind, deaf, dumb with anger; but as usual, she had calculated the limits of his control. She always calculated everything to a hair's tolerance, but it was possible that this time she had overextended herself a bit.

"You may go," she was saying and attempting to roll sideways off the dais. He gave a sudden, blood-curdling war cry, following it immediately with another even shriller. Anyone who heard it would think that he had gone (or been sent) over the edge. She shrank back into herself a little, but recovered well.

"I'm mad with love, Gisela," he said, scrabbling after her over the mounded furs. "My lovely, my golden one."

"Morrien, wake up." She caught him on the side of the head with an open handed blow that made his ears ring, perhaps as a gesture to bring him to his senses. They tumbled from the dais as he grappled with her. For her lesser size, she really wasn't bad as a fighter, he noted; it was all he could do to restrain her and undo the strings of her tabard. He kept a glassy look in his eyes and kept on mumbling mindless things about Gisela. She could only blame herself that she had pushed him too far and driven him to this (or so he hoped). He twined his fingers in her hair in the pretext of caressing it and brought her head down smartly against the stone floor, not enough for damage, just enough to stop this infernal wrestling match. He hoped she hadn't presence of mind left to realize how premeditated that act seemed. Her eyes went a little blank and he could do anything he wanted, so for awhile he did, though it wasn't as enjoyable as he'd hoped. Then he gave her what she had professed to want, but not friendly, not gentle as she had ordered. All with the excuse of his feigned madness, though possibly by that time he had achieved a kind of madness of his own, and perhaps he would never be sure at this point just who had been raped.

Riska limped a little as she led the way into the tunnel and when she moved, she moved carefully. "I had some terrible dreams last night," he said, glad that the darkness masked his expression; he could not have taunted her so in the light.

"Your dreams are not my concern," she said coldly. "I slept . . . well. What is it you remember of your dream?"

"I dreamed of an enemy. Someone I wanted to kill."

"Sorry." He enjoyed the way she recoiled when he *accidentally* bumped against her, but, as he was beginning to realize with more and more clarity, he must not carry these games too far. She was not stupid and with the least flicker of suspicion, she would leave him here to wander about until he died. She'd probably enjoy the idea of it.

Morrien crouched at the opening into the palace. His

nerves were pulled tight by the waiting. His troops were in position at the hundred egresses of Ultebre. Down the tunnelways the word was passed. "Down the tyrant, Amery." Ultebre, the queen city, was almost in their hands. Morrien burst out amidst general confusion; Riska had insisted she be at his side, as second. He didn't object; perhaps some enthusiastic Ultebren would settle his dilemma by killing her. Though he supposed he would regret her death. Here, even in the palace itself, defense was poorly organized. He supposed their strength had been concentrated along the walls with their turrets and wonderful war machines, unfortunately now facing the wrong way for a proper defense.

His sword was drawn, but he saw little combat, his troops going before him, so easily it seemed putting to rout the confused palace guard. He kept hearing the plaintive question, "Where are they all coming from?" *Like insects from the walls and rats from the sewers,* he thought. An inner chamber was fiercely guarded and Morrien joined in the close fighting, thinking that perhaps Amery was here. The defense cut down or scattered, they battered down the door. Amery's body lay sprawled across some cushions. His guard had given him the time to be quite dead, but hardly peaceful looking, the skin cyanotic, flecks of foam drying around the mouth.

"He was wise," observed Morrien.

"Cut off the head," said Riska. "Have it displayed on a pike at the city's gate. The body you can throw into the sewers for the rats to squabble over." Soldiers rushed to carry this out, as a messenger entered to tell them that Jos'l had escaped, gotten out of the city in the confusion of its fall. "Then don't waste time standing here puling. Get the word out—one hundred gold pieces for the return of Jos'l . . . alive."

Kyren and Morrien exchanged looks as she left. "Now that we are in control, the savage is of no further use. She is a positive danger. And you know it well."

Morrien gave a gesture of dismissal, but Kyren caught his eye and a look of understanding passed between them.

After many days had passed Riska confronted the guards at the door of the fine new house that Morrien had provided for her. They crossed their pikes as she approached. "Your ladyship is not to go out alone," said one of them. "The streets still hold some danger. The conquest of the city still goes on in isolated areas."

She laughed rudely. Though the sound of it made him shuffle in embarrassment, it didn't change the position of the pikes.

"Say I do not go out . . . by Morrien's order."

She wheeled about and walked disconsolately through the richly furnished rooms. At first this seemed a part of what she had won. There had been parties; Morrien had even been here once though he had looked rather grim. The baths, the servants, the fine clothes, these had distracted her somewhat. But it hadn't taken her that long to realize that no matter how fine the quarters, when you couldn't leave them, you were in prison. And Morrien's grim face might mean more than responsibility for reorganizing the government of Ultebre.

The assassin was dressed in dark clothing so he was halfway across her bed chamber before she detected him. Her only warning was the light rippling down the knife blade. His hand arched back, down, struck the mounded fabric on the dais. It was not really luck that she had decided to sleep on the floor. He was just discovering that he had murdered the bedclothes when she hit him from behind with a brass lamp. She turned him over with a foot, but didn't recognize him, though she had had a fleeting hope when she had struck him that it would be Kyren, and an unexpressed fear that it was Morrien. She shouted and threw the lamp against the wall with a metallic crash. When the guard entered, he tripped over the sprawled body of the assassin and called out for his companion as she had hoped. As they crouched over the assassin, she slipped from the room and made for the unguarded door, no longer a fine lady, nor a prisoner, but free and everything they thought her—perhaps even worse.

Morrien entered his sleeping chamber wearily, releasing his cloak from his shoulders to let it fall on the floor. A servant rushed to attend him, but Morrien spoke curtly, sending him away.

A dagger struck the inlaid wood of the floor and vibrated rattlingly between Morrien and Riska, who stepped from the shadows. "I came to return this," she said and lifted her lip off white teeth in a smile.

He still had a knife at his belt, if he wished to draw it, but he seemed oblivious of the weapon. "It seemed the only solution. I only wanted you in a safe place, out of the way, but Kyren—"

"You knew he hated me. You knew what he would do."

"I don't know. I suppose so. I had even thought of making you my lady, to rule with me." There was a silence as their eyes met, then Riska broke it with a laugh that Morrien joined in.

"I see. The allies one makes in war can become an embarrassment in time of peace. Times change and people do not." She turned to go.

"I will have to set men to exploring the caverns. I can't be as blissfully ignorant of history as Amery was."

"Their windings are many and deep, and I know secrets by which the very walls may be changed. It will be long before you may say you have found them all out. And a human life is short."

"All things considered, yours may be shorter than most."

"Perhaps . . . if you don't guard the ways too strongly, you may waken to someone who will lie down with you—like someone who comes in a dream. In the morning, some trinket or some treasure may be missing. I hear there are thieves in Ultebre."

AGBEWE'S SWORD

Charles R. Saunders

It was never my intention that Amazons *be an "all women's" anthology. The concept of anthologies akin to Pamela Sargent's* Women of Wonder *series is extremely valid, their execution important. Yet for this particular anthology the only valid criterion seemed to be that which was outlined in the market report: "Powerful images of women in heroic fantasy." Sex of the author was not a determinant of this factor.*

That men are largely incapable of writing about powerful women is a terrible indictment of our society. I received stories about bungling, ineffectual, sexy or "cute" amazons who were dependent on men, fainted at the drop of a pin, or behaved like fatuous children—or, conversely, lopped off breasts, murdered men and babies, and all but held their swords outward from the crotch. I'll leave it to wiser analysts than I to divine how it came that only men devised characters such as these.

Exceptions exist, certainly. A couple of likely candidates couldn't complete stories in time, as they were overburdened by deadlines—a powerful reason; yet women who were equally pressed made that extra effort, and with stories they felt. The very idea of writing about amazons appealed more to women; hence a woman-dominated anthology is not a surprise, even if a reverse of the standard.

Charles R. Saunders is the greater exception. We'd been correspondents well before such successes as his two consecutive appearances in Year's Best Fantasy; *we'd supported each others' projects; I felt confident about his work. So I was extremely disappointed when the deadline passed and no story! A long-distance call from Toronto was my first contact with Charles outside of letters; apologetic, he asked for an extra week. I was ornery and made no promises. Two weeks later I re-*

84

ceived "Agbewe's Sword." A superb piece—but it was submitted to an ostensibly finished and manless anthology.

With borrowed calculator I tallied the total words already in the book—and wouldn't you know it: I could barely squeeze in one more tale.

So Amazons *has its token male contributor . . . Charles R. Saunders writes "as good as any woman."*

In precise unison they moved, dozens of lithe-thewed women in orderly rows, stretched across a sunwashed field. The afternoon glare sheened from indigo-black bodies clad only in brief leather loincloths and brass ankle-rings. Dancer's grace imbued their smooth motions—but these were no dancers. They were *ahosi,* women warriors of Abomey. Their lives depended upon their mastery of the maneuvers they practiced.

Guile was their primary weapon: the subtle twist of a shield that sent a swordpoint sliding harmlessly by; the quick feint of a swordarm followed by a sudden swift lunge once the foe was off balance; the slight shift of the head that gave the enemy's spearpoint only air for a target—all these deceits required a swiftness of reflex and suppleness of physique that was the mark of the *ahosi,* acquired only through hours of training such as this.

More than the usual military grimness masked the faces of the *ahosi* as they leaped, whirled, and thrust with imaginary weapons. Only the light tread of bare feet on crushed grass broke the silence of the practice field . . . until the staccato voice of a *kposu*-of-ten barked: "Dossouye! If you move that clumsily on the battlefield, you'll have an Ashanti spear between your ribs before you know it!"

Dossouye, a tall, lanky *ahosi* of the Brown Spider clan, bit her lip in embarrassment and struggled to regain the swift rhythm of the others' movements. But it was difficult, more difficult than ever before during her three years as an *ahosi.* She had taken longer than most to slip into that detached state of consciousness wherein the mind surrenders to reflex and the need for conscious control of nerve and sinew vanishes. That surrender was impossible for her this day, for the dream she'd endured the previous night continued to trouble her thoughts.

"Halt," came the command from the *khetunga*, commander of Dossouye's company of *ahosi*. Confused, Dossouye and several others around her stumbled in mid-motion before recovering to stand at rigid attention. The exercise period was less than half over; why should the *khetunga* stop them now?

Surreptitiously, hoping her *kposu* didn't notice, Dossouye glanced out of the corner of her eye down the column of lean, sweat-glossed bodies, and she saw the reason the *khetunga* had halted the practice. And, seeing it, she felt a stab of apprehension.

Next to the *khetunga* stood a bizarre figure who, but for his station, might have been more an object of ridicule than fear. He was shorter than the *khetunga*, and his portly, robe-swathed form compared poorly against the sturdy commander's. Further, one side of the man's head was shaved bald as a black egg, while the hair on the other grew in an unruly, bushy mass. But it was this singular coiffure that proclaimed his rank. He was a Half Head, a messenger of the Leopard King, and thus of a status surpassing even a commander of *ahosi*.

The *khetunga* frowned while the Half Head spoke to her. Dossouye was too far down the column to make out the words, but the commander's tone was clear. She was probably arguing that the *ahosi* needed every moment possible for preparation for the next battle against the invading Ashanti.

Still frowning, the *khetunga* stepped away from the Half Head when their conversation was done. Raising her voice so that it carried across the field, she said, "Toxisi, Esusi, Kyauni, Aloko, Dossouye: you are to go with the Lord Half Head to the Kunnah Palace. Da Gwebenu, the Leopard King, has need of you."

Glancing nervously at each other, the five *ahosi* came forth from the ranks and stood before the Half Head.

"Our clothes . . ." began Nyauni.

"No need for that," the Half Head said impatiently. "Come quickly now."

Dossouye fell into step with the other *ahosi*. She was hard-pressed to keep her apprehension from showing on her face. First the dream; now this mysterious summons from the Leopard King. Not only that, she thought uneasily as they marched through the streets of Alodah, but the other four *ahosi* the *khetunga* had named were, like herself, members of the Brown Spider Clan. Why, she asked herself repeatedly. Why?

The five *ahosi* knelt in the posture of prostration, their foreheads touching the painted floor of the throne room. Carved wooden columns supported a high ceiling, and hangings of colorful appliquéd cloth hung on sun-brick walls. Though the room was large and cool, sweat beaded on Dossouye's brow. When the Half Head had ushered them into the presence of the Leopard King, Dossouye had noticed those who sat by the monarch's stool, and awe had swept through her at the sight of such an assemblage of the people-of-name of Abomey. The glimpse she had caught of them before she folded into prostration had been fleeting—but more than enough.

"Rise," said the *kpulu*, the king's Linguist. As one, the five *ahosi* stood.

The Linguist sat on a silver-inlaid stool several inches lower than the king's. Directly behind him sat Da Gwebenu, the Leopard King, a bull-shouldered man of more than medium height. A headpiece of plumes and metal, and flowing appliquéd robes proclaimed his rank. Beneath his chin, a tuft of kinky gray beard contrasted with the black of his face.

On stools to either side of the king sat Hwesunu, who was the *ganulan*, or commander of the men's army, a man whose broad chest was weighted with necklaces made from the teeth of enemies he had slain; Akalundu the *azaundato*, the chief sorcerer; and Nyina, the *akpadume*, the Queen of Spears, who held higher rank even than the *khetunga* among the *ahosi*. Unlike most women of Abomey, who wore no clothing above the waist, the *akpadume* was clad in a robe that bared her left shoulder, but draped far down over the right, covering an arm that was no longer there.

Dossouye knew this woman well. It had been her mother who had struck the blow that had cost the *akpadume* most of her forearm years ago in a quarrel over the man who later became Dossuye's father.

Nyima glared ferally at Dossouye. The young *ahosi's* eyes did not waver. Dossouye had long suspected that the *akpadume* had had a hand in the death of her parents—both slain by Mossi assassins who had themselves been killed before they could be questioned.

The king said something in a tongue unintelligible to any save his Linguist.

"Da Gwebenu commands that you answer truthfully the questions Akalundu will ask," the Linguist translated.

The *ahosi* stood perfectly still, as discipline demanded. But the *akpadume* must have detected stirrings of anxiety and curiosity among the warriors. She scowled reprovingly, but said nothing as the *azaundato* rose and spoke.

"You will each tell me exactly what you dreamed last night," he said. The strings of amulets and *gbos* sewn into his robes clashed and clattered as the old man walked toward the row of *ahosi*. Dossouye felt a sudden foreboding that was close to panic.

"Dreams?" said Kyauni, always quick-tongued. "I dreamed nothing. Nothing I can remember. I never remember my dreams."

Akalundu looked at Kyauni. Fearless in battle though she was, Kyauni trembled beneath the *azaundato's* scrutinizing gaze. It was common knowledge that the sorcerer possessed a *gbo* that unerringly revealed the truth or falseness of a person's words. Kyauni knew that she spoke the truth—but would the *gbo* believe her?

Kyauni relaxed visibly as the *azaundato's* eyes left hers. The old man moved without further comment to the next *ahosi* in line. Toxisi. Toxisi had the disposition of a lioness, with a physique to match. But now, before the burning gaze of the *azaundato*, she sweated profusely and appealed to Nyima: "Must I tell, *akpadume?*"

"Will you defy the wish of the Leopard King and disgrace me as well?" Nyima shouted, rising in outrage from her stool.

A helpless, resigned expression descended upon Toxisi's blunt features.

"All right," she said. "I—I dreamed I was on the sleeping-mat with . . . with Lord Hwesunu!"

In less serious circumstances, Toxisi's admission might have provoked lewd laughter. The *ahosi* were, as all knew, technically wives of the Leopard King. They wore the same brass ankle-rings that identified the king's scores of official wives—but Da Gwebenu had never lain with an *ahosi* as he did with the others, and he never would. Any other Abomean who dared to sample the charms of a woman warrior risked the punishment meted out for Royal Adultery: public beheading. Often the soldiers of the men's army joked that it was more than love of Abomey that fired the *ahosis'* lust for battle. . . .

Hwesunu permitted himself a slight grin before Nyima's voice echoed through the throne room.

"This is war," Nyima shouted. "The Ashanti wash their spears in our blood and you dream of adultery. Do you think the enemy will run from pregnant *ahosi*? Perhaps ten rods broken across your back will teach you to keep your mind on warfare."

A shudder shook Toxisi's muscular frame. Ten rods would leave her back a raw, bleeding mass of meat for the vultures.

"Surely, *akpadume*, you wouldn't deprive your forces of a valuable spear simply because of a dream?" said Hwesunu. Nyima glared at him.

"Don't tell me how to. . . ."

The king spoke. There was no need for the Linguist to translate; Da Gwebenu's tone was clear. Nyima fell silent.

Dossouye was next. As the eyes of the *azaundato* blazed into all three of her souls, she knew that she could not lie, no matter how desperately she wanted to. Haltingly, she began.

"I was in the Hills of Sogbaki. It was night. I was walking . . . walking along a twisted path that led to a cave near the summit. The cave was dark, but there was a . . . brightness of some kind shining out of it. I was afraid . . . but something within the cave was *calling* to me. I went into the cave, and followed the light to its source. There, I saw a brightly glowing sword, cast in the shape of Dangbe the serpent. Standing behind it was a woman. She was wearing the armor of an *ahosi*. She pointed toward the glowing sword. I knew that she meant that I must take it up. I was still afraid, but I bent down to pick the sword up. Then I awoke."

Dossouye cast her gaze downward when she finished. Aka-lundu stepped back, the whites of his eyes bulging in his seamed black face.

"Do you know who the woman in your dream was?" he asked.

"She was Agbewe, the first *ahosi*, who was beloved of Anansi the Spider and ancestress of the clan of the Brown Spider."

"And the sword?"

"Was Agbewe's sword, gifted to her by Anansi. Agbewe used it in the final battle of the Mizungu War, when the people of Nyumbani rose to drive the white devils back to their island in the Western Ocean. Agbewe laid down her sword when the war was done, and nothing has been seen of it for a thousand rains since."

"*Bokono*-dream," Akalundu whispered. "I, too, dreamed of Agbewe and her sword . . . and the cave . . . and a woman of the *ahosi*. But her back was to me; I could not make out the face. The dream is *bokono*, a dream of divination, for no one other than the Leopard King and the others here knew of it, and they have told no one. I knew only that the *ahosi* in the dream had to be of the Brown Spider clan; that is why you were summoned here."

Dossouye's shoulders straightened, as if a weight bowing them had been lifted. To either side of her, her companions moved back, even the formidable Toxisi. Before now, Dossouye had been a kinswoman and an *ahosi*; no more, no less. Now, they knew that the hand of Mawu-Lesa, the dual god of Sun and Moon, had touched her. Dossouye was now a person-with-name, and the other *ahosi* were her equals no longer.

Not everyone acknowledged Dossouye's new status.

"You had a *bokono*-dream, yet dared to tell no one about it?" snarled Nyima. Her face was twisted into an ugly mask of spite.

"Am I a sorceress, to interpret the meaning of dreams?" Dossouye shot back. Then, softly, "No. That is not the truth. I said nothing because I was afraid."

"Well spoken, child. It is rare that words of such honesty are uttered in this room."

Time stood still in the throne room of the Kunnah Palace. It was the Leopard King who had spoken, not in the Royal Speech for the *kpulu* to translate, but in the common tongue of Abomey. Had the walls of the palace fallen flat in the next instant, the *ahosi* and the people-with-name gathered in the room would not have been more shocked.

"Hwesunu, Nyina, the rest of you *ahosi*, leave us," Da Gwebenu continued. "You also," he told the *azaundato* and the Linguist. "We must talk, this daughter of Agbewe and I. And you, Toxisi . . . fight well against the Ashanti in the coming battle, and I am certain your *akpadume* will reconsider your punishment. Now go."

Quickly the others prostrated themselves, then left the throne room. Their gait was a stunned shuffle, like the shamble of slaves about to be sacrificed to the Leopard

King's ancestors. As she passed beneath the carved lintel of the doorway, Nyima paused and directed a glare of murderous hatred toward Dossouye. Dossouye did not react. The king's speaking of the common tongue had left her as confused as the others.

"Sit, child," the king said, indicating Nyima's stool. Dossouye found herself committing without hesitation an act that would otherwise have earned her a very painful death. But it was the Leopard King's command. She sat.

Da Gwebenu looked at her. She stirred uncomfortably beneath the soft brown gaze of the man who held ultimate power in Abomey. She knew what he saw: a tall, gangly woman, taller even than Toxisi but lacking Toxisi's powerful thews. Her legs seemed too long for her body, her shoulders were wide and bony, her breasts no more than slight swellings on a narrow chest; all left naked by the bit of leather that was her only garment. Dossouye did not guess what else the king saw: the coiled, serpentine tension in her limbs, the onyx-hard determination in her dark eyes, the adamant set of her heavy-lipped mouth now that she had acknowledged the destiny she had dreamed.

"You are an *ahosi*," the king said at last. "Well do you know the peril that besets Abomey now. The Ashanti are expanding northward; they struck without warning across the Gulf and captured Oidah, our only port city. Our allies refuse to aid us; the Ashanti have bought them off with their accursed gold. Fools! They fail to realize the danger they'll be in if Ashanti conquers us. They're merciless—the envoys I sent down to Kumasi to discuss peace with the Asantehene were returned here in pieces! We *must* drive the Ashanti back across the Gulf. And we could do it, were it not for the *gbo* their sorcerer unleashed upon our forces."

An inward tremor crept through Dossouye at the memory of the awful battle at Oidah. The *ahosi* and the men's army had recovered from the abruptness of the Ashanti attack, and were beginning to prevail over the legions of the Asantehene. Then came disaster. The Ashantis' sorcerer, a renegade from far Ife, had called down the lightning of Shango. White bolts had seared downward from a black sky, decimating the Abomey ranks. Dossouye had only barely thrown herself aside from the flaming death that left her companions lumps of charred flesh and blackened bone. She had fled from

Oidah like the others, shameless in her terror of the power of
the dan-Ife.

"Akalundu has no *gbo* to match the lightnings of Shango,"
the king continued. "All these weeks we have sat here in Alodah, preparing for a counterattack we fear to make, wondering what the Ashanti will do next. But now—the Sword of
Agbewe possesses a *gbo* that may well match the dan-Ife's.
You and you alone, Dossouye, must seek the blade of your
ancestress, and use it against the dan-Ife while we attack the
Ashanti forces holding Oidah. Will you do this thing, Dossouye?"

"The Hills of Sogbaki are very close to Oidah. There will
be many Ashanti soldiers there. And I am to go alone?"

Coldness crept into the Leopard King's eyes. "You are,
then, still afraid?"

Dossouye's sharp laughter startled the king. "Afraid? Here
I sit on the stool of the *akpadume*, speaking with the Leopard
King in common tongue about the fate of Abomey . . . there
is nothing of fear in me now, Great King. Nothing at all."

"I see," said Da Gwebenu. He paused, noting that even in
her sitting position, the young *ahosi's* spare frame seemed
taut as a crouching panther's. Her face remained impassive,
but her fervor was apparent in her eyes. Da Gwebenu sighed,
as if Dossouye's burden were also his.

"You will leave tonight," he said calmly. "A war-bull will
take you south to the fringe of the territory occupied by the
Ashanti. From there, you must proceed on foot to the Hills.
In three days we will march on Oidah. Whether you have
found the sword or not, we will attack. It is better to die
fighting than live with the foot of the Asantehene on our
necks."

"I have your leave to go now, Great King?"

Da Gwebenu nodded assent. Dossouye rose from Nyima's
stool and bent her body in prostration. Then she got up and
departed from the throne room. The Leopard King stared
thoughtfully at the doorway through which her straight, slim
back had passed. And he mused, "If this one lives through
what is to come, she'll be a far greater threat to me than any
Ashanti. . . ."

Dossouye knelt in a grove of tall, straight-trunked palm
trees. The moon shone silver through serrated black fronds.
The grove was like many others scattered along the outskirts

of Alodah. It was a *fedi* grove, and beneath each palm was buried thin wooden tubes containing the umbilical cords of generations of Abomeans. The *fedi* beneath which Dossouye prayed was the watcher of her fate, the guardian of two of her three souls, the *selido* and the *semedo*. The *selido* was the soul that spoke before the judgment of Mawu-Lesa, while the *semedo* was the soul that made Dossouye one with her ancestors. The third soul, the *djautau*, belonged only to the individual, and thus needed no guardian.

Dossouye prayed to Mawu-Lesa, and all the ancestresses that stretched in an unbroken line to Agbewe and beyond.

She prayed for life.

When she was done, she rose from her knees and went quickly to the place where her war-bull was thethered. The horned giant, trained as the people of the Soudan trained horses, nuzzled her hand as she untangled its reins from a thick bush. War-bulls were the product of an ancient cross between ordinary cattle and the fierce buffalo of the forest, retaining the docility of the former and the fearlessness of the latter.

Dossouye vaulted into the saddle and urged the war-bull onto the road to Oidah. Before long, she and her mount melted into the blackness of night.

A pair of eyes, narrow and malignant, turned from Dossouye's retreating form to the *fedi*-palm beneath which the young *ahosi* had prayed.

Dossouye crouched motionless behind a screen of brush as a patrol of Ashanti soldiers marched past. Moonlight glinted from helmets shaped in the semblance of snarling leopards and iron corselets decorated with outlines of circles to resemble a leopard's spotted hide. In their own tongue, they were called *asufos*—killers.

Though her heart pounded like a funeral drum, Dossouye knew that the *asufos* could not hear it. She held herself as still as a jungle cat lying in ambush. Since she had abandoned her war-bull near the first burnt-out village she had encountered outside Oidah, Dossouye had encountered more and more patrols. Each time, her keen senses and catlike quickness had carried her to safety before the *asufos* could spot her. This time, though, she had barely leaped into the brush before the *asufos* were upon her.

The round, humped silhouette of the Sogbaki Hills bulked

close to Dossouye's refuge. Beyond them the walls and lights of Oidah were visible in the moonlit gloom. Impatience battled against iron discipline as she listened closely to the retreating tramp of the *asufos'* boots. Only a ruined millet field now lay between her and her destination. Silently she prayed to Mawu-Lesa that no other *asufos* would come up the path while she sprinted across the burnt stubble of the field.

A loud rustle sounded only a few feet from Dossouye. Startled, she jumped, inadvertently shaking the brush again. She swore vehemently as she heard a shout from one of the Ashanti. They would be coming back now . . . *asufos*, as Dossouye well knew, were thorough. Although there were only five of them in this patrol, they would search the brush until they found the source of the commotion.

What *had* made the disturbance, Dossouye wondered furiously as the footsteps of the *asufos* came nearer. A civet? A hare? Some misplaced monkey? Speculation was useless; her concern now was to avoid the *asufos*.

She knew she could not crouch where she was forever. Sooner or later the Ashanti would discover her; they would leave no inch of the brush uncovered in their search. Her only chance lay in maneuvering out of the brush while the *asufos* worked their way farther in. Then she'd risk all in a furtive dash across the field. Despite the moonlight, her dark skin and the blackened leather harness would afford some camouflage against the night . . . even her ankle-rings had been smudged to dull their gleam.

Soundlessly Dossouye crept toward the perimeter of the spiky foliage. Behind her she heard the thrashings of the *asufos*, who had evidently not been trained in the techniques of stealth. They were nowhere near her—no! One was slowly beating his way toward her while his fellows swept farther inward. Only one, thought Dossouye as she unsheathed her sword. . . .

The *asufo* blundered closer. Dossouye could see his sword probing at the brush as she maneuvered like a phantom until she was behind him. He passed only inches from Dossouye . . . but failed to see her. The *ahosi* uncoiled like a striking cobra. One hand reached under the *asufo's* chin and jerked his head upward; the other slid the razor-edge of her sword swiftly across his throat. The *asufo* gurgled, then slumped forward bonelessly. Dossouye eased him down; she wanted no crashing fall to alert the others.

Dossouye listened. The other *asufos* had completed their first sweep; now they were turning to retrace their steps. Dossouye knew that the time to make her run across the field was now. Stepping over the corpse of the *asufo* she had slain, she parted the last screen of brush between her and the field.

Something hard and unyielding cracked against the back of her head. Red bursts of pain exploded in her skull as she pitched forward, slumping against the brush. Consciousness loosened, threatening to float free. Dimly the *ahosi* heard the shouts and crashings of the four surviving *asufos*. She stumbled to her feet and strove to stiffen her legs beneath her. Terror stabbed through her reeling mind—had the *asufo* she'd killed risen from the dead to strike her down?

The Sogbaki Hills blurred before Dossouye's eyes. She took a lurching step forward . . . then the clank of iron sounded behind her. Hard hands seized her; then she was jerked roughly about to face her captors. The four *asufos* glared madly at her, shouting in Ashanti. One of them shoved her head downward. Blearily she stared into the empty eyes of the slain *asufo*, staring beneath the snarling leopard helm.

A heavy fist blotted her vision. Her head rocked back; her limbs refused to obey her brain's frantic commands to move as the *asufos* dragged her from the brush. Dossouye knew what the *asufos*, who hated women warriors, did to captive *ahosi*. She knew that she would welcome the end of her life long before it came.

Dossouye's head was clearing. An *asufo* was lashing her left wrist to the shaft of a spear driven deeply into the ground. Dossouye cursed Mawu-Lesa for lifting the veil of impending unconsciousness; now she'd be fully awake and aware during the outrage the Ashanti were about to perform. Already the flesh on her stomach and between her breast bled from the *asufos'* carelessness in hacking her harness away from her body. They had stripped off their own armor, the better to enjoy the feel of the flesh of a woman who thought she was a man. Through the undisguised terror that now flooded her thoughts came a counterpoint of bitterness. She, the "savior" of Abomey, who had sat by the side of the Leopard King, was about to be ravished like a peasant woman captured for sport.

But she would still die like an *ahosi*. As the *asufo* who was tying her arm pulled it toward the spear, Dossouye stiffened her muscles. The arm moved no farther. At the same time, she held her thighs rigid as another Ashanti struggled to force them apart. Snarling in impatience, he pulled harder. Suddenly Dossouye relaxed her thigh muscles. The *asufo* fell forward. Dossouye's knees slammed full into his face. The *asufo* rolled away, yelping in pain as blood spurted from his nose.

A third *asufo* smashed his spearbutt into the pit of Dossouye's stomach. Her body bent double; a low, agonized moan escaped her throat. The *asufo* raised his spear again . . . and staggered backward as a spear thrown from the brush tore into his chest. Black faces twisted in rage; the two still on their feet whirled toward the brush. One of them groaned and fell, a spearpoint ripping through his abdomen. The other stopped and flung his own weapon toward the spot in the foliage from where the spear that killed his companion had been propelled. No outcry of pain rewarded his cast. But a high, piercing shriek of agony brought him spinning about. His mouth gaped open in astonishment at what he saw.

Summoning strength from somewhere within her wracked body, Dossouye had freed her left hand, torn the spear that had held it from the ground, and driven its point into the groin of the *asufo* she'd stunned before her mysterious savior had struck. Now she stood, a naked, bloody vision of vengeance. Her victim writhed spasmodically and howled like a madman as blood poured between the fingers he clutched to his wound.

The last *asufo*, weaponless and bare of armor, saw that Dossouye was reeling, hardly able to stay on her feet. But she still held a spear in her hands. Weakened as she was, the *ahosi* could still deal death. Her eyes burned with a demonic flame; her lips curled back from her teeth, set in a rictus of rage and pain.

Remembering the spears that had brought death from the brush, and his comrade's shrill screams echoing in his ears, the Ashanti succumbed to the emotion the *asufos* were reputed to have conquered—fear. He wheeled and fled, running toward the encampment from which he and the others had been sent on patrol.

Dossouye steadied herself, aimed, then hurled the heavy Ashanti spear. She almost fell with the effort. Arcing through the night, the weapon took the fleeing *asufo* full in the back. The Ashanti cried out and went down in a tangle of limbs, the spearshaft whipping back and forth as he fell. Then he lay still.

Searching along the ground, Dossouye recovered her sword, which the *asufos* had left near her discarded harness. From the ruined harness she salvaged only a belt. Then she went to the *asufo* she had unmanned. His shrieks still tore through the night. Dossouye cut his throat. His cries might already have alerted other Ashanti soldiers. Dossouye had no time to rest, or even to heave up the bile that swirled in her bruised stomach. What strange force was it, she wondered, that could betray her in the brush, yet mysteriously save her again? Was it some *gbo* of the dan-Ife sorcerer that had struck in the brush, only to be countered by the influence of Agbewe's Sword? *Who had hurled those spears?*

Dossouye shook speculation out of her mind as she sheathed her sword, gathered up a fallen spear, and turned to the black, looming hills. Striving not to stagger, she began the final step of her quest, hoping that no Ashanti followed her into the hills.

The entrance to the cave greeted Dossouye like a huge, open mouth, fanged with outcrops of rock, exactly as it had appeared in her dream. Dizzy as she was from the punishment she had taken, Dossouye had easily made her way up the twisted, narrow path leading to her destination—she had done it before. The dream had truly been *bokono*; she knew now that she had not been chasing an illusion. But this knowledge brought Dossouye only a small measure of relief.

A pale glow radiated from within the black depths. Stepping cautiously across the rocky floor, Dossouye approached the source of the white-gold glow. She knew what she would find—a natural dais of stone, upon which the scintillant, snake-shaped Sword of Agbewe would rest. Would Agbewe herself be hovering behind the dais, beckoning her descendant to claim the wondrous weapon, as she had done in the dream?

Dossouye came to the dais. Duplicating the image graven into her memory only a few days before, the luminous blade reposed on rough stone. But the woman standing behind the dais was not Agbewe. . . .

"I cannot lift it," Nyima hissed between clenched teeth. "The sword won't let me touch it . . . not so long as *you* remain alive."

Dossouye looked at her. The *akpadume* wore leather armor blackened for camouflage as Dossouye's had been. A cuplike leather sleeve encased the stump of her left arm. From its blunt end an iron spike projected. A strap belted across her back held an empty javelin-quiver.

Nyima's eyes met Dossouye's. At another time, Dossouye might have quailed before the raw flame of the *akpadume's* hatred. Now the *ahosi's* own hatred flared forth in one savage, fluid motion as her spear shot toward Nyima's breast.

But swift as Dossouye's cast was, Nyima reacted with equal quickness. Her truncated left arm moved in a dark blur. The iron spike clanged against the advancing spear-point; the deflected weapon clattered off the cavern wall.

In the weird glow cast by Agbewe's Sword, Nyima leaped from behind the dais, drawing her sword in the same motion. Dossouye barely brought her own blade up in time to blunt Nyima's thrust.

"Your blood will cool the *gbo* of Agbewe's blade," Nyima said. "With your death the cycle will be complete. Your death I will savor even more than your mother's. I paid the assassins who slew her and your cursed father. Mine will be the hand that slays you!"

She lunged forward, driving the iron spike toward Dossouye's side. Dossouye twisted her body aside, but not before the sharp point tore a crimson furrow across her ribs. Despite Nyima's handicap, it was Dossouye who fought at a disadvantage. Even with one arm, the *akpadume* was as formidable a warrior as any in Abomey, male or female. Worse, Nyima was rested, and fully-clad for battle, while Dossouye was naked, bleeding, and staggering from the abuses she'd already suffered this night. She stumbled backward, driven by Nyima's relentless attack. Hard-pressed to parry the *akpadume's* slashing strokes, Dossouye realized to her dismay that Nyima was toying with her.

New lines were added to the crimson tracery on her skin as Nyima's point licked repeatedly past Dossouye's weakening defense. Her wounds were not deep, but precious blood drained from each of them, exacting an inexorable toll. With each caress of blade against flesh, Nyima's harsh features split in a sadistic smile. Dossouye longed to obliterate that smile in a smear of blood—but she could hardly hold up her sword.

Then, with a deft flick of the wrist, Nyima disarmed her. Dossouye's sword landed with a clang a dozen feet away.

Dossouye knew she was finished. Even in prime condition, she could never have reached her weapon before Nyima ran her through. Triumphantly, the *akpadume* stood between the *ahosi* and the dais.

"My sword will impale you now, bitch-spawn," she said. "I could not allow the *asufos* to take you, though your terror when they began to force your knees open was beautiful to behold. With you dead, I will be the one to wield the *gbo* that will defeat the Ashanti. The glory will be mine, not yours. Now, bitch-spawn—your life for my arm!"

As Nyima leaped forward, Dossouye moved—not toward her own sword, but to the one on the dais. Uncoiling her long legs, she dove to Nyima's left. A stiff jab of her hand pushed the iron spike aside. With a screech of wrath, Nyima whirled, swinging her blade in a deadly shimmering arc.

But Dossouye had already touched the hilt of Agbewe's Sword. Dark fingers curled eagerly around bright metal. Time slowed . . . an awesome energy coursed through the *ahosi's* battered frame. Nyima's blade swept slowly, slowly toward Dossouye, who was sprawled awkwardly across the dais. Yet Agbewe's Sword swung as if of its own volition, and scythed through Nyima's good wrist.

Still clutching the swordhilt, the *akpadume's* severed hand dropped to the cavern floor. Nyima's screams echoed hollowly in Dossouye's ears. The *akpadume* lunged desperately with the iron spike, its point plunging toward Dossouye's eyes. Again Agbewe's Sword shifted in the *ahosi's* hand. The blade cut through leather, flesh, and bone as if through butter. Blood jetting from both arms, Nyima tottered, then crumpled to the floor.

The brilliant glow of the serpentine blade suffused Dossouye's drawn features as she stood over the fallen *akapadume*. Energy flowed into her lean frame; no longer did she feel weak from the steady seepage of blood from her wounds. Yet she knew no sense of triumph when she gazed down at the writhing form of Nyima. She knew that the *akpadume* had become mad—and for the mad she felt only pity.

A spasm shook Nyima's body, then she lay still. But she was not dead. Her eyes glared upward into Dossouye's, and her voice quavered not at all as she spoke:

"It is not over yet, bitch-spawn. Agbewe protects her own . . . but you are already dead. You have been dead since the day you departed Alodah . . . the day I cut down your *fedi*-palm—"

Nyima's eyes filmed into the glistening opacity of death, her lips set forever in a smile of satisfaction.

Dossouye's limbs wavered, the strength lent by Agbewe's Sword gone as though it were illusion. The shining blade slipped forgotten from her fingers. Her *fedi*—dead. Two of her souls—dead. With their guardian gone, her *selido* and *semedo* were no more, leaving her only the *djautau*. Even though she still moved, breathed, thought, she was dead.

"*My souls. . . .*" Dossouye whispered before a curtain of blackness fell. Then she slumped limply across the dais.

Slowly, fitfully, consciousness returned to Dossouye. It was as if something were dragging her unwillingly up from oblivion. To Dossouye, death was infinitely preferable to the extreme pain that insinuated in every muscle she could move. Yet the summons to awareness continued insistently.

Dossouye's eyes flew open. Light intruded only dimly in the black cavern, but it was brighter than before. It was daylight, filtering in from the mouth of the cave.

The Sword . . . painfully Dossouye turned her head, looking past the grisly corpse of Nyima. The serpent-shaped blade lay on the rocky floor. In its white luminescence, Dossouye could see a vague shape, pointing downward with a ghostly finger.

Dossouye closed her eyes.

"Do you mock me, ancestress?" she said weakly. "My souls are gone . . . how can I wield your Sword when the *semedo* that connects me to you is dead?"

A voice spoke softly inside Dossouye's head.

"I grant you my own *semedo*, daughter. But you must grasp the Sword yourself; I cannot give it to you. You *must*. Can you not hear the sound of battle outside the cavern?"

Faint sounds reached Dossouye's ears—the clangor of arms; the bellows of war-bulls; the shrieks of the dying—and above that, the rumble of distant thunder.

The thunder . . . the *gbo* of the dan-Ife who aided the Ashanti. His devastating sorceries were about to begin anew, and there was no one to forestall the lightning of Shango but herself.

"Come," the smoky wraith of Agbewe demanded. "Come. . . ."

Dossouye rolled herself off the dais and fell onto the body of Nyima. Her hands slid sickeningly in the blood pooled around the sneering corpse. On hands and knees, Dossouye crawled over the dead *akpadume*, inching painfully toward the shining blade and the wavering form of her ancestress. She cursed the dream that had led her here; she cursed the old feud between her parents and the *akpadume*; she cursed th soft-eyed Leopard King. . . .

Her fingers closed on the hilt of Agbewe's Sword.

On the plains beneath the Sogbaki Hills, combat raged like a tempest of blood and iron. The *asufos* had held their ground against the initial arrow-storm of the Abomeans. They had withstood the awesome charge of the cavalry—troops of men and *ahosi* mounted on war-bulls. Then the Ashanti had counterattacked with their own cavalry mounted on *ikengas*, fleet animals descended from antelope domesticated centuries ago. While not as massive as the Abomean war-bull, the *ikengas* were swifter by far, and their darting forays played havoc with the Abomean mounted formations.

But the Abomeans refused to retreat. Now the foot-troops entered the fray. Despite the inexplicable disappearance of their *akpadume*, the *ahosi* fought with their customary cunning and ferocity along the Ashanti flanks, while the men's arm hammered at the center. The pain between Oidah and the Sogbaki Hills became a scarlet morass as warriors from both sides bartered their lives in blood.

Slowly the Abomeans were prevailing, their battle-fury fueled by their determination to rid their land of the hated invaders. The *asufos*, remorseless as the leopards their accouterments mimicked, littered the ground with Abomean corpses for each stubborn foot they retreated. But retreat they did, for Da Gwebenu had called upon the full array of his kingdom's forces. If the Ashanti retreated into Oidah, the Leopard King would lay siege to his own city; destroy it brick by brick until no more Ashanti lived in Abomey. His army shared this grim conviction.

Weapons crimson to the hilt, the Abomeans advanced from the shadow of the hills. From his vantage point, the Leopard King observed—and prayed to Mawu-Lesa that Dossouye would soon appear with the Sword of Agbewe. Already there was a discernible darkening in the sky, and the thunder of Shango muttered like distant war drums.

The sky grew darker; the thunder increased in volume, overriding the clash of weapons and the wails of the wounded and dying. In the press of combat, soldiers from both armies paused to look up as the white spears of Shango coruscated across the clouds. The *asufos*, remembering the carnage the fires from the sky had wrought in the last battle, grinned mercilessly beneath their fanged helmets and slashed into the Abomeans with renewed ferocity. The Abomeans, recalling the horror of the burning death that had ravened among them, fell back in dismay. Then, remembering that the Leopard King had told them of a *gbo* that would dispell the dan-Ife conjurings, male and female warrior alike met the resurgent Ashanti like a wall of iron.

"Back!" came the command from the Ashanti officers. As they had done before, the *asufos* retreated, clearing a wide space between themselves and the Abomeans. Hidden in a veil of swirling black traced with patterns of fire, the sky seemed to sink onto the earth.

Panic clawed at the hearts of the Abomeans. The dan-Ife's clouds had gathered; a few moments more, and flaming bolts would incinerate them—and there was no sign of the *gbo* Da Gwebenu had promised.

"Charge into them!" yelled Hwesunu in a lion's roar. "Let Shango's lightning take the *asufos* with us!"

The *ganulan's* armor was hacked and dented; his war-bull trembled with fatigue. Still he dug his heels into the war-bull's heaving sides, and the huge beast lurched forward. Heartened by their commander's example, the others started forward . . . then stopped short, raising their shields in front of their faces as a blinding burst of light flooded the battle-field.

The blinking Abomeans stared at each other, astonished that none had fallen in the blaze. The Ashanti were equally incredulous.

"There!" several voices cried at once, pointing toward the Hills of Sagbaki. While thunder rolled overhead, both armies looked to the hills, eyes wide in disbelief. At the summit of the hills a shaft of brilliant white-gold light shot skyward, rending the storm clouds asunder.

Those closest to the hills could make out a dark figure within the column—a tall female form, naked but for belt and anklets, wounds etched like red glyphs against the ebony of her skin—and a serpent-shaped sword raised high above her head. Whips of lightning crackled across the sky, lashing against the radiant shaft. But the shaft absorbed the flaming bolts, even as the clouds that spawned them dissipated into ragged remnants in a blue sky.

Still the shaft of light blazed, changing direction, streaming toward a weirdly garbed, gesticulating figure silhouetted atop the northern wall of Oidah. The man waved his arms frantically; his shouted incantations could be heard above the sudden silence of the battlefield. The dan-Ife's magic availed him nothing; the shaft struck with blinding, concussive force. When the afterglow of the explosion faded, the dan-Ife was gone . . . along with a small portion of the wall he was standing on.

The white-gold light had vanished—but the work of the figure on the hill was not yet done. Before anyone in either army could react, she drew back her arm and hurled the glowing sword out toward the battlefield. Trailing radiance like a comet, the serpentine weapon arched far across the sky, farther than human muscles could have flung it. Straight toward the massed Ashanti forces it flew, not stopping until it plunged into the heart of the commander of the *asufos*.

As if wielded by the hand of an invisible *ahosi*, the Sword of Agbewe rose up and swooped down again and again, each time leaving a dead *asufo* in its wake. The blade remained clean and luminous, the blood of its victims hissing off in a cloud of crimson steam.

At the precise moment that Hwesunu roared out his command to attack, the iron discipline of the Ashanti army snapped like a dry twig beneath the foot of an elephant. Dropping their weapons, they turned as one and fled for the harbor where their ships were moored. The gates of Oidah slammed open—the *asufos* left behind to garrison the city poured out like a herd of antelope fleeing lions. No lion, though, could have matched the wild cruelty of the Oidah civilians who pursued the Ashanti, pulling down as many as they could catch and dismembering them with whatever their hands could grasp.

What had begun as a battle, two determined armies clashing like finely honed swords, ended in butchery. Of the three-score ships that had carried the Ashanti invasion force, only two returned to their homeland across the Gulf of

Otongi. By the time the sun rose the next day, no Ashanti remained alive in Abomey.

While his soldiers were cutting down the remnants of the *asufos*, the Leopard king had ventured into the Hills of Sogbaki, seeking Dossouye. After Agbewe's Sword had inflicted its initial damage, it had returned to the summit where Dossouye awaited, her body still limned by a nimbus of pale light. Da Gwebenu had seen the Sword settle gently into Dossouye's hand. Then Dossouye had disappeared.

Climbing with a determination that overcame the disadvantage of his years, the Leopard King followed the route Dossouye had taken the night before. It was the only path that could be climbed by humans. Only the lack of forage for sheep and goats had forestalled the discovery of the cave and the Sword long ago by some curious herdsman. The path had been trod first by Agbewe, centuries ago; then Dossouye, and now the Leopard King.

What he intended to say to Dossouye when he found her, Da Gwebenu did not yet know. Nor had he decided whether he could allow her to live. After her deed this day, her potential as an ally was exceeded only by her threat as a foe. . . .

He reached the end of the path—and half-collapsed against an outcrop of rock when he saw that the end was marked by a newly fallen pile of boulders, blocking what appeared to have been the entrance to a cave. In front of the boulders, two brass ankle-rings glimmered in the dying sunlight. They had been severed cleanly, more cleanly than a master blacksmith could have done.

Of Dossouye, the Leopard King found no other sign.

The *fedi*-palm lay like a long black corpse in the dark grove. Only a jagged stump yet stood, mute testimony to the destruction of Dossouye's souls. The other *fedi* seemed to bow their trunks in mourning, their fronds hanging like leafy shrouds. Dossouye stood silent and alone before the dead tree, a shadow among shades. With clothing, weapons and mount salvaged from the battlefield, she had fared northward with all the unobtrusive stealth of a fugitive.

She was an *ahosi* no longer. The last deed she had performed with Agbewe's Sword before hurling it back into the cave had been to cut away the ankle-rings that bound her to the Leopard King. She would serve him no longer, because she was no longer Abomean.

Gazing at the fallen palm, Dossouye smiled—but there was neither mirth nor joy in the expression. She did not understand why she still lived. Like all Abomeans, she had believed that the *selido* and *semedo* were anchors to the vital, invisible, infinite world of the gods and the ancestors. Without this link, the individual could not claim kinship with the spiritual essence of Abomey. The *djautau,* which died when the individual died, was not believed capable of sustaining life without the provenance of the other two souls. One whose *fedi* was destroyed by fire, lightning, or disease was considered a living ghost, and his claim to property, status, even spouse and children became void. Such unfortunates had never been known to live long following the passing of the *seledo* and *semedo.*

Yet—Dossouye remained alive, suffering no more than the aching discomfort of the wounds she had bound with strips torn from the garments of the dead. There was no emptiness within her; no chasm inadequately filled by her *djautau.* The horror engendered by Nyima's account of the murder of her souls was gone. To Dossouye, the downed tree evoked only slightly more emotion than any other log in the forest.

But because of this log, there was no place in Abomey for the greatest heroine the kingdom had known since the days of Agbewe herself. When the Abomeans discovered that their land had been saved by a person who should have been dead, they would find themselves faced with the choice of abandoning thousands of years of belief—or slaying Dossouye.

Dossouye knew which choice her people would make. The Leopard King and the *azaundato* would see to that. Already she had heard that a group of *ahosi*, led by Toxisi, had been ordered to seek out any clues to her whereabouts.

Exile was the only alternative. Others, mainly *ahosi* fleeing execution for Royal Adultery, had made their way to the Soudan empires to the north, or the teeming city-states of the West Coast, where they sold their swords as mercenaries. Dossouye would do the same. And she would prosper. The trials of the past days had forced her to plumb depths of will and strength far deeper than she had ever dared to believe possible. Despite the loss of two souls, Dossouye had become more than she was before Agbewe had visited her dreams.

Turning from the dead *fedi*, Dossouye mounted the war-bull that would carry her out of Abomey. A straight, slender figure wrapped in cloths to conceal her bound wounds, she glanced once more at the tall palms that guarded generations of decaying umbilical cords. Then she dug her heels into the beast's sides, urging it toward the north.

She never saw the tiny green *fedi*-sprout, hidden by the shadow of the fallen tree.

JANE SAINT'S TRAVAILS

Part One

One threat to "theme" anthologies is a sameness among entries. An editor needs to be on guard lest a book feature tales of too similar a cut. In bringing the present collection to fruition, this was less a problem than I'd expected. I could fill three volumes without duplication! Stories such as these have waited so long to be written that there has accumulated in the minds of authors a wealth of characters and plots each unlike all others.

I have high expectations of heroic fantasy. I don't believe it has to be the endless barrage of hastily written imitations whose themes, characters, plots, and even cover illustrations fade into each other without separate identity—minor variations on a two chord theme, feeding incestuously on its own clichés. To witness stagnation such as that is saddening. Heroic fantasy has been trapped too long in the attitudes and styles of the Nineteen-thirties to fifties. Some fine stories were written then, yes—but imagine if science fiction had grown so little since Doc Smith. Then imagine what heroic fantasy would be now if it had evolved as steadily as science fiction!

The most unique tale among all these comes from the British author of The Hieros Gamos of Sam and An Smith *(Doubleday, 1969), whose short stories have appeared in countless major anthologies. "Jane Saint's Travails (Part One)" is a surrealistic adventure—comparable only to the classic works of surrealist painter and author Leanora Carrington. There will be zealot loyalists who'll condemn the piece as polluting heroic fantasy with higher ideals of breadth and experimenta-*

107

*tion . . . but the wise will realize that heroic fantasy, no
less than the best of science fiction, is an arena of limitless scope and potentiality.*

Jane Saint held out her arm for the injection. It was a
tranquilizer and she did not want it, but there were laws. She
concentrated all her energies ready to use them. The police
doctors were chatting. An orderly spoke to her.

"I must say you are calm, usually they. . . ." She looked
him into silence with gray-eyed contempt. Death by drowning. She had chosen it. Her missions had been treason, and
this was the result of betrayal. But there were still things that
she could do. The drowning was not violent; she should be
able to go through. If she did not make it, then she would
never see her three little girls again, or find the kodebook that
her group needed. One last chance.

She composed herself once more, and each time her fear
broke loose she had to begin at the beginning. According to
official doctrine there was no such thing as a soul. They had
better be wrong. She sent a mental message to her children:
"Mother's coming soon." And that was all there was time for.
They came and lifted her into a tank and manacled her to
the bottom, filled it with water at blood heat. She felt it
gently creeping up to her ears, lapping her lifted chin. Things
could not be better for she would be in a womb. An amniotic
spaceship.

They closed the lid on the vision of her cloud of red hair
streaming like blood, needing flowers to be Ophelia.

Down she went into the heights.

She did all she knew of to ensure a journey to and in another world, in place of the usual extinction of light. Even
so, it was without memory of where and why that she noticed a telephone box on the desolate moor which she
tramped, and decided to use it to ascertain her whereabouts.
There was no habitation within sight in this windswept world
of peatbogs; it was only relieved by an upheaving of rock,
and by sky on the move, wracked yet determined not to relin-
quish any secret—a Brontë land, relieved by puce spewings
of *Erica*, torsioned bonsai.

The operator, stating that it was against the rules, said that she knew that farther up the road there was shelter. The box was in Glun Cloud, which was not famous.

She came to the track upward, and soon saw the tower against a Sublime Sky. She wrestled with an inner turmoil which she knew to be despair. The sight of the tower did not fill her with joy; it looked hostile. It stood on raised ground, with steps cut from the rock leading up to it, spiraling around the mound, and the whole resembled an immense phallus, although she knew that there were days when everything looked like that.

She mounted the steps and banged on the great door which opened immediately, knocking her over as it swung outward. Swearing and cursing about design she arose to face a peasant. It was a female peasant dressed in sacking, with greasy hair and warts, obviously medieval Germanic.

"What do you want?" demanded the peasant, in a strong Yorkshire accent.

"Sanctuary, sanctuary," said Jane, gloriously beautiful as Notre Dame, somehow feeling herself as hunched and gnarled.

"Come in then, and warm thyself." There was a great brick oven in the corner with wonderful fires raging beneath and a glow from the ashtrap.

"Take off your things and dry them." Jane had hardly noticed the rain, and her white operation gown was already steaming, clinging to her body like stone drapery. She declined.

"It's very kind of you to have me in. I was told that I might stay over and that you could help me on my way." She was not certain about that, she now only *thought* that the telephonist had told her that. Perhaps it was the right thing to say. "I'm looking for my children, and for a kodebook." Memory had returned, although not all her reason.

"The Kodebook? You must be from Earth?"

"Yes. I'm in an important rescue team. They need the kodebook." It was a relief that she had recalled her mission.

"Your children will probably be in the Valley of Lost Children. We might be able to help, but first you must help us. We are making an Anthroparion, and we need a few drops of the blood of a good woman."

Jane laughed. "But I am not that woman. Your recipe will curdle if you use my blood."

"Well let's try it anyway. There's nobody else. Mine won't do, for certain. When Anthroparion is made he will be able to help you on your way, they can answer all questions." Very useful! Jane tried to be patient and wait. After all, it was more than possible that this zone was Timeless.

From the opposite corner of the room the other half of "we" shambled out from a narrow closet, dusty and unattractive; an old, selfish man. There were ingrained foodstains on him and his teeth were horrible.

"Are you the new apprentice?" he asked Jane, ogling her beauty. Before she could reply "no," the old woman had answered "yes."

"Well come here then, I've a few things to show you." He had all the air of a flasher in a mac; he was fatherly and furtive and much too pale. As she watched, he mixed salt and soot and sulphur, boiled them up and produced gold.

"Crikey!" said Jane, understandably. He took it over to the closet, and flushed it down the oubliette.

"We don't make it for its own sake you know, it's only for practice." He grabbed her hand and while she was worrying about that, he pricked her finger and got a drop of blood on a filter paper. He threw that into a glowing crucible and then poured all his unholy mix into a bottle, which he sealed with a stopper.

"Now we cook him." And into the great oven went the bottle and then the old woman came near and began to take off her clothes.

"Time for bed," he said, taking off his clothes also. Jane was embarrassed.

"You can sleep over there, under the bench while we make this baby. Don't mind us." Jane went and crept under the bench with her back to the couple and her ears stopped against the lengthy sounds of copulation. She realized just as she fell asleep that there was something else she must remember, or ought to know.

Melanie, Dolores, and Sybil clung to one another in the Valley of Lost Children, chilled by the wails of others, by the gray mists and by the hard white rocks.

"I think I hear Mother saying she will come to us soon," said Sybil, only half-convinced. The others did not reply. They might be merely lost, or lost forever. There were girls who had been waiting here for a million years, waiting for

Mother, or for Life to Begin. They needed a clue as to how to escape, so they used the only power left to them which was wishing. They wished very hard and nothing happened. Then they tried hoping, for Melanie thought of that distinction and it seemed important. As they hoped, they had the idea of digging down into the pebbles, which they did, finding a ring which they pulled, which opened a door into the rock revealing a cave. They entered the cave and the door sealed itself behind them. Inside, it was as bright as day and delightfully warm.

They were afraid, but determined. They walked on around a corner and came into a chamber containing the most enormous woman they had ever seen, reclining like a stranded whale. She was so comfortable and smiling they felt all their problems and miseries floating away.

The woman's hands were held in a caressing pose, and they were large enough for a baby to sit in the palm of each. Her limbs were immersed in rolls of solid flesh, her skin taut over nourished fat. Her eyes were hypnotically kind.

"Come to Mother," she said softly, and they went forward. Her hair was like fibrous rootlets of trees uprooted after a gale, earth clinging to it with a fresh smell. There was a creaking noise of something expanding.

The huge finger beckoned. Dolores began to cry, incoherently certain that they must not proceed. She tugged her sisters hard, trying to turn away.

"We want *our* mother," she managed at last, and the other two suddenly seemed as if they woke up. They had a sense of terror, and without thinking they fled away down the tunnel.

"Keep on hoping, don't forget," said Sybil.

"Nil desperandum," said Melanie.

"Excelsior," said Dolores. And indeed the tunnel was leading upwards.

Jane Saint was watching the presumably alchemical process, seated by the great fired oven. She was remembering her other life in swatches like fabric samples, colored and indecisive. Why was she searching for her three lost children? She could not recall losing them; she could not recall having them. It was something ingrained, like instinct—perhaps it *was* instinct. She wondered how old she was, felt certain that it was not less than fifty. Therefore the children were surely not so very little? A late motherhood? Illegal. She got up and

went to look at herself in the window against the evening,
and knew that she looked young and beautiful by any standards. Had she ever had a husband? Why had they put her in
the tank to drown? She must be a criminal. What was the
Kodebook?

"Look, something is manifesting!" screeched the old
woman. She had flung back the oven doors, and inside the retort glowed. Jane surmised that it should have melted, so hot
was the fire. They carefully pulled out the tripod holding the
retort, maneuvering with iron rakes until the thing stood on
the hearth. Inside, there was a slow cloud of bloody smoke,
and claws and scales appeared in it, denoting something not
human. As Jane watched, she recalled a dream in which
much of this had occurred. Was the other life a dream, or
was this? It seemed for a moment or so that she was falling
between two stools.

The thing in the retort was complete, and the old man
came over from his bookshelves to look. He was skinny and
bent with an eye that rolled upward from time to time when
he scowled, and stringy hair that he never cut or brushed.
Jane loathed him.

"Ask it the passwords!" he roared. He always either roared
or mumbled, a sign of a deceitful nature, Jane believed.

"Kodebook Seven," said the old woman, and the hairs on
Jane's arms stood up with interest.

"There's no such thing," spoke a little voice in the retort.
"Kodebooks belong to people without hearts and brains. The
Koran, the Bible for example out of many, are all without
value in that they only seem to offer a good way of life.
There shall be no more Kodes."

"Sounds like Blasphemy," said the old man, grinning.

"Sounds like good sense to me," said the old woman, thinking of how all females have been judged evil Eve and sinful
Salome. A book biased to half the world must be about half
rubbish—or rather more. But she did not speak, and neither
did Jane, for both knew that it is better to keep the trap shut
in certain circumstances. The old man took the stopper out of
the retort and bid Anthroparion to come out. He took no notice when the old woman pointed out that this was not Anthroparion, but a demonic presence. It didn't seem to matter
anymore. It had leathery wings, a scaly tail with a horny
point, little sharp teeth in a monkeyish head, and gilded

feathers or scales which shone in the firelight. It appeared to be wearing pink nail varnish. It spoke to Jane.

"I have seen your daughters. They have been tested and found strong enough to be women. They are on their way home and do not need you."

"I haven't the faintest idea what you are talking about," said Jane, shivering.

"It doesn't matter, I'm just trying to calm your fears. You thought you were on an important mission, but you were not. There are no great missions anymore. In this land we have achieved only shadowy dreams, so how could we help you achieve more than that?" Jane realized that she had expected miracles of what was after all only another reality. She could not now recall the political problem she had been dedicated to—but she was realizing that there was another one, more important.

"I'm hungry," announced the thing. "My name is Zilp; it's meaningless. Once, I had an exotic Hebrew name but they've given all that up as racialist." Nobody got that.

The old woman went to drag out a sack of flour to prepare some scones. She beckoned to Jane to get on with it, but Jane declined, saying that she needed some fresh air. Her personality must be changing! At one time she would have made not only scones but cakes and batch bread and currant biscuits and scotch pancakes. Now they could damn well make themselves.

Going down the steps of the tower, she wrestled with Guilt. After all, a woman's place is in the tower.

At the bottom of the steps was a desert—no wonder so many turned back. It was a temptation. But, ahead also were temptations, coming toward her in the form of a man. Zilp was watching from the window.

The male figure approached and Jane saw that it wore a doublet and hose in dark velvet with white sleeves slashed over gold. It had long fair hair and regarded itself inwardly, which was to be seen from the noble and absent-minded expression on its face. She felt that she could throw herself into the river for love of such a one. Thank heavens this was a desert!

It seemed for a moment that the figure led a white horse, but she was fascinated to observe that the whole scene changed. The man was in fact wearing farm-laborer's jeans, was naked to the waist, barefoot, his chest covered in a ba-

roque pattern of dark hair, his features clear as if cut from
Siena marble. He was hardworking, proud of it. She could
bear him ten children as well as keep the house perfect and
sit up all night with ailing calves, breaking off to take him ale
in the field and to cook huge repasts. But before she could offer herself, he changed again. Zilp came out of the tower and
hopped over to Jane who ignored him. He pulled at her dress,
whining not to take notice of them, for they were merely the
work of a sorcerer, mere shifted shapes.

The man now had on a hairy tweed suit and wore a thin
pale beard, smoked a knobbly pipe and had untidy hair,
leather patches on his elbows and stout stitched shoes on his
feet. His eyes were distant with academic problems and male
thoughts, kind and strong and yet vulnerable, absent-minded
and clever and remote and yet like an uncle, all at once. He
smelled of nicotine and peat and book-bindings. Her heart
began to beat faster and she shut her eyes in bliss. When she
opened them again there was a very young man in tight jeans
and a tee-shirt, lean and innocent, with a little bit of acne
marring his immature visage. She glanced at Zilp who
clutched his head in despair. Why would he mind her giving
herself to one of these? She could see no harm in it.

"Test them out by shifting shape yourself," advised Zilp. "I
can help you to change your shape to some other kind of
woman, and you will see these men reveal themselves for
what they are." Jane shrugged and said why not, for she did
not believe him. She knew love at first sight when she saw it,
and she could have all or any of them.

The man before her now was taller and obviously very
strong and powerful, all dressed in black, which set off his
close-cropped pale hair to perfection, and his broad shoulders
carried a long leather overcoat which was open to reveal a
black silk shirt, black trousers and jackboots polished by
somebody else. He had a gun and a dagger and an iron cross.
Jane could hardly resist running to him and kneeling at his
feet, she itched to undo her own clothing. But her shape was
changing.

She was a little shorter, a little fatter, her face was a little
less firm, her breasts a little smaller and a little less perky.
Her hair was shorter and full of gray, and her eyes were less
bright and her ankles a little thicker. The man blinked and
stared at her and passed his hand over his eyes, clicked his
heels, bowed and turned to go. The youth appeared and

stared at her with empty eyes, the farmer assessed her for work capacity. Then the first man rather roughly suggested that she retire to a nunnery.

"Do you believe me now?" asked Zilp smugly, preening his gilded feathers or scales. One fell out and Jane picked it up. Of course she believed him, for in a way she had always known it was like this, but had not wanted to know. There had been nothing else to live for.

"Come on back to the tower, Jane. Tea's ready." Zilp took her hand in his sympathetic claw, and sadly she ascended the steps with him.

"But I shall have no friends, nobody will love me any more," she said, beginning to cry.

"Yes you will, people will love you. Those weren't friends, they were only vampires."

Scones were handed round, and a massive pot of tea, and Jane tried to cheer up. The question was: what to do now? She had failed to find her lost girls, if she had ever had any, she had failed to find the Kodebook, if there was such a thing and if it was worth having, and she had failed to get herself a handsome prince, if they were what they seemed to be. Failed, failed on all counts.

The old man must have been reading her thoughts.

"You'll be all right, girly, if you keep your head clear. Things are changing. They are changing here, just like there, but it takes centuries for things to *really* be different. It's that kind of world."

He handed her another scone. He didn't seem so sinister, now; he seemed more sincere. Perhaps he was changing too.

"Go back and start to change things. Start to do a bit of something real, instead of barraging up the old order. You probably thought you were some kind of revolutionary, but you were in the service of those who would cheat you of your existence, I bet." Jane would bet, too. She felt utterly duped.

"Well, I can't go back. I'm dead, remember."

"No, no. Dead is dead—how could you be here or anywhere if you were dead. You are in a coma. They reprieved you, but kept you in storage until they made further investigations. Right, Zilp?"

"Right. You can go back. It will be like waking up."

"Not drowned?"

"No. After all."

"But what shall I do when I get back, I won't know what to say, I don't know. . . ."

"Just don't tell them any of this; keep your secrets until you get sorted out, that's my advice." It seemed like good advice. Zilp brushed the crumbs off his monkeyish jaws, and offered to go with her part way. He thought it a good idea to simply walk for a while and see what turned up. You could never tell how long it would be before "returns" took place. So, after all the leave-taking and thanking had been done with, they went out into the desert again, but this time Jane could see an oasis on the horizon.

Zilp told her how to change her shape. It was easy. She would be able to test things out whenever she wanted to in the future.

"It is well that you did not have children, especially girls. You would have filled them up with a right load of romantic nonsense, would you not?" Jane had to agree, and laughed aloud. He kissed her hand, and took off in flight, flapping slowly against the lemon-colored sky.

Jane walked on to the oasis, wrestling with the problem of hoping, while not hoping for any particularity.

A burning sense of mission was a great help in keeping a person going; she felt pain at the idea of relinquishing it, but knew what vanity it was to think that she could have ever saved the world. But there were plenty of useful things to do, still. There must be.

Understanding a great deal less than she ever had before, but with great futures stirring within her, Jane Saint just kept walking, and hoped.

When they were resuscitating her, the orderly found a feather of pure gold in her left hand.

THE SORROWS OF WITCHES

Margaret St. Clair

Garish covers aside, all but the coyest allusions to sexuality in fantasy and sf have been taboo from the pulp era to fairly recent years. Presently the opposite has become fashionable: violent, exploitative sex scenes inserted at random. Various social psychologists have attempted to explain why hypocritically puritanical societies are repeatedly wont to degrade sexuality as immoral while simultaneously providing a massive market for its commercialization. To this day, relatively few authors strive seriously and intelligently for a mature handling of themes dealing with human sexuality.

Two men are generally and erroneously credited with bringing the genre out of its prepubescence: Michael Moorcock with the early New Worlds series, and Harlan Ellison with the Dangerous Visions collections. However, if we look at what was written before these landmark anthologies, we discover two women first breached the barriers: the late Miriam Allen deFord, and the author at hand, Margaret St. Clair. Each investigated human and alien sexuality before it was the mode, though neither received the fanfare allocated male mimics.

Author of Dancers of Noyo, Dolphins of Altair, The Shadow People, Change the Sky and Other Stories, and Message from the Eocene, Margaret St. Clair graces Amazons with a distinguished tale of war, governorship, and the sexuality of a sorceress queen. "The Sorrow of Witches" is a perfectly crafted tale, rich in irony.

Who cares for the joys or sorrows of witches? In both they are set apart from ordinary humanity. If witches are glad, it is because they have purchased joys beyond the common at the cost of their souls. And if they suffer in ways that we cannot know, when their dark lords desert them, it is no more than the wicked things deserve. Yet they are women, with the hearts of women, for all that.

Morganor was a queen of Enbatana, one of the great Enbatanid line of necromantic queens. From her earliest years she had studied the mantic arts with her grandmother, her mother being dead; and by the time she was twenty she had attained an unheard-of mastery of unholy things. Those of her subjects who hated her—and there were a few—swore that she had her power from the rotting mummy of a monkey that she fed in abominable ways at the dark of the moon, and that she was attended always by the writhing spirits of two men whom she had slain in torture. It was certain that no wizard of her time or before it could approach her in invocation, the lore of philtres, and the power to summon up and dismiss.

But for all her necromantics she was a wise queen, and the land throve under her. The faïence of the workmen of Enbatana went wherever white-winged ships could sail; the webs of the women of Enbatana brought a great price in any marketplace. No child in Enbatana went hungry, no old man or woman thought with dread of what the morrow might bring.

Morganor had many lovers. They were won, it was said, not so much by the glamour of her queenship or the power of her philtres as by the wonderful beauty of her person and the sweetness of her voice, which was like the notes of a golden lyre. She tired of her lovers quickly, and left them, and they were forbidden to feel jealousy.

But in the queen's twenty-third year there came an embassy to her court from the land of the burnt faces. Among the soldiers who attended the embassy was a captain named Llwdres, a huge man like a lion, with a bronzed face. And Morganor, as if her stars had enjoined it on her, fell desperately in love with him.

She wooed him shyly at first, with gifts of fruit and little presents. Then, when she met no response, she showed him favor openly and sent him queenly gifts.

Morganor could scarcely believe it when he continued cold and averse. She bit her lips in vexation and set herself to brew a sovereign philtre, and this philtre she gave him to drink as he sat at table by her side. With kindling eyes she saw him put the golden cup down empty from his lips. But Llwdres might have drunk clear water for all the good she had from him.

Then indeed was Morganor desperate. She rose hastily and went to her apartments. Up and down she paced, gnawing her white wrists and tearing her dark hair. Remember, from her birth until this moment no wish of hers, possible or impossible, had gone ungratified. Llwdres' stubborn refusal seemed to her out of the order of things, perverse, unnatural, intolerable.

At last she called the chief of the palace guard to her and gave him orders. Llwdres was to be taken to a dungeon and whipped. He had ignored her soft words, her smile and her love-presents, had he? She would see what physical pain could do. Then she threw herself down on a long divan and wept.

The minutes went by—so many that Morganor, who had ordered but twenty lashes, grew afraid. She had risen to her feet and started to the door when a terrified servant, beating the ground before her with his head, stammered out that Llwdres had been put to death.

Morganor felt that her heart would stop beating. She ran through the palace like a madwoman. When she reached the dungeon she saw by the winking light of the torches that Llwdres' limbs had been severed from his body; he had died painfully. And she saw, without understanding it, that another body was dangling by a noose from a crenation in the dungeon walls, the body of the chief of her palace guard. He had hanged himself.

Morganor realized then, too late, that she had given Llwdres for punishment to a man who had been her lover for a pair of nights. He had trembled and turned white when she had told him she wanted no more of him. Why had she not seen how jealous he was? Unbearable jealousy had driven him to kill Llwdres. And after that he had hanged himself.

Morganor knelt by the body of her beloved and gathered the severed limbs to herself, like Isis in search for dead Osiris. She covered them with tears and kisses. Then she had them lifted up carefully and borne to her apartments. And after that, for many days and nights, she wept.

She wept until her hair was sodden with weeping. She could have put out the coals of a great fire had she shaken her hair over it. But at last her old nurse came to her, a book of enchantments in one hand and in the other Morganor's rings and bracelets of sorcery, and she said in a quavering voice, "Queen of the Enbatanians, how long will you weep for your beloved and lament? Have you forgotten that you are the daughter of queens and the mistress of all mantic arts?"

Morganor was as if deaf at first, but at last she roused herself. She called her maids, and they bathed and annointed her. She purified herself with incense and put on garments of virgin samite. She donned her rings and bracelets, her pectorals of sorcery. And she opened many volumes from her shelves of books.

Nontheless, it was a dreadful task she had set herself. To rouse the dead after a fashion is not difficult; it lies within the province of any hedgerow sorcerer. False life may be infused into them, and they be set to striding about stiffly with unseeing eyes. Or demons, great strange spirits may be made to enter and animate them. But Morganor would have none of this. Llwdres must live again as he had been in very life. And this goal, Morganor knew, lay at the very limits of sorcery.

She labored for many days, and without success. She had arrested decay in Llwdres' body by a great spell, but for the rest he was mere lifeless flesh. She stopped for a day, waiting out an inauspicious aspect of her stars, and during this time she sent a dire enchantment against the soul of the slayer of her beloved. Wherever he was, in whatever dim after-world, he should pay for it, he should pay! Then Morganor returned once more to her work.

On the twenty-sixth night, as she stood in a triple circle and the palace lights burned blue, a mighty spirit appeared to her. He proposed a bargain to her. If she would surrender much of her mantic power—nay, the greater part—it could be done, and Llwdres could live again. There was also another sacrifice—but the demon would not name what.

Morganor turned pale, but she nodded. She erased the circle around her, and gave to the spirit all her symbols and arcana of power save for two elementary volumes and a simple gold amulet. The mighty spirit, free from the constraint Morganor had put on him and his whole tribe, beat his wings together in a paroxysm of delight and darted like a river of fire through the roof. And Llwdres, lying on his bier, stirred.

He stirred and mumbled words. After a moment he sat up and looked at her. And he smiled.

For, whether the necromancy of the mighty spirit had changed Llwdres' nature, or whether, as Morganor thought, he had only refused her before from country pride and fear to be ruled by a woman as great as Morganor was, this time he loved her with all the strength and ardor of a man. They met in an embrace like the coupling of eagles. And Morganor had such joy at the fulfillment of her love that she annointed the posts of her bed with nard from Punt, and kissed the bed covers. Joy shone in her face as if a lamp had been lit within the flesh.

She kept her resurrected love with her for a month, and all those days were to her as one day. With each embrace he gave her, her love for him grew. She dreamed of setting him beside her on the throne of Enbatana as king, but she knew this was impossible. Her people were proud in a perverse way of their necromantic queen, but they were a stiff-necked and narrow-minded folk. If she set a dead man over them as lord—and there were certain inescapable signs that Llwdres, though he lived now, had once been dead—some of them would rise against her, and some would be true. There would be war within Enbatana then, and all the bitterness of civil strife. Already gossip, though wide of the mark, was beginning to seep through the palace and out into the streets.

On the thirty-first day, therefore, Llwdres consenting, Morganor cast him into a deep sleep most like that sleep of death from which he had arisen recently. For his bed he had a massive chest wrought and inlaid with gold, and this chest Morganor kept always in her bedchamber. Whenever it seemed to her safe, she would rouse her captain, using what remained to her, of her mantic art, and they would hold love dalliance. And this unhallowed commerce wrapped her senses in such a blaze of sweetness that she had eyes for no other man.

But always her councillors urged on her to wed. They presented her with petitions written on velum, respectful in phraseology but peremptory in tone, in which they spoke of her daughterless state, and the evils which befall the kingdom left without a queen. When Morganor cursed them royally, the councillors bowed to the ground and drew up new petitions to present to her. At last Morganor, acknowledging the justice of what they said, gave in.

She told the council to pick what mate for her they

pleased. Puffed with self-importance, they went fussily to
their task, and pitched at last on a neighboring princeling
named Fabius, a man famed for his virtue (here Morganor
laughed), and his piety. From the picture they showed her,
he was well-enough made, with a girlish, small-featured face.

The marriage was celebrated with more rejoicing among
the people than there was in Morganor's heart. She but endured her new consort for the sake of her realm, though he
was a well-intentioned man. To her he was a small flame
bleached by Llwdres' lordly sun.

In time a child was born to Morganor. It was certainly the
child of her consort, since those who have been dead, however ardent they are, can kindle no new life. But Morganor,
in the unfailing sweetness of her love for Llwdres, felt that
her womb had been enchanted and that her child was begot-
ten by her own true love and none else. She was happy in her
motherhood. Then Enbatana was afflicted by two dry years.

The drought in itself would not have harmed the land. The
vast granaries which Morganor's mother's mother's mother
had built, Morganor herself had consolidated and enlarged.
Enbatana might have suffered a dozen worse years and
known no dearth. But the nomads to the north of Enbatana,
always on the edge of starvation, saw their scanty pasturage
dry up and the sands begin to blow. Soon they were in motion like a deadly storm sweeping onward from the desert's
heart.

Morganor, wise queen, hated war. She tried to treat with
the nomads, to settle them on the marches of her land as hus-
bandmen. But they broke treaty after treaty, and Morganor
saw at last that they were fierce and faithless men who
despised the tasks of husbandry and civic life. Their only art
was to destroy what others had built, to turn fruitful land to
desert under the hungry jaws of their sheep and goats. They
gathered on the borders of Enbatana as many as locusts, and
their sunken eyes were dark with battle lust and hate.

Morganor assembled her council and asked for plans. One
said one thing and one another; all trembled and uttered dole-
ful prophesies. Fabius, the virtuous Fabius, advised prayer
and fasting and sacrifice. So Morganor once more roused her
lover, this time for counsel, not dalliance. And Llwdres
proved himself as skillful and brave in war as he had been in
love.

He told Morganor to levy armies with the grain tithe lists

ranging battle plans. Then, the armies being assembled, the
as base. He told her how to judge her generals and captains,
which to trust and which to dismiss, and how to lay long-
queen and her dead leman rose out at their head.

While the do-nothing king hugged the capital and prayed
and fasted, there were many battles. The terror of the times
had relaxed all ordinary rules of conduct, and Morganor
spent many a brief, alarm-broken night in her lover's arms.
The men of Enbatana, for all their lack of practice in war,
fought with desperate bravery. Morganor herself was wounded once, in her right thigh. And it was said in aftertimes by
grave historians that Enbatana was saved in her darkest hour
by a dead man and an accursed necromantic queen.

There was one great battle, a nightmare of confusion and
blood and dust. Llwdres bore the royal standard in it and
fought as a lion fights. When the battle was over, nearly half
the men of Enbatana were dead. But the nomads had died to
the last man.

Morganor remembered prudence then. She cast Llwdres
once more into the sleep that was so like death and, giving
out that he had died of wounds received in battle, had him
placed in state on a bier in her train. When they reached the
capital he was conveyed secretly to her apartments and
placed once more in the gold-wrought chest.

But Fabius, like a virtuous man, was jealous of his honor.
Rumors reached him. He conceived suspicions. One night,
when Morganor had been long asleep and Llwdres slept un-
breathing in the chest, he came to her apartments with his
bodyguard.

"Accursed witch!" he shouted at her as she blinked up at
him with sleep-dazzled eyes. "Where is the man with whom
you defile my bed?"

Morganor was for a moment utterly puzzled. Fabius had
never been real to her. She did not know what he meant. "I
have never defiled it," she said in a sleep-roughened voice.

"No?" He strode stiffly about her bedchamber, looked under draperies and pulling out hangings with his sword. At last
he said to his attendants, "The dog must be here. We will
drive him out. Fire the room."

One of his men touched a torch to a length of drapery that
hung beside Llwdres' chest. Flame shot up instantly and
spread over the ceiling in a gush. And Morganor screamed.

She sprang from her bed and darted toward the shelf that

held her last tools of the mantic art. In her mind was only one thought, to put out the fire by magic before it could fasten on Llwdres' enchanted limbs. She feared not merely his death but some horror which should transgress the bounds of the possible. The mighty spirit had warned her of another sacrifice. But two of Fabius' guards caught her and held her; for all her struggles and imperious cursing she could not get free.

Then Morganor, turning to her consort, said, "Let me go, and I will confess it. Let me go, and I will swear never to defile your bed again."

Fabius looked at her narrowly. His face was flushed with his poor triumph. "Do you swear it on your royal honor?" he demanded. The flames were already licking around the chest.

"I swear it," Morganor said.

"Release her," Fabius ordered his men.

They let go the queen's wrists. The room was full of smoke and fire. Morganor ran through it, choking, and seized her books and amulet desperately. She gasped out a spell, traced figures in the air, cast a powder toward the fire. And the flames died down sullenly.

Morganor saw that the chest, though charred, was unhurt. She ran to it and cast her arms about it, sinking on her knees. Except for that, she was too spent to move.

Fabius came toward her, naked sword in hand. "So that was where the dog was, was it?" he said bitterly. "Out of the way, witch. I am going to kill him now."

Morganor got slowly to her feet. "Consort of the queen of Enbatana," she said in a clear voice, "do you hope to sit again on the lower throne by my side?"

Fabius wavered. Then he recovered himself. "I avenge my honor," he said.

"Your honor will not avail you when my people tear you in pieces," Morganor said. "They remember who saved them in battle, and who fasted and prayed. Therefore I charge you solemnly as you hope to consort with me and beget other children on me: do not open the chest." This she said because she knew that if Fabius saw who slept in the chest, there would be civil war.

Their eyes met. His eyes were hawk's eyes, but Morganor's were the eyes on an eagle. At last he said, "So be it. But remember, my queen, your royal oath."

"I remember," Morganor said.

When he and his men had gone she went over to a window and stood looking out. The sky was paling; it would not be long before dawn. She saw the greater infortune regarding her malevolently from her tenth house, and she thought of the configurations of the stars and the varied fortunes of men. Then she went to the chest and, for the last time, awakened her love.

They sat for some hours together, talking quietly, their hands joined. There could be no love between them, because of Morganor's great oath. Only, before she lulled him into sleep again, Llwdres gave the last of many kisses to his queen's lips. Then Morganor went out to her lawful consort, and thenceforward day and night were alike to her, and both wearied her.

But the body of her beloved she had conveyed by those she trusted most to a great mountain to the east of her domain, a mountain at whose heart there was a chamber cut out of solid rock. The attendants left Llwdres in the chamber, as the queen had ordered them, and sealed it with masonry. And there the captain lies in his enchanted slumber until a greater necromantic queen or a more fortunate of Morganor's line shall come to awaken him.

FALCON BLOOD

Andre Norton

Although the 1970's have seen radical changes and improvements in the attitudes and quality of science fiction and adult fantasy, prior to the present decade this potentially visionary genre imposed many serious limitations upon itself. There remain many boundaries to transcend. Until the recent past, however, there weren't even a noticeable percentage of authors willing, able, or allowed to feature women as central characters.

Fan and critic Jennifer K. Bankier observed in the science fiction journal Algol that Andre Norton, "was writing books with strong, competent, heroic women in them long before other authors even began to consider the possibility." Ordeal in Otherwhen, Ms. Norton's first novel with a female protagonist, was considered radical by her publisher—as indeed it was at the time. Since then, powerful women have been common to her work. Recommended are: Storm Over Warlock, Moon of Three Rings, Ice Crown, Exiles to the Stars, The Book of Andre Norton, Android at Arms, Dread Companion, Breed to Come, Trey of Swords, Zarsthor's Bane, Spell of the Witch World, and all other Witch World books and stories.

In spite of the hassles of changing residence and a general funk that had slowed down her writing, Ms. Norton yet conveyed an enthusiasm when I contacted her about Amazons! It was an example of the kind of high energy and commitment this collection sparked at every level of creation—the experience of which was my own greatest reward.

"Falcon's Blood" continues Andre Norton's tradition of strong women especially in her Witch World series. Herein we gather important historic information about a certain Witch World race, and are given images of two powerful women—one evil, one heroic—and one man whose cultural myths encompass a paranoia so intense as to justify irrational hatred of women.

126

Tanree sucked at the torn ends of her fingers, tasted the sea salt stinging in them. Her hair hung in sticky loops across her sand-abraded face, too heavy with sea water to stir in the wind.

For the moment it was enough that she had won out of the waves, was alive. Sea was life for the Sulcar, yes, but it could also be death. In spite of the trained resignation of her people, other forces within her had kept her fighting ashore.

Gulls screamed overhead, sharp, piercing cries. So frantic those cries Tanree looked up into the gray sky of the after storm. The birds were under attack. Wider dark wings spread away from a body on the breast of which a white vee of feathers set an unmistakable seal. A falcon soared, swooped, clutched in cruel talons one of the gulls, bearing its prey to the top of the cliff, where it perched still within sight.

It ate, tearing flesh with a vicious beak. Cords flailed from its feet, the sign of its service.

Falcon. The girl spat gritty sand from between her teeth, her hands resting on scraped knees barely covered by her undersmock. She had thrown aside kilt, all other clothing, when she had dived from the ship pounding against a foam-crowned reef.

The ship!

She got to her feet, stared seaward. Storm anger still drove waves high. Broken backed upon rock fangs hung the Kast-Boar. Her masts were but jaggered stumps. Even as Tanree watched, the waters raised the ship once more, to slam her down on the reef. She was breaking apart fast.

Tanree shuddered, looked along the scrap of narrow beach. Who else had won to shore? The Sulcar were sea born and bred; surely she could not be the only survivor.

Wedged between two rocks so that the retreating waves could not drag him back, a man lay face down. Tanree raised her broken-nailed, scraped fingers and made the Sign of Wottin, uttering the age-old plea:

> "Wind and wave,
> Mother Sea,
> Lead us home.
>   Far the harbor,
> Wild thy waves—
>   Still, by thy Power,
> Sulcar saved!"

Had the man moved then? Or was it only the water washing about him which had made it seem so?

He was—This was no Sulcar crewman! His body was covered from neck to mid thigh by leather, dark breeches twisted with seaweed on his legs.

"Falconer!"

She spat again with salt-scoured lips. Though the Falconers had an old pact with her people, sailed on Sulcar ships as marines, they had always been a race apart—dour, silent men who kept to themselves. Good in battle, yes, so much one must grant them. But who really knew the thoughts in their heads, always hidden by their bird-shaped helms? Though this one appeared to have shucked all his fighting gear, to appear oddly naked.

There came a sharp scream. The falcon, full fed, now beat its way down to the body. There the bird settled on the sand just beyond the reach of the waves, squatted crying as if to arouse its master.

Tanree sighed. She knew what she must do. Trudging across the sand she started for the man. Now the falcon screamed again, its whole body expressing defiance. The girl halted, eyed the bird warily. These creatures were trained to attack in battle, to go for the eyes or the exposed face of an enemy. They were very much a part of the armament of their masters.

She spoke aloud as she might to one of her own kind: "No harm to your master, flying one." She held out sore hands in the oldest peace gesture.

Those bird eyes were small reddish coals, fast upon her. Tanree had an odd flash of feeling that this one had more understanding than other birds possessed. It ceased to scream, but the eyes continued to stare, sparks of menace, as she edged around it to stand beside the unconscious man.

Tanree was no weakling. As all her race she stood tall and strong, able to lift and carry, to haul on sail lines, or move cargo, should an extra hand be needed. Sulcarfolk lived aboard their ships and both sexes were trained alike to that service.

Now she stooped and set hands in the armpits of the mercenary, pulling him farther inland, and then rolling him over so he lay face up under the sky.

Though they had shipped a dozen Falconers on this last voyage (since the Kast-Boar intended to strike south into

waters reputed to give sea room to the shark boats of outlaws) Tanree could not have told one of the bird fighters
from another. They wore their masking helms constantly and
kept to themselves, only their leader speaking when necessary
to the ship people.

The face of the man was encrusted with sand, but he was
breathing, as the slight rise and fall of his breast under the
soaked leather testified. She brushed grit away from his nostrils, his thin lipped mouth. There were deep frown lines between his sand-dusted brows, a mask-like sternness in his
face.

Tanree sat back on her heels. What did she know about
this fellow survivor? First of all. the Falconers lived by harsh
and narrow laws no other race would accept. Where their
original home had been no outsider knew. Generations ago
something had set them wandering, and then the tie with her
own people had been formed. For the Falconers had wanted
passage out of the south from a land only Sulcar ships
touched.

They had sought ship room for all of them, perhaps some
two thousand—two-thirds of those fighting men, each with a
trained hawk. But it was their custom which made them utterly strange. For, though they had women and children with
them, yet there was no clan or family feeling. To Falconers
women were born for only one purpose: to bear children.
They were made to live in villages apart, visited once a year
by men selected by their officers. Such temporary unions were
the only meetings between the sexes.

First they had gone to Estcarp, learning that the ancient
land was hemmed in by enemies. But there had been an unbreachable barrier to their taking service there.

For in ancient Estcarp the Witches ruled. and to them a
race who so degraded their females was cursed. Thus the Falconers had made their way into the no-man's-land of the
southern mountains, building there their eyrie on the border
between Estcarp and Karsten. They had fought shoulder to
shoulder with the Borderers of Estcarp in the great war. But
when, at last, a near exhausted Estcarp had faced the over-
powering might of Karsten, and the Witches concentrated all
their power (many of them dying from it) to change the
earth itself, the Falconers, warned in time, had reluctantly returned to the lowlands.

Their numbers were few by then, and the men took service

as fighters where they could. For at the end of the great war, chaos and anarchy followed. Some men, nurtured all their lives on fighting, became outlaws; so that, though in Estcarp itself some measure of order prevailed, much of the rest of the continent was beset.

Tanree thought that this Falconer, lacking helm, mail shirt, weapons, resembled any man of the Old Race. His dark hair looked black beneath the clinging sand, his skin was paler than her own sun-browned flesh. He had a sharp nose, rather like the jutting beak of his bird, and his eyes were green. For now they had opened to stare at her. His frown grew more forbidding.

He tried to sit up, fell back, his mouth twisting in pain. Tanree was no reader of thoughts, but she was sure his weakness before her was like a lash laid across his face.

Once more he attempted to lever himself up, away from her. Tanree saw one arm lay limp. She moved closer, sure of a broken bone.

"No! You—you female!" There was such a note of loathing in his voice that anger flared in her in answer.

"As you wish—" She stood up, deliberately turned her back on him, moving away along the narrow beach, half encircled by cliff and walls of water-torn, weed-festooned rocks.

Here was the usual storm bounty brought ashore, wood—some new torn from the Kast-Boar, some the wrack of earlier storms. She made herself concentrate on finding anything which might be of use.

Where they might now be in relation to the lands she knew, Tanree had no idea. They had been beaten so far south by the storm that surely they were no longer within the boundaries of Karsten. And the unknown, in these days, was enough to make one wary.

There was a glint in a half ball of weed. Tanree leaped to jerk that away just as the waves strove to carry it off. A knife—no, longer than just a knife—by some freak driven point deep into a hunk of splintered wood. She had to exert some strength to pull it out. No rust spotted the ten-inch blade yet.

Such a piece of good fortune! She sat her jaw firmly and faced around, striding back to the Falconer. He had flung his sound arm across his eyes as if to shut out the world. Beside him crouched the bird uttering small guttural cries. Tanree stood over them both, knife in hand.

"Listen," she said coldly. It was not in her to desert a helpless man no matter how he might spurn her aid. "Listen, Falconer, think of me as you will. I offer no friendship cup to you either. But the sea has spat us out, therefore this is not our hour to seek the Final Gate. We cannot throw away our lives heedlessly. That being so—" she knelt by him, reaching out also for a straight piece of drift lying near, "you will accept from me the aid of what healcraft I know. Which," she admitted frankly, "is not much."

He did not move that arm hiding his eyes. But neither did he try now to evade as she slashed open the sleeve of his tunic and the padded lining beneath to bare his arm. There was no gentleness in this—to prolong handling would only cause greater pain. He uttered no sound as she set the break (thank the Power it was a simple one) and lashed his forearm against the wood with strips slashed from his own clothing. Only when she had finished did he look to her.

"How bad?"

"A clean break," she assured him. "But—" she frowned at the cliff, "how you can climb from here one-handed—"

He struggled to sit up; she knew better than to offer support. With his good arm as a brace, he was high enough to gaze at the cliff and then the sea. He shrugged.

"No matter—"

"It matters!" Tanree flared. She could not yet see a way out of this pocket, not for them both. But she would not surrender to imprisonment by rock or wave.

She fingered the dagger-knife and turned once more to examine the cliffs. To venture back into the water would only sweep them against the reef. But the surface of the wall behind them was pitted and worn enough to offer toe and hand holds. She paced along the short beach, inspecting that surface. Sulcarfolk had good heads for heights, and the Falconers were mountaineers. It was a pity this one could not sprout wings like his comrade in arms.

Wings! She tapped her teeth with the point of the knife. An idea flitted to her mind and she pinned it fast.

Now she returned to the man quickly.

"This bird of yours—" she pointed to the red-eyed hawk at his shoulder, "what powers does it have?"

"Powers!" he repeated and for the first time showed surprise. "What do you mean?"

She was impatient. "They *have* powers; all know that. Are

they not your eyes and ears, scouts for you? What else can they do beside that, and fight in battle?"

"What have you in mind?" he countered.

"There are spires of rock up there." Tanree indicated the top of the cliff. "Your bird has already been aloft. I saw him kill a gull and feast upon it while above."

"So there are rock spires and—"

"Just this, bird warrior," she dropped on her heels again. "No rope can be tougher than loops of some of this weed. If you had the aid of a rope to steady you, could you climb?"

He looked at her for an instant as if she had lost even that small store of wit his people credited to females. Then his eyes narrowed as he gazed once more, measuringly, at the cliff.

"I would not have to ask that of any of *my* clan," she told him deliberately. "Such a feat would be play as our children delight in."

The red stain of anger arose on his pale face.

"How would you get the rope up there?" He had not lashed out in fury to answer her taunt as she had half expected.

"If your bird can carry up a finer strand, loop that about one of the spires there, then a thicker rope can be drawn in its wake and that double rope looped for your ladder. I would climb and do it myself, but we must go together since you have the use of but one hand."

She thought he might refuse. But instead he turned his head and uttered a crooning sound to the bird.

"We can but try," he said a moment later.

The seaweed yielded to her knife and, though he could use but the one hand, the Falconer helped twist and hold strands to her order as she fashioned her ropes. At last she had the first thin cord, one end safe knotted to a heavier one, the other in her hands.

Again the Falconer made his bird sounds and the hawk seized upon the thin cord at near mid point, With swift, sure beat of wings it soared up, as Tanree played out the cord swiftly hoping she had judged the length aright.

Now the bird spiralled down and the cord was suddenly loose in Tanree's grasp. Slowly and steadily she began to pull, bring upward from the sand the heavier strand to dangle along the cliff wall.

One moment at a time, think only that, Tanree warned

herself as they began their ordeal. The heavier part of the
rope was twisted around her companion, made as fast as she
could set it. His right arm was splinted, but his fingers were
as swift to seek out holds as hers. He had kicked off his boots
and slung those about his neck, leaving his toes bare.

Tanree made her way beside him, within touching distance,
one glance for the cliff face, a second for the man. They
were aided unexpectedly when they came upon a ledge, not
to be seen from below. There they crouchd together, breathing heavily. Tanree estimated they had covered two thirds of
their journey but the Falconer's face was wet with sweat and
trickled down, to drip from his chin.

"Let us get to it!" he broke the silence between them, inching up to his feet again, his sound arm a brace against the
wall.

"Wait!"

Tanree drew away, was already climbing. "Let me get aloft
now. And do you keep well hold of the rope."

He protested but she did not listen, any more than she paid
attention to the pain in her fingers. But, when she pulled herself over the lip of the height, she lay for a moment, her
breath coming in deep, rib-shaking sobs. She wanted to do no
more than lie where she was, for it seemed that strength
drained steadily from her as blood flowing from an open
wound.

Instead she got to her knees and crawled to that outcrop of
higher rock around which the noose of the weed rope
strained and frayed. She set her teeth grimly, laid hold of the
taut strand they had woven. Then she called, her voice
sounding in her own ears as high as the scream of the hawk
that now hovered overhead.

"Come!"

She drew upon the rope with muscles tested and trained to
handle ships' cordage, felt a responding jerk. He was indeed
climbing. Bit by bit the rope passed between her torn palms.

Then she saw his hand rise, grope inward over the cliff
edge. Tanree made a last great effort, heaving with a reviving
force she had not believed she could summon, falling backward, but still keeping a grasp on the rope.

The girl was dizzy and spent, aware only for a moment or
two that the rope was loose in her hands. Had—had he
fallen? Tanree smeared the back of her fist across her eyes to
clear them from a mist.

No, he lay head pointing toward her, though his feet still projected over the cliff. He must be drawn away from that, even as she had brought him earlier out of the grasp of the sea. Only now she could not summon up the strength to move.

Once more the falcon descended, to perch beside its master's head. Three times it screamed harshly. He was moving, drawing himself along on his belly away from the danger point, by himself.

Seeing that, Tanree clawed her way to her feet, leaning back against one of the rocky spires, needing its support. For it seemed that the rock under her feet was like the deck of the Kast-Boar, rising and falling, so she needs must summon sea-legs to deal with its swing.

On crawled the Falconer. Then, he, too, used his good arm for a brace and raised himself, his head coming high enough to look around. That he was valiantly fighting to get to his feet she was sure. A second later his eyes went wide as they swept past her to rest upon something at her own back.

Tanree's hand curved about the hilt of the dagger. She pushed against the rock which had supported her, but she could not stand away from it as yet.

Then she, too, saw—

These spires and outcrops of rock were not the work of nature after all. Stones were purposefully piled upon huge stones. There were archways, farther back what looked like an intact wall—somber, without a break until. farther above her head than the cliff had earlier reached, there showed openings, thin and narrow as a giant axe might have cleft. They had climbed into some ruin.

A thrust of ice chill struck Tanree. The world she had known had many such ancient places and most were ill-omened, perilous for travelers. This was an old. old land and there had been countless races rise to rule and disappear once more into dust. Not all of those peoples had been human. as Tanree reckoned it. The Sulcar knew many such remains, and wisely avoided them—unless fortified by some power spell set by a Wise One.

"Salzarat!"

The surprise on the Falconer's face had become something else as Tanree turned her head to stare. What was that faint expression? Awe—or fear? But that he knew this place, she had no doubt.

He made an effort, pulling himself up to his feet, though he clung for support to a jumble of blocks even as she did.

"Salzarat—" His voice was the hiss of a warning serpent, or that of a disturbed war bird.

Once more Tanree glanced from him to the ruins. Perhaps a lighting of the leaden clouds overhead was revealing. She saw—saw enough to make her gasp.

That farther wall, the one which appeared more intact, took on new contours. She could trace—

Was it illusion, or some cunning art practiced by the unknowns who had laid those stones? There was no wall; it was the head of a giant falcon, the fierce eyes marked by slitted holes above an out-thrust beak.

While the beak—

That closed on a mass which was too worn to do more than hint that it might once have been intended to represent a man.

The more Tanree studied the stone head, the plainer it grew. It was reaching out—out—ready to drop the prey it had already taken, to snap at her. . . .

"No!" Had she shouted that aloud or was the denial only in her mind? Those were stones (artfully fitted together, to be sure) but still only old, old stones. She shut her eyes, held them firmly shut, and then, after a few deep breaths, opened them again. No head, only stones.

But in those moments while she had fought to defeat illusion her companion had lurched forward. He pulled himself from one outcrop of ruin to the next and his Falcon had settled on his shoulder, though he did not appear aware of the weight of the bird. There was bemusement on his face, smoothing away his habitual frown. He was like a man ensorcelled, and Tanree drew away from him as he staggered past her, his gaze only for the wall.

Stones only, she continued to tell herself firmly. There was no reason for her to remain here. Shelter, food (she realized then that hunger did bite at her) what they needed to keep life in them could only lie in this land. Purposefully she followed the Falconer, but she carried her blade ready in her hand.

He stumbled along until he was under the overhang of that giant beak. The shadow of whatever it held fell on him. Now he halted, drew himself up as a man might face his officer on some occasion of import—or—a priest might begin a rite.

His voice rang out hollowly among the ruins, repeating words—or sounds (for some held the tones of those he had used in addressing his hawk). They came as wild beating cadence. Tanree shivered. She had a queer feeling that he might just be answered—by whom—or *what*?

Up near to the range of a falcon's cry rose his voice. Now the bird on his shoulder took wing. It screamed its own challenge, or greeting—so that man-voice and bird-voice mingled until Tanree could not distinguish one from the other.

Both fell into silence; once more the Falconer was moving on. He walked more steadily, not reaching out for any support, as if new strength had filled him. Passing under the beak he was—gone!

Tanree pressed one fist against her teeth. There was no doorway there! Her eyes could not deceive her that much. She wanted to run, anywhere, but as she looked wildly about her she perceived that the ruins funneled forward toward that one place and there only led the path.

This was a path of the Old Ones; evil lurked here. She could feel the crawl of it as if a slug passed, befouling her skin. Only—Tanree's chin came up, her jaw set stubbornly. She was Sulcar. If there was no other road, then this one she would take.

Forward she went, forcing herself to walk with confidence, though she was ever alert. Now the shadow of the beak enveloped her, and, though there was no warmth of sunlight to be shut out, still she was chilled.

Also—there *was* a door. Some trick of the stone setting and the beak shadow had concealed it from sight until one was near touching distance. With a deep breath which was more than half protest against her own action, Tanree advanced.

Through darkness within, she could see a gray of light. This wall must be thick enough to provide not just a door or gate but a tunnel way. And she could see movement between her and that light; the Falconer.

She quickened step so that she was only a little behind him when they came out in what was a mighty courtyard. Walls towered all about, but it was what was within the courtyard itself which stopped Tanree near in mid-step.

Men! Horses!

Then she saw the breakage, here a headless body, there only the shards of a mount. They had been painted once and the color in some way had sunk far into the substance which formed them, for it remained, if faded.

The motionless company was drawn up in good order, all facing to her left. Men stood, the reins of their mounts in their hands, and on the forks of their saddles falcons perched. A regiment of fighting men awaiting orders.

Her companion skirted that array of the ancient soldiers, almost as if he had not seen them, or, if he had, they were of no matter. He headed in the direction toward which they faced.

There were two wide steps there, and beyond the cavern of another door, wide as a monster mouth ready to suck them in. Up one step he pulled, now the second. . . . He *knew* what lay beyond; this was Falconer past, not of her people. But Tanree could not remain behind. She studied the faces of the warriors as she passed by. They each held their masking helm upon one hip as if it was needful to bare their faces, as they did not generally do. So she noted that each of the company differed from his fellows in some degree, though they were all plainly of the same race. These had been modeled from life.

As she came also into the doorway, Tanree heard again the mingled call of bird and man. At least the two she followed were still unharmed, though her sense of lurking evil was strong.

What lay beyond the door was a dim twilight. She stood at the end of a great hall, stretching into shadows right and left. Nor was the chamber empty. Rather here were more statues; and some were robed and coiffed. Women! Women in an Eyrie? She studied the nearest to make sure.

The weathering which had eroded that company in the courtyard had not done any damage here. Dust lay heavy on the shoulders of the life-size image to be sure, but that was all. The face was frozen into immobility. But the expression. Sly exultation, an avid . . . hunger? Those eyes staring straight ahead, did they indeed hold a spark of knowledge deep within?

Tanree pushed aside imagination. These were not alive. But their faces—she looked to another, studied a third—all held that gloating, that hunger-about-to-be-assuaged; while the male images were as blank of any emotion as if they had never been meant to suggest life at all.

The Falconer had already reached the other end of the

hall. Now he was silent, facing a dais on which were four figures. These were not in solemn array, rather frozen into a tableau of action. Deadly action, Tanree saw as she trotted forward, puffs of dust rising from the floor underfoot.

A man sat, or rather sprawled, in a throne-chair. His head had fallen forward, and both hands were clenched on the hilt of a dagger driven into him at heart level. Another and younger man, lunged, sword in his hand, aiming at the image of a woman who cowered away, such an expression of rage and hate intermingled on her features as made Tanree shiver.

But the fourth of that company stood a little apart, no fear to be read on *her* countenance. Her robe was plainer than that of the other woman, with no glint of jewels at wrist, throat or waist. Her unbound hair fell over her shoulders, cascading down, to nearly sweep the floor.

In spite of the twilight here that wealth of hair appeared to gleam. Her eyes—they, too, were dark red—unhuman, knowing, exulting, cruel—alive!

Tanree found she could not turn her gaze from those eyes.

Perhaps she cried out then, or perhaps only some inner defense quailed in answer to invasion. Snake-like, slug-like, it crawled, oozed into her mind, forging link between them.

This was no stone image, man-wrought. Tanree swayed against the pull of that which gnawed and plucked, seeking to control her.

"She-devil!" The Falconer spat, the bead of moisture striking the breast of the red-haired woman. Tanree almost expected to see the other turn her attention to the man whose face was twisted with half-insane rage. But his cry had weakened the spell laid upon her. She was now able to look away from the compelling eyes.

The Falconer swung around. His good hand closed upon the sword which the image of the young man held. He jerked at that impotently. There was a curious wavering, as if the chamber and all in it were but part of a wind-riffled painted banner.

"Kill!"

Tanree herself wavered under that command in her mind. Kill this one who would dare threaten *her*, Jonkara, Opener of Gates, Commander of Shadows.

Rage took fire. Through the blaze she marched, knowing what must be done to this man who dared to challenge. She was the hand of Jonkara, a tool of force.

Deep within Tanree something else stirred, could not be totally battered into submission.

I am a weapon to serve. I am—

"I am *Tanree*" cried that other part of her. "This is no quarrel of mine. I am Sulcar, of the seas—of another blood and breed!"

She blinked and that insane rippling ceased for an instant of clear sight. The Falconer still struggled to gain the sword.

"Now!" Once more that wave of compulsion beat against her, heart high, as might a shore wave. "Now—slay! Blood—give me blood that I may live again. We are women. Nay, *you* shall be more than woman when this blood flows and my door is opened by it. Kill—strike behind the shoulder. Or, better still, draw your steel across his throat. He is but a man! He is the enemy—kill!"

Tanree swayed, her body might be answering to the flow of a current. Without her will her hand arose, blade ready, the distance between her and the Falconer closed. She could easily do this, blood would indeed flow. Jonkara would be free of the bonds laid upon her by the meddling of fools.

"Strike!"

Tanree saw her hand move. Then that other will within her flared for a last valiant effort.

"I am Tanree!" A feeble cry against a potent spell. "There is no power here before whom Sulcar bows!"

The Falconer whirled, looked to her. No fear in his eyes, only cold hate. The bird on his shoulder spread wings, screamed. Tanree could not be sure—was there indeed a curl of red about its feet, anchoring it to its human perch?

"She-devil!" He flung at her. Abandoning his fight for the sword, he raised his hand as if to strike Tanree across the face. Out of the air came a curl of tenuous red, to catch about his upraised wrist, so, even though he fought furiously, he was held prisoner.

"Strike quickly!" The demand came with mind-bruising force.

"I do not kill!" Finger by finger Tanree forced her hand to open. The blade fell, to clang on the stone floor.

"*Fool!*" The power sent swift punishing pain into her head. Crying out, Tanree staggered. Her outflung hand fell upon that same sword the Falconer had sought to loosen. It turned, came into her hold swiftly and easily.

"Kill!"

That current of hate and power filled her. Her flesh tingled, there was heat within her as if she blazed like an oil-dipped feast torch.

"Kill!"

She could not control the stone sword. Both of her hands closed about its cold hilt. She raised it. The man before her did not move, seek in any way to dodge the threat she offered. Only his eyes were alive now—no fear in them, only a hate as hot as what filled her.

Fight—she must fight as she had the waves of the storm lashed sea. She was herself, Tanree—Sulcar—no tool for something evil which should long since have gone into the Middle Dark.

"Kill!"

With the greatest effort she made her body move, drawing upon that will within her which the other could not master. The sword fell.

Stone struck stone—or was that true? Once more the air rippled, life overrode ancient death for a fraction of time between two beats of the heart, two breaths. The sword had jarred against Jonkara.

"Fool—" a fading cry.

There was no sword hilt in her hands, only powder sifting between her fingers. And no sparks of life in those red eyes either. From where the stone sword had struck full on the image's shoulder cracks opened. the figure crumbled, fell. Nor did what Jonkara had been vanish alone. All those others were breaking too, becoming dust which set Tanree coughing, raising her hands to protect her eyes.

Evil had ebbed. The chamber was cold, empty of what had waited here. A hand caught her shoulder, pulling at her.

"Out!" This voice was human. "Out—Salzarat falls!"

Rubbing at her smarting eyes, Tanree allowed him to lead her. There were crashing sounds, a rumbling. She cringed as a huge block landed nearby. They fled, dodging and twisting. Until at last they were under the open sky, still coughing, tears streaming from their eyes, their faces smeared with gray grit.

Fresh wind, carrying with it the clean savor of the sea, lapped about them. Tanree crouched on a mat of dead grass through which the first green spears of spring pushed. So close to her that their shoulders touched, was the Falconer. His bird was gone.

They shared a small rise Tanree did not remember climbing. What lay below, between them and the sea cliff's edge, was a tumble of stone so shattered no one now could define wall or passage. Her companion turned his head to look directly into her face. His expression was one of wonder.

"It is all gone! The curse is gone. So she is beaten at last! But you are a woman, and Jonkara could always work her will through any woman—that was her power and our undoing. She held every woman within her grasp. Knowing that, we raised what defenses we could. For we could never trust those who might again open Jonkara's dread door. Why in truth did you not slay me? My blood would have freed her, and she would have given you a measure of her power—as always she had done."

"She was no one to command *me*!" Tanree's self-confidence returned with every breath she drew. "I am Sulcar, not one of your women. So—this Jonkara—she was why you hate and fear women?"

"Perhaps. She ruled us so. Her curse held us until the death of Langward, who dying, as you saw, from the steel of his own Queen, somehow freed a portion of us. He had been seeking long for a key to imprison Jonkara. He succeeded in part. Those of us still free fled, so our legends say, making sure no woman would ever again hold us in bond."

He rubbed his hands across his face, streaking the dust of vanished Salzarat.

"This is an old land. I think though that none walk it now. We must remain here—unless your people come seeking you. So upon us the shadow of another curse falls."

Tanree shrugged. "I am Sulcar but there was none left to call me clan-sister. I worked on the Karst-Boar without kin-tie. There will be no one to come hunting because of me." She stood up, her hands resting on her hips and turned her back deliberately upon the sea.

"Falconer, if we be cursed, then that we live with. And, while one lives, the future may still hold much, both good and ill. We need only face squarely what comes."

There was a scream from the sky above them. The clouds parted, and, through weak sunlight, wheeled the falcon. Tanree threw back her head to watch it.

"This is your land, as the sea is mine. What make you of it, Falconer?"

He also got to his feet. "My name is Rivery. And your

words have merit. It is a time for curses to slink back into shadows, allowing us to walk in the light, to see what lies ahead."

Shoulder to shoulder they went down from the hillock, the falcon swooping and soaring above their heads.

THE RAPE PATROL

Michele Belling

Some while ago, Joanna Russ mentioned a story by one of her creative writing students at the University of Washington. She said it was an absolutely superb story, but too unsettling to the status quo to find an easy market. My interest was piqued, but Joanna had no idea where a past student might be.

Time passes.

As I am dependent on the city buses, I meet many interesting people enroute about Seattle. Most people tend to sit quietly, rigidly—so I suppose a few view me as some kind of "character" merely for failing to ride along as a silent lump. Many, however, are simply relieved for someone to reach out of the void with a human voice.

Occasionally I find my openness has invited a religious fanatic or other mental deficient to prattle loud, embarrassing, disgusting commentary—giving me insight into why most people don't communicate with each other on buses. But more often, I have extremely pleasant exchanges with a wide variety of other bus dependants, sometimes making friends of lasting importance. One such was Michele Belling, who actually knew me by my writing (this is still a rare, surprising, and of course pleasing occurrence). She too wrote fiction, and I said I'd like to see some of it. I gave her my address.

A few days later, a manuscript was delivered to my door. I read it with an eerie combination of repulsed fascination and righteous glee. Something familiar clicked in my head and I realized: this is the story Joanna was talking about!

Michele Belling's vision of "The Rape Patrol" is fantastic, but plausible. Even her vision of women's supernatural power rings with possibility. This story will

143

*startle you—but I'll wager you'll read it again and again.
It elicits too many contradictory reactions to understand
one's own experience in a single reading. Be warned.*

Heidi and I were at her house drinking white wine and
playing 500 rummy when the phone call came.

"Well," I was saying, laying down three nines, "castration
is not the answer. It's this castration anxiety, the impotence
complex, that triggers these things to begin with. So you take
away his penis and he'll stick something else in. Worse, he'll
do it with a vengeance." I poured myself another glass.

"Yeah. And you can't just hospitalize them, 'cause then
they'll just come back." Heidi picked up a card and the corner of her mouth angled back. "And come back and come
back." She put down the card. "It's grim."

"What? Your game?"

I like Heidi. She's a big woman, six feet tall. She has broad
shoulders and broader hips. She was brought up on the farm
with three older brothers and she has muscle. She has short
blond hair. She's very gentle.

"Answer that, will you?" She scratched the side of her
head and drew another card, raising her eyebrows.

I picked up the receiver from the wall phone behind me.
"Yeah," I said, "Heidi's house."

"Diane," said the woman on the other end. "This is Joesy.
Another rape. This one in broad daylight. Luckily the woman
had our number and got to a pay phone before she passed
out. Cass and Barbara are over there with her now talking it
through and fixing up her face. Fortunately she knows who it
was and could give us some idea where to look for him. Her
description, by the way, correlates perfectly with that west
side rapist we missed two weeks ago. That description we got
from that black woman?"

"I know the one. Where are you now?"

I'm over here with Agnes keeping an eye on him. He's in
a house with about four other men. Corner of Chapin and
Seminary, about three houses south west. We're in the blue
car. Wait about an hour until it gets good and dark and call
me back. 932-5836. If he moves from here I'll notify you."

"Okay." I took down the number. "I'll call Maria."

"Good. Thanks. See ya."

I put the phone down and told Heidi. Then I called Maria and gave her the info. We are seven women known as the Rape Patrol. We handle crimes against women: rape, beatings, muggings, and murder. There are three or four auxiliary members who act as seconds and backup women and provide extra woman power as needed; but the core group of seven decides policy. Right now we are in a minor policy crisis concerning the penalty for rape. It's the second time this disagreement has arisen. It's a touchy subject.

Heidi got up and went into the bedroom and came back out with her mountain boots. Her eyebrows shot up and she shrugged mutely and grinned at me. "It was a pleasant afternoon," she said, sat down, and started putting on the boots. I'm always amazed at her strength. She has been with us from the beginning, although she joined the patrol a week or so later than I did. We have been operating now for about thirteen months and so have whittled our strategy and tactics to a keen-edged efficiency. We have extensive files, mostly in Joesy's head—she's got a photographic memory—and this is a necessity, for many of our cases, especially muggings, go unavenged. At first. But now we are discovering patterns of recurrence. We may not get the man on the first or even the second offense, but we invariably get him on the third. Invariably.

Myself, I am a knife artist. I can hit any target of any size, moving or static, at a range of up to 130 feet. I have also a second degree black belt in Karate. I am twenty-five years old. My mother contracted spinal meningitis after being kicked in the back by a rapist when she was thirty-five, and so I have lived with that.

Heidi made us a couple of roast beef sandwiches and we played a few more hands. We finished off the wine. An hour later I called Joesy at the pay phone. They were still there. Heidi and I got in my car—it's nondescript, there are dozens like it in town—and drove over there.

We parked the car four blocks away and walked over to where Joesy and Agnes were parked, watching the house. We got in the car. Maria was already there. We greeted each other. Joesy turned around in the front seat and handed us a sketch of our man. "He's got red hair and blue eyes and he's about five eleven," she said. "His name's Jim Sutter. He's in

that house." She pointed across the street. "The white house."
I nodded and handed back the sketch. Joesy looked at Agnes,
who continued to watch the house, binoculars in her lap. She
turned again and looked us all carefully in the eyes, myself,
Heidi, Maria. "He stopped her on the street and asked her
for a match. There was nobody else around so when she had
her eyes off of him he twisted her arm around her back and
threw her on her face in an alley, scraping her face on the
pavement. When she tried fighting back he punched her in
the face and head and pulled a knife on her. Then he did it
and when he was through slammed her head against the
pavement for good measure. She's pretty messed up. She's got
a concussion." She glanced at the house. "He's in there playing cards with four other men. I figure you three can go in
the front door. Agie and I will go around the back and when
we hear you we'll come in, unless he tries running out the
back door, in which case we'll have him. Sound okay?"

"Wait a minute," said Heidi, "is that where he lives?"

"Oh, sorry, yes, that's his house. Possibly he lives there
with one or two of the other men. It's a pretty big house."

Heidi nodded.

"Is there a basement?" asked Maria.

"Yeah but no outside door."

"Sounds good to me," said Heidi.

"Check." I said.

"Fine." said Maria.

"Okay," said Joesy. Agnes turned around and we all
looked at each other then, sharing a quiet moment. Sharing
trust.

"Let's go," said Maria.

We piled out of the car and crossed the street to the house,
Agnes and Joesy walking ahead of us. We waited on the
front walk to give them time to get in position. Maria and I
looked at each other. I like working with her. She has a third
degree black belt in Karate and a black belt in Kung Fu.
She's quick and always on target. We work on the same
rhythms and in a tight spot our minds often go in synch.
Now the three of us walked quietly up the front porch steps
and stood in front of the door. I looked in the window. Sutter
was on the floor with four other men playing cards with the
TV on. We were pretty evenly matched. We were to tackle
the defense and clear a path for Agnes and Joesy. We pulled
on our ski masks and our gloves. The masks are a little re-

stricting but in a situation like this a necessity. I nodded at Heidi and she leaned back and kicked the door open with her foot. She was still feeling the wine. The door smashed back against the wall and we were inside, three of the men scrambling to their feet. Sutter got up so fast spinning around that he fell forward on his hands then high-tailed out of the living room. "Holy shit" somebody said. Heidi flung her arms wide and caught a man backhand on the jaw, sending him crashing into the television. I leapt in the air and came down feet first on the back of the man nearest me as he tried to stand up from the floor. Somebody picked up a chair and brought it down on Heidi but she caught it by a rung and kicked him in the balls. Hard. He doubled over soundlessly and fell on the floor. The big man in front of me picked up a bottle and swung it thudding against the back of Heidi's head at the same time I connected with a fast kick to his kidneys. It dulled the impact but Heidi staggered forward tripping over the man she just downed. Not to hurt these clowns they're not the ones we want. There was a fish tank on a shelf and I jerked it over ripping out the plugs and sloshing fish and water and threw it in the man's lap. I could hear Agnes and Joesy coming in the back. He caught it in the stomach and fell backward, slipping on the cards but the man behind me was up and I flipped him hard against the wall. Maria was in the corner laying the other guy out over the television. She spun around and grabbed the guy with the fish tank under the ears and he shouted "ah" and sprawled. The man was up from the wall and swinging but I ducked and hit him in the larynx. He gasped for breath and grabbed at his throat, tripped over his own feet and fell backward. Heidi was trying to stand. I went over and helped her to her feet while Maria ran out of the living room. "You all right?" I asked her.

"Yeah," she said, shaking her head and staggering. "How come I always get hit?"

I let go of her. "C'mon," I said.

We ran into the kitchen and Maria said "Psst" from the top of the stairs. I took the stairs three at a time. The bathroom door was broken open. He had apparently locked himself in and used a length of clothesline to swing out over the garage roof. Agie and Jo were gone. "I'll get the car," said Maria.

"Which way?"

"Out over that fence," she said, pointing, and bounded

down the stairs, disappearing out the back door with Heidi. I
ran down after her and flew out the back door, tore across
the lawn, hit the middle of the cyclone fence and clawed my
way to the top, jumped down, crossed another back yard,
vaulted a board fence, sprinted down a driveway, and came
out on Seminary. Running blindly and by intuition I veered
to my right, across the intersection and up Chapin to a long
alley that ran for blocks behind houses and shops. Then I
heard Agie's whistle, high and shrill, drift down the alley
from the school yard. Started down then stopped myself and
ran back out on Chapin. The car was coming in my direction. They had the yellow light on. I waited and stepped into
the glare of the headlights and jerked my thumb a few times
in the direction of the river. They backed the car and turned
down Seminary. I took off down the alley running at break-
neck speed, zigzagging around trash cans, breathing through
clenched teeth. I ripped off my mask without breaking stride
and was hit in the face with a blast of cold air. I pulled it
deep in my lungs and put on an extra burst of speed. At the
dress shop I darted between a couple of buildings to my right
and plunged into a backyard. I know a shortcut. Leapt a picket fence. Ducked through an arbor. And came out on another
narrower alley. Ran down it, gasping for breath, and hit second
wind as I reached the school yard. Nobody there. Still running, I reached the playground and was about to whistle
when I saw a figure dash out of a back yard a block over.
Then another figure in hot pursuit. I took out my knife and
ran down the walkway behind the school, crossed Oak, ran a
block, heard scuffling, then silence, turned the corner and saw
Joesy getting to her feet on the sidewalk. She saw me and
flung out an arm. I took off again, down Elm, down another
alley, and came out on Front Street. Out of the corner of my
eye saw Sutter and Agnes disappear behind an old store
front. This block is condemned houses, boarded up shops, decaying warehouses, and the river behind them. I ran around
to the other side of the store and opened my knife. Behind
the store was a wide stretch of unpaved parking lot, filled
with rocks and broken glass and surrounded by buildings.
Across the lot was a small warehouse. Agnes came out of a
building to my right and at the same time Sutter darted
around a corner of the warehouse and into an open basement
doorway. I was across the lot by the time he got the door
shut and I flung my whole weight against the door. We

struggled like that on either side of the door, both of us push-
ing. I kicked it. Too late, heard the bolt slide, then another
one. Agnes was behind me. "I'll check inside," she said, and
went around the front of the warehouse. I waited in front of
the door. After a while she came back around, flashlight in
hand. "There's no other entrance," she said, "that I can see."

"Well, we'll have to wait." I snapped my knife shut and
put it away.

Agie put her fingers between her teeth and let out a
whistle. In a few minutes, Joesy, Heidi, and Maria came
around the back of the store and into the parking lot. He's
in there," I said, "and there's no other way in." Heidi tried
the door a few times with her foot, unsuccessfully. It was
thick planks with steel reinforcements.

"Let's check inside again," suggested Maria.

I wanted a look for myself too so Joesy, Maria and I took
the light and went around the front of the building. It fronted
right on the river. A strip of broken sidewalk edged a steep
bank that crumbled down to the quiet black water, the bank
worn back by the river tides, covered with debris and jagged
rocks, a washed up tree branch. The air was damp. The front
door of the warehouse hung open on one of its hinges. We
stood in the doorway and Maria flashed the powerful light inside. The front part of the room was covered with rubble,
broken boxes and plaster. A beam had fallen down bringing
part of the ceiling with it. She slid the light over the floor,
over broken glass, rusted cans, shattered beer bottles and
rags, across the boarded windows. Glided the beam up and
down corners. Checked the ceiling. Walked inside, feeling her
way with the light, watching the ceiling. Cleared the floor
with her boot. "The floor's cement," she said.

"What's that over there?" Joesy pointed to a corner.

Maria shone the light on a row of old shelving and a stairway that led up. he walked over behind the broken beam
and inspected around the stairway, flashed the spotlight up
the stairs, and disappeared through a low doorway, ducking
under a timber.

"Be careful." said Jo.

In a few seconds she came back out, flipped the light
around the room again and came outside. "Nothing, there's
no way down."

We went back around to the others. We tried kicking the

door in twos and threes. No give. We stood in a semicircle around the door, looking at each other.

"Could we smoke him out?" asked Agnes. We looked at the door. About an eighth of an inch between the bottom of the door and the ground.

"We could burn the door," suggested Heidi.

"We could hack through the cement," said Joesy.

"We could hack through the door."

We looked at it. It was a possibility.

"We could call Judith." said Maria.

We looked at each other. We all nodded. Maria left the parking lot. We waited. Heidi looked at me and cast her eyes upward.

"Like a rat," I muttered.

After about ten minutes Judith came, pulling her car down the old driveway right into the parking lot. She turned it off in a corner of the lot and got out, shutting the door but leaving it unlatched. Maria walked in after her and rejoined us. Judith came around the back of her car and opened the other door. We watched her. She's a thin woman with long black hair and large green eyes. She was dressed in a salvation army suit coat and baggy black levis. A wisp, I thought, watching her. She pulled something off the front seat that looked like a pair of chicken feet and stuffed them in a small white cotton sack with draw strings. She shut the door, latching it with a soft click, turned around and faced us. First she looked at me, then at Maria. "He's in there," said Maria, pointing at the door.

Judith just stood there, facing the door, held out a hand and waved it almost imperceptibly back and forth in front of her. All of us stepped back, spread out in a wide half-circle, flanking the space between Judith and the door, Heidi and I to her left, the other three women to her right. Judith walked forward holding the bag by its drawstrings. Her eyebrows were knit up into the middle of her forehead. She reached the door and took the chicken feet, or whatever they were, out of the sack and shook them over the door, over the ground in front of the door. Shook them all around the base of the door, like a madwoman, all the time murmuring something. Then she put them back in the sack and pulled the drawstrings, put the sack in the inside pocket of her coat, and brought out a small vial. She unscrewed the cap and backed away from the door, sprinkling the contents of the vial in a pattern on the ground in front of it. When it was empty, she screwed the top back on the vial, put it away, and walked backward until she stood about sixty feet from the door. Then she pulled the sack out of her pocket again and took out the chicken feet.

The man came out of the doorway on his hands and knees, screaming.

"Sh," said Judith.

He crawled forward on his knees, clawing the air and writhing his upper torso wordlessly. Judith walked forward to meet him. He saw her and moaned, fell forward on his elbows, ducked his head between his arms, and crawled toward her on his elbows and knees. Judith stopped. He crawled to her feet and hunched there shivering and pissing his pants. She held out the chicken feet a moment more and looked at him, her eyebrows knitted to the middle of her forehead in compassion. She put the things back in the sack and glanced around at us. We closed in on him, Heidi and Maria pinning his arms behind his back and holding his legs down, keeping him in a kneeling position. He offered no resistance.

Judith put the sack in her coat pocket and turned away. She walked to her car and got inside, latching the door gently. I followed her. She rolled down her window. We just stared at each other silently. "Thanks," I said.

She sat there a second with her eyebrows knitted up unconsciously like that. "Love him," she said. She started the car and backed it around and pulled out of the lot.

I walked back to the group. They were waiting for me. Sutter was quiet, dazed, his chin on his chest. Agnes stepped in front of him. I stood next to her. We take turns at this. Judge, jury, and executioner. "James Sutter," she said. He didn't look up. Joesy, behind him, grabbed him by the hair and pulled his head back so he was looking directly at Agnes. She had her mask off. "James Sutter," she said, "did you rape Sylvia Livingston on the night of April 11, 1975?" He closed his eyes. "Did you rape Carol Neith this afternoon?" He started struggling. Sometimes they answer yes. "You have been accused of rape by those women," she said and held out her hand to me. He gave up struggling. I brought out my knife, opened it, and gave it to her. When he saw that he started struggling again. Heidi held his jaw shut. "The penalty for rape is death," said Agnes, watching him and holding the knife. "I do this in the name of your victims and in the name of all Women," she said and slit his throat from ear to ear. The blood sprayed out covering her pants. He gurgled. Agnes closed the knife and gave it to me. They held him a little longer, then let him drop forward on his face.

I walked the block to the car and got the sign that said RAPIST in stenciled letters, brought it back and placed it on the corpse. then we all headed back to the car and got in, Agnes driving.

"Can we go home and unwind," asked Maria, "and meet on this tomorrow?"

Everyone agreed. "I have to work tomorrow," said Agnes, looking at her pants.

"Tomorrow evening?"

"Okay," said Agie. "My house?"

We agreed. Agnes went around the long way and left Heidi and me off at my car. We shook hands all around, expressed our gratitude, and I drove us back to Heidi's place.

We went inside. I fell down on the couch and sighed. Took off my gloves. Took off my shoes. Heidi went in the kitchen and shook the empty wine bottle ruefully, put it under the sink, and opened the refrigerator. I put on a Mozart quartet. Heidi made sandwiches.

BONES FOR DULATH

Megan Lindholm

*There were many harrowing moments in putting to-
gether this anthology. The following story provided such
a moment, because the tale ended with a scene too similar to the ending of another manuscript I wanted to include. That other story was by Phyllis Ann Karr, and
featured characters from her novel, Thorn and Frostflower. I kept both authors in unfair suspense as I
weighed the two stories, and weighed them—but my
heart couldn't part with either even though I knew they
oughtn't appear together. My decision was made for me
when Phyllis' publisher informed that she oughtn't use
the same characters in short story sales elsewhere. The
story was withdrawn with apologies, and painful as it is
to lose a good story, it was a relief to have the impossible dilemma obviated.*

*Megan Lindholm's story was important to the anthol-
ogy for another reason as well, since it lent to the
theme-balance I was striving for in compiling Amazons!
I wanted, if at all possible, to include at least one story
each dealing with issues of a powerful woman with a
male nemesis, a female nemesis, dealing with rape,
child-rearing, and in interpersonal relationships with
other women, and with men. Of course the latter was
commonly submitted: pair-bonded amazon and war-lord
. . . but the stories were generally awful, or the
women comparatively objectified and subjugated so that
it was really a story about the man.*

*As it turns out, one of the rarest visions in storytell-
ing of any sort is that which successfully portrays
strong women and strong men in relationships that are
not ridden with power plays, manipulation, and inequal-
ity. Megan Lindholm, a resident of Kodiak, Alaska, in-
troduces us to Ki and Vandien who, in the face of*

*others' expectations, yet define their bond as friendship
and only coincidentally share a bed.*
　　Megan plans a novel about these two.

Ki set the wheel brake, wrapped the reins about the
handle, and leaped from the wagon box in one fluid motion.
She dashed forward past the team, caught herself, and
proceeded more cautiously. She was not certain where the
edge of the concealed pit began. A wild thrashing came from
its unseen depths.

"Vandien?"

A muffled curse and the shriek of a trapped animal were
the reply.

"Vandien!" Ki called, more urgently.

"WHAT?" he demanded angrily through the sounds of
struggle. Still unsure of her footing, Ki stretched out on the
snowy ground. Now she could peer into the pit which had
abruptly swallowed her companion. She saw a tangle of horse
and man thrashing about below.

"Are you all right?" she asked anxiously.

"NO! Will you shut up? This beast is trying to kill me!"

"Cut its throat!" Ki suggested helpfully.

"No! It cost me fifty dru, and I'm not letting my money go
so easily." Vandien was breathless with the effort of staying
on top away from stamping hooves.

The yellow horse heaved and squealed again, slamming
Vandien's leg once more into the side of the pit. Ki could see
its problem. One of its legs had been broken by the fall. Ad-
ditionally, it was impaled on the ugly spikes set in the bottom
of the pit.

"Kill it before it kills you, Vandien. The pain is driving it
mad. We'll never get it out of there alive. Besides, it was
never worth fifty dru in the first place. I told you that when
you bought it.

"No! And shut up!"

"Vandien." Ki chided softly. "The beast is suffering."

She saw the flash of drawn blade, heard a sudden spattering of blood. Gradually the thrashing stilled.

"Damn," came Vandien's voice ruefully. "Ki, you owe me a horse."

"What?" Her voice was distant.

Vandien looked up. She had disappeared. He had a lovely view of an overcast sky. Lips compressed, he drew his leg with difficulty from where the dying horse had trapped it against the side of the pit. It tingled strangely. Was that horse blood down his thigh, or his own? He had been buffeted about so much it was difficult to separate any one pain.

"Ki!" he called in sudden alarm. "Ki, where in damnation are you? Get me out of here!"

A rope came snaking down. "It's tied to the wagon. Can you climb up or shall I haul you out?"

"I can't climb. I've hurt my leg."

Her slim figure was outlined against the sky. Tall boots dug into the side of the pit as she lowered herself. Fur vest and breeches gave her a feline appearance accented by her lithe movement. She rappelled down to land with a light thump on the hindquarters of the dead mount. Vandien gasped lightly in pain from the jolt.

"Where are you hurt?" Ki asked gently. She squeezed his shoulder reassuringly. "Vandien, you're shaking!"

"In my place, you'd shake too. I took one of those spikes in my leg. I fear it was poisoned. My whole leg hums."

Ki moved about to stare at the long gash in his leggings that bared his skin, and the long gash in his skin that bared meat and oozed blood. Carefully she touched one of the spikes. Her finger came away daubed with a dark substance.

"Those spikes aren't wood," Vandien noted. "More like something's old toenails."

"Gah!" Ki wrinkled her nose in distaste. "Vandien, you have a way with words Let's get you out and clean that gash."

"Don't forget my saddle and gear," he cautioned.

"I won't," she replied, looping the rope under his arms.

Out of the pit, Vandien sat in the snow and looked queasily at his wound. The strange tinging had stopped. He touched the edge of the gash cautiously. Nothing.

"Ki!" He could hear her struggling to uncinch his saddle. "Ki, you owe me a horse!"

"How in damnation do you figure that?" Ki demanded.

"You were the one who wanted to use Old Pass instead of

Marner's Road. If we hadn't come this way, I'd still have a horse under me."

"It cut six days off our time, didn't it? Besides, I don't recall pressing you to join me on this haul."

"You owe me a horse," Vandien asserted firmly. "Ki, I can't feel my leg," he added plaintively.

"I'll be right there."

She scrambled out of the pit and hauled up his gear. She knelt beside him in the snow to consider the wound. Ki shook her head in bafflement.

"I'll clean and bind it, and then we had best find who set that trap and what poison they used. And what they were hoping to catch in it. If there's game big enough to warrant a trap that size in this pass, I doubt I shall want to use it again. Come."

She slipped her arm about him and helped him to stand. Leaning heavily on Ki, Vandien limped toward the wagon. The two huge gray horses eyed him with mild reproof. It took most of his strength to mount the box and clamber into the enclosed sleeping area in the front half of the wagon.

"I'll toss your gear in back with the freight."

Vandien nodded and lay still, listening to his heart pump poison through his body.

"Who sets pit traps in Old Pass?"

Ki had wormed her way through the motley crowd in the tap room of the inn. She stood at the Innmaster's elbow. He glanced at her angry face, and his eyes slid away.

"My patrons call for ale. I must serve them."

One of Ki's hands snagged the Innmaster's sleeve as the other settled on the hilt of a broadsword, incongruously large on her. The Innmaster caught her meaning, for he abruptly plopped down on a stool next to her, wiping his sweaty face on his apron.

"Dulath sets pit traps in Old Pass," the Innmaster admitted reluctantly. "He is not for talk with strangers. The god's traps are why Old Pass has not been used much lately. What did you lose to him?"

"A good friend. Nearly." Ki glared at a listener who swiftly looked away. "I hauled him out, but he is poisoned by a gash from a spike. Even now he sweats and turns on my bed-skins. I must see this Dulath and ask him what poison he used. And I should like to know what he hopes to trap with his pits in the middle of wagon paths."

The Innmaster's hands had become claws on the table edge. He licked dry lips. "You left his pit empty?"

Ki noticed several sets of eyes flicker toward her at his question. "Aye, or nearly so. There's a yellow nag in the bottom, such as it was. Dulath is welcome to such game if he relishes it. Innmaster, I need a room for my friend to rest in while I seek Dulath."

The Innmaster heaved to his feet. "No room. Sorry." He turned away.

Ki's browned hand shot out, seized the Innmaster's large wrist. With surprising strength, her fingers bit into the tender area between wrist and hand, causing the Innmaster to yelp in sudden pain.

"He needs a room. It is cold in the wagon, and he is in pain." She sounded very reasonable.

The Innmaster attempted to twist out of her grip; he gasped when her fingers only tightened.

"A room," Ki reminded him pleasantly. Abruptly she loosed her hold on the Innmaster's wrist and rose to keep a knife from piercing her. Simultaneously, she felt a hand seize both collar and hair.

"This way," came a voice at her ear. Ki complied. Out in the frosty air, the grip loosened, but did not let go.

"That your wagon?"

Ki nodded, unable to speak for the thought of the knife.

"Get on it."

The point of the knife followed her ribs up onto the box, only moving away when she seated herself and gathered the traces. Ki glared down at her antagonist. His face was without malice. He was, in fact, but a youth, younger than Ki, but taller by more than a head. He shrugged, not unkindly.

"My father means no ill to you. But if your friend has taken Dulath's poison, he is a dying man. And we let no rooms to the dead. Now be on your way."

"Be on my way where?" Ki demanded angrily. "The boneyard? Or shall I let him stiffen first?"

The youth's face softened. "Try Rindol. His cottage is back that way, the one of wood chinked with moss. He is skilled in herbs, and takes in the sick and weary. I have heard, though I do not credit it, that once he healed a man of Dulath's poison. But that was not in my lifetime, nor yours. Try there, stranger. And bear us no malice for what must be."

Ki made no reply, but merely shook the reins. The grays stirred; the wagon moved off.

"Ki?"

She did not glance back at the door that led into the wagon. "Shut the door, Vandien. It will do no good to chill yourself."

"No wind could chill me now, Ki. My blood burns within me. My left side is gone numb."

"Save your strength. We go to find a healer. Now shut the door." Ki's face was white, and the team wondered at the trembling of the reins.

At Rindol's cottage, Vandien swayed over Ki, a doll stuffed with sand, as she half dragged, half helped him from the wagon. She straightened under his weight, his arm across her shoulders. She glanced down at his leg, appalled at the swelling that threatened to burst the bandaging. Then she felt part of his weight taken off her, as a wizened old man, disfigured by pox, took Vandien's other arm.

"This way, this way," he shouted cheerfully, in spite of their proximity. "Rindol can always tell who comes to call on him. The lame, the diseased, and the maimed. And the poisoned!" he added shrewdly. "Where got he this pretty token?"

"In a pit trap this morning," Ki said as they maneuvered Vandien through the low door. "A pit trap of one called Dulath. I am told you can heal him. How much will it cost?"

"In this way, and onto that pallet. Pull the skins about him so. No, man, do not fight us. You may feel warm, but your body is chilled to the bone. Let an old man who knows have his way. So. Now, woman, stand aside. There is hot tea on the hearth. Warm yourself. You can do no more here. Let me see the damage now."

Ki wandered across the room to the hearth and poured herself a mug of tea. Her forehead was creased in thought. Now they would surely lose the time they had gained by using Old Pass. And she didn't like the way the old man had sidestepped the question of fee. She had little enough coin, and Vandien's had gone for his ill-fated horse. She had no hope of money until she delivered her freight to Yuri, days and miles away. Damn the man! What call did he have to go plunging himself into pit traps anyway?

Vandien cried out wordlessly under Rindol's probing fingers. Ki winced in sympathy, knowing such sounds were not wrung from him easily.

"At least there is still some feeling!" she observed aloud.

"Save your breath, woman," the old man advised. "The pain has chased his mind out of his body. And his soul soon to follow. I can ease his passing; Waters of Kiev will keep him from feeling the worst. And later, cutting the tendons prevents the body from twisting up as badly as it might. Or, if you wish, I can make his passing more swift. Which shall it be?"

Ki stared at him in consternation. "Cut his tendons? Waters of Kiev? Gods, man, that's the same kind of healing we practiced on his horse earlier today. If that's what I wished, I would do it myself with a blade. Many's the time he's tempted me to," she added softly. "But I am of no mind for that now. No, Rindol, I wish him cured, not killed."

"If the poison be Dulath's, that be impossible. They all die, that take that poison, if they be not already dead when they meet it. That be our custom now. The villagers throw their dead into his traps, to stave him off their livestock. Before the eggs hatch, they return, to burn both bodies and spawn. A tidy method don't you agree?"

Ki rubbed her forehead wearily. A madman. The youth at the inn had sent her to a madman. Or at best an eccentric, his mind under the weight of many years. Best to seek her answers in simple questions.

"Then all die who take Dulath's poison?" she asked.

"Aye . . . or almost. There was a one, upon a time. A hero. He set forth to slay Dulath, paid well by the village. But during the battle, he fell into Dulath's pit. His squire pulled him out and brought him here. The hero did not die, but it was none of my doing. He claimed the credit himself, saying he lived because he had lapped Dulath's fresh blood from his blade. That's as may be, I suppose. Never paid me, either. Left in the middle of the night, and the whole village saying I was to. . . ."

Ki waved him to silence, tried to sift his scrambled words for a thought that might help.

Across the room Vandien lay pale and still unconscious. He could be dying. He probably was, for that seemed the only thing the citizens of this cursed town could agree on. Still, what hunter would use a poison with no cure? She must see Dulath.

"Where can I find this Dulath? I would have words with him," she asked abruptly.

Rindol looked up from slurping hot tea. "Dulath? She will be in the higher peaks today, or mayhap she has returned to her trap to partake of her catch."

"She?" exploded Ki. "Whence comes this 'she'? I would speak to Dulath!"

Rindol continued to eye her mildly. "She, he, it is all one to that kind. As for speaking to him, well, the mouth that leaves such gaps in his prey is not for talking. For Waters of Kiev and tendon slitting, I ask but five measures of grain. My goats fancy it."

Ki's mind was reeling. She sorted her thoughts frantically. "I'll find Dulath at the pit trap?" she asked. The old man nodded. "Waters of Kiev will make Vandien a dribbling idiot. Give him none of that, and do no tendon slitting. I'll give you three measures of oats to keep him here, warm and dry, and ease his pain in any way that will not do him harm. I go to find Dulath. I'll pay you on my return, provided Vandien is intact."

Ki gestured Rindol to silence before he could further confuse her. Sher rose and with a strange reluctance, crossed the room to Vandien.

She rested a cautious hand on his hair, but he did not stir. The scent of him rose up to her, a scent like herbs and moss crushed underfoot on a damp morning. She brushed the dark curls back from his forehead. His skin appeared drained of blood, and his face was cool, too cool to her touch.

"Keep him alive for me!" she told Rindol brusquely, and turned to leave.

"Ki!"

She turned back instantly. Vandien's eyes were dull but intelligent.

"Take the rapier from my gear. Use it, if you have need."

"I have my broadsword. I know it, but your rapier is still strange to me."

"Take it. That clubbish sword of yours does not even frighten anyone. Take the rapier."

"I am a child with it. You yourself say I have no skill with it in spite of your lessons."

"You are better with it than many who believe themselves skilled. Take it. I shall not tell you again."

She nodded once, and departed.

Evening became night without warning. Ki had no hours to waste awaiting daylight. She had paused but once, to kindle the torch she now carried. It billowed about her hand uncomfortably. She cursed herself for not bringing an extra one. And she cursed the yellow horse for being dead. Even its bony frame would have made a better mount than broad gray Sigurd. Her hips ached from bestraddling him. But her trip was near an end. She slowed Sigurd. The torch was small help to pierce the night. She had no wish to land in a pit on top of a dead yellow horse.

She need not have worried. Wise Sigurd halted of his own, snorting in disgust at the smell of his dead comrade. Ki slid from his back gratefully. She could trust him to stand.

She advanced cautiously to the edge of the pit. Where would this Dulath be? She peered in.

The yellow horse was not alone. Added to him was the ribby body of an aged man and the corpse of a young woman. Ki gagged, then swallowed convulsively. She backed away from the sight. She gasped in cold air to regain herself. There had been truth in the old man's babblings. The villagers threw their dead into Dulath's pits. Who then, or what, was Dulath, to be appeased by such thoughtfulness? Ki felt no curiousity.

Snow crunched, not on the trail, but above, up the side of the pass. Ki was not alone. She held her ground, uncertain if flight was necessary or wise.

Dulath was white. At first she could not separate him from the snow. It was as if he materialized in one piece within the circle of her torchlight. He paused once, perhaps noticing her, but almost immediately moved on, deeming her of no consequence.

Dulath had no head; he had no front, nor back, nor sides, by any standards Ki knew. His body was roughly ellipsoidal, fringed by dangling orbs that could have been eyes, though they ignored the light of the torch. Beneath each orb hung a spike like a fleshy icicle. Ki had seen those spikes before. His back was smooth, and at least as broad as Sigurd's. He moved on a multitude of skinny jointed legs, some of which ended in finger-like appendages. He entered the pit with the ease of a caterpillar crawling down a twig. The scuttling of legs in the snow was the only sound.

Ki was shaking. The whites showed all around Sigurd's

eyes. "Stand," Ki whispered to him. Suppressing her fear she advanced to the pit.

Within the pit. Dulath feasted. He perched lopsidedly on the tangled frozen bodies. Ki watched in nausea as a great parrot-like bill on the underside of Dulath's body closed with a crunch on the plump buttock of the dead woman.

It made no chewing motions or feeding sounds. There was only the rattling of its spidery legs and the crunch of the great bill nipping off hunks of frozen flesh. Eventually, it had its fill. Dulath then squatted busily. A questing ovipositor descended from its now sagging underbody. With blinding speed, it punched into the bodies of the dead, leaving a neat depression and a glistening white egg. Soon the bodies were specked with the shiny orbs. Ki seemed to come out of a trance as the torch scorched her fingers. Her hand jerked, the torch fell. It streaked into the pit, to fall next to Dulath and his nursery.

Ki heard an angry rattling of castanets. The white body of Dulath surged up over the edge of the pit and at her. She had threatened the nest.

In the stingy light of a waning moon, some of the appendages rose off the ground to become weapons. Opposed claws clicked at her. Ki dragged her rapier free of its sheath and fell into the stance Vandien had schooled her to.

"Present the narrowest target possible," she seemed to hear him say. "Get behind your blade." Dulath came on, clicking. He struck suddenly for her face, and she parried it wildly. Her darting blade thrust his appendage aside. She lunged then in an automatic riposte. Her blade rang against Dulath's hard back, and she retreated hastily.

"Fingers and wrist, fingers and wrist," cautioned Vandien. "Are you a reaper of wheat or a reaper of men?"

She backed away from Dulath, and he, encouraged, struck again. Her blade reacted before her mind, whistling in to strike at the questing appendage. With a snick a segment of it flew away into the snow. Ki felt Dulath squeal in a voice above her hearing level. Heartened, she lunged, but again her rapier only skittered off Dulath's back. Ki fell back, then attacked again. Her rapier tasted air. Dulath had wearied suddenly of this game, especially with a foe that fought back. Scuttling backwards, he disappeared into his pit-nest.

Ki fought a sudden trembling. The icy air froze the sweat that damped her hair. In sudden hope she examined the blade of her rapier; no trace of blood. The legend of Dulath's blood curing his poison was now her only chance. But that blood was not easily shed. Her blade would not pierce his back armor and hewing off his appendages would not gain her a drop. Getting at his soft underbelly was a possibility. Still mulling on that, she clambered onto Sigurd and turned his head back to Rindol's. She would need a vessel in which to catch the blood. How she would get the blood she did not know.

Ki stepped into Rindol's hut blinking the night from her eyes and shaking the cold from her clothes. Vandien lay as she had last seen him. She unfastened her cloak and shed it as she moved to his side. He did not stir.

His lashes lay on his cheeks, veiling his dark eyes. The ruddiness of his wind-weathered face contrasted strangely with the pallor of his poisoned body.

"Vandien?" Ki called him softly, as if he wandered in some immeasurable distance.

"Ki?" he mumbled, and turned his face to search for her, but his eyes did not open.

She lifted the coverings and looked at his leg. Rindol had removed the useless bandagings. There was no bleeding. The gash gaped wide and raw amidst the swelling of his thigh. She lay a hand on it softly as if to cure him with a touch.

Vandien stirred and his hand moved to her breast. Startled, Ki jerked away. His eyes opened, and, though sunken in his face, seemed to laugh at her. The gentleness of the cuff she gave him made it almost a caress.

"Do you think of nothing else, even when you're poisoned?"

"Even when I'm dying. Besides, what's a man to do when a woman sends her hand creeping up his thigh?" He tried to laugh and groaned instead.

"You're not dying," Ki asserted without sympathy. "Where's Rindol? I have need of him."

Vandien nodded toward a curtained door. His eyes closed. Even as Ki turned toward the door, Rindol parted the hangings.

"Not a widow yet!" he greeted her cheerfully.

"We are but friends. But I do not expect to lose him. I have questions, old man. Answer, but please do not chatter at me. How long do those poisoned by Dulath live?"

"It depends," the old man shrugged. "A child or a goat,

seldom more than a day. But a man such as he may last, oh, four perhaps. Why, he has not even begun to arch yet. I remember one fellow, took close to a week. . . ."

"Enough! Dulath has laid her eggs and fed. How soon before he digs his next pit?" Ki scowled as she found herself using the mixed pronouns of the old man.

"That too depends. The villagers will burn the pit tomorrow, to keep the eggs from hatching. One god is enough, it seems. Dulath will wait a day, at most two, before digging again. But do not fret; there will be a pit for your man when he goes. . . ."

Ki was hard put to refrain from striking him. Instead she made an abrupt gesture for silence.

"I'll sleep, then, for a while. Rindol, might I buy a goat from you?"

"It depends," the old man began shrewdly. Then, marking the look Ki gave him, he became direct. "Twenty dru."

Ki hefted the purse at her belt, frowning.

"Five dru. And this ring," she pulled it from her hand, "for the goat. Now I sleep."

Ki slapped the ring and coins into his hand before he could object. Then she went out the door, to return with her bedding. She dumped it on the floor next to Vandien. He stirred slightly and opened his eyes.

"Ki, you owe me a horse."

"Shut up," said Ki, without malice, and went to unfastening her boots.

Vandien awoke to the dim light of dawn coming in the open door. A gust of wind carried in a few flakes of snow, and the pocked old man. Rindol shuffled across the room, and tumbled an armful of wood to the hearth.

"You be awake!" he informed Vandien. Rindol ran a pale tongue over his remaining teeth, and leaned unpleasantly close over Vandien. "How does the leg feel?"

"It doesn't." Vandien was appalled at the weakness of his own voice. Yesterday he would have sworn that no man could feel worse than he did. Today he knew better. Once, during the night, he had awakened, and turned his eyes down to his wound. He would not look again. Surely that blackening leg, so immensely swollen it resembled a rotting log, could not be his. Surely Fate would not visit this upon Vandien, her favored child. Surely it could not be himself lying here in a madman's hut, watching his body rot away from him.

Rindol looked about cautiously, then leaned his whiskery face closer. "I have Waters of Kiev. It would give you respite. Why should you not slip away in the memories of love thrusts and sword play? When you died, you wouldn't even know it!"

"No." Vandien wished he didn't have to speak. Why couldn't the old wretch leave him alone?

"So says the woman. But a poor wife she is to you, sir! Does she sew a shroud or make you death song? No! She sits outside and makes pot meat of a goat!"

"What?" Vandien struggled to understand, his mind slipping.

"Aye! She squats in the snow, to skin and bone a goat. What wife thinks of filling her stomach when her husband is dying? I'd beat her for you myself, were I a younger man!"

"Not wife. Friend. Go away." Vandien tried to turn his face away. He couldn't.

"She will buy no Waters of Kiev for you! Yet she finds coins to buy a goat. Still, I would not see you suffer. You wear a ring, sir. A simple one, true, but I am a man of charity. Give it me, and the Waters of Kiev are yours. Waters of peace, of wondrous dreams, of youth, remembered with the clarity of each passing moment! Waters of Kiev, to ease your passing. What say you?"

"Vab freeze you," muttered Vandien, and sank into darkness.

A thin smoke rose from Dulath's pit. The smells of roasting meat would have been appetizing, had Ki not known what meats were roasting. A small group of villagers kept vigil over their smouldering relatives. Ki and Sigurd paused.

"What do you seek, woman?" asked one.

"The new pit of Dulath. A man is dying." Ki shuddered inwardly at the implications the villagers would give her words.

"Farther up the pass where it is narrowed by a slide. She has dug there, so none may pass unless they pay her toll. Praise Dulath! He cares for our dead! They live in her!"

Ki set her heels to Sigurd and cantered past. She did not trust her tongue to reply.

She found the pit fresh and empty. Her knowing eyes

could see the marks of the many scrabbling legs that had dug it. In the bottom there bristled a profusion of the spikes. This pit Dulath had not covered, trusting to its location.

It was a barren area; nothing but the wall of the pass and the jumble of loose stone. Ki led Sigurd behind a tangle of boulders and settled to her watching. Now time might betray her. For wait she must, to be sure her gift to Dulath would be on the top of the pile, to be certain he would eat of it and not merely choose it for eggs. How long before Dulath would return to feed? For Vandien's sake, she hoped it would be soon.

Ki was still crouching among the boulders and snow when the colors of the day faded. By twilight, what was not black was gray. There had been but one visitor to the pit, some petty official of the village who had unceremoniously tumbled in the rags and bones of a beggar. He had not seen Ki.

The wind was rising. Ki pulled her cloak tighter. The wind stealthily ran icy fingers up her back. Ki's legs ached from crouching. But she needed the cold. If she was to succeed, her bundles must remain tightly frozen until she used them.

The sound could have been the rattle of small stones stirred by the wind. But Ki knew what it was. On stiff legs she stumbled to the edge of the pit with her bundles. From each she took a roll of goat meat tied with soft twine. She tossed them gently into the pit so that they landed atop the bony body. Surely Dulath would choose them for his meal. Ki was gambling Vandien's life on it.

She had scarcely regained her hiding place before Dulath came into view. Ki lit no torch; she would risk no chance of disturbing him before he fed. Dulath scuttled out of the snowy hills, pale creature, native of some far world. He moved through the moonlight on his clicking legs, undulating around boulders. He flowed into the pit.

For one chill moment, Ki knew remorse. This was no creature of evil, no demon or god. It was only a beast, following the dictates of its instincts. It alone of its kind remained in this perpetually frozen pass, seeking only to feed and reproduce in its own way. Whence it had come, Ki would never know. Of its beginnings, none would ever speak. Its end would be all she could witness. Then she heard the crisping sound of its feeding. Vandien came to mind. The poison had overwhelmed the left side of his body. His sword arm lay motionless and swollen on the bed skins. A desperate sleep possessed him, seeming to exhaust him more than the most frantic bout of sword. Which of these two would she choose to live? Remorse died within her, replaced by a cold watchfulness. Her chance would be brief; she must not miss it.

The feeding sounds ceased. Now Dulath would be implanting her eggs in the frozen corpse. Ki sent up a prayer, to what god she hardly knew, that Dulath had consumed the parcels of meat. Now would come another waiting. How long would Dulath remain guarding her nest? And how long would it be before Dulath's body heat freed the gifts Ki had worked into the meat?

She had learned from the Pelashi, a woefully poor tribe of the Northern Stretches. They subsisted by trapping food and hides. Each animal furnished the means to capture the next. The supple bones of each were saved, bent and tied in an arch, and frozen. The ends were sharpened. Once frozen, the ties that held the bone could be removed, and the bone buried in a chunk of meat. Left on a game path or near a den, the frozen chunks of meat with their hidden bones were swallowed up by the predator. The heat of the animal's body did the rest. As the bones thawed they straightened, piercing the animal from within.

There were times when it did not work. If the animal chewed the meat, the bones were broken or discarded. But Ki could not afford to consider that chance; Vandien would die if Dulath refused the bones. Dulath must swallow the bones whole. Ki willed it.

There was a scrabbling from the pit. Dulath came bounding over the edge, arching and twisting in an effort to dislodge the bones within. Again Ki felt rather than heard his high scream. He scuttled into darkness.

Ki followed hastily. She must be close when he died, to harvest the blood. Thonged about her neck was the squat vessel with its tight stopper.

She followed the sounds of his flight. She caught a glimpse of him dodging crazily among the scattered boulders of the slide. Ki drew Vandien's rapier as she ran. She could not let Dulath go far. Once she had the blood, she must make all haste to Rindol's. Ki scrambled through the loose stone.

Dulath reared up! From behind a boulder he rose to meet her. A pincer darted at her face. Ki leaped back as it snicked through a fold of her heavy cloak. The rapier's blade flashed through the pincer. But tonight Dulath was in pain. He would not flee. Two new pincers rose to challenge her blade. Ki parried the thrust of one, but did not sever it. The other seized a fold of her cloak and drew her nearer. She struck at it, severing it at a joint. But two other pincers had already risen to replace it. She felt her cloak seized in two, then three places. As swiftly as she struck the claws away, others seized her.

The claws gave a sudden twitch, jerking her onto her knees. She tried to catch herself on one hand, gripping her rapier with the other. She skidded over frozen ground to find herself under the pale body of Dulath.

The parrot beak gaped at her, snapped. Ki twisted aside, struck upward with her blade. But the claws retained their grip on her cloak and limited her movements. She saw the underbody of Dulath loom, heard the snap of his beak. A fold of her jerkin ripped away.

Panic came to her aid. With a strength not her own, she tore her arm free from her crippling cloak. She jabbed deep and tore through the bulging underbody. Ki pulled her rapier free of tangling entrails and stabbed again. Dulath's pincers clattered together as he screamed piercingly. Blood rained down upon Ki.

Ki jabbed up again, to keep the pale body from settling upon her in death. With her free hand she tore loose the vessel, pulled the stopper with her teeth. She waved it frantically to catch the wildly spattering blood. Ki had expected it to be red and warm. It was a creamy white and hot enough to scald her. A gout of it spashed her hand and she felt the vessel grow heavy.

A final jabbing slash lifted Dulath's body high. Ki butted her way through a wall of spiny legs. A single flying pincer snatched a lock of hair from her head. She had no time for pain. Vessel clutched in one hand, rapier in the other, Ki raced for her horse.

Sigurd snorted at the foul smell as Ki threw herself on his back. That he kept his footing coming down out of the boulders was to his credit alone. Ki gave him no directions except her battering heels. Sigurd's great feathered hooves struck sparks from stones. Behind the scrabbling of pincers faded. Sigurd's hooves beating on snow and stone and the hammering of Ki's heart filled her ears.

There were the lights of the cottage, its dark shape, and finally its door. Sigurd halted after he realized Ki had left his back. He sent a rebuking whinny after her. Why was he being treated so ill? But the slam of the door was his only answer.

The poison had begun its work on Vandien's muscles. His heels and head were attempting to meet behind his back. Vandien's eyes stared into hell. Rindol bent over him, tugging at the ring on his unresisting hand. A clear flask with water of the palest rose rested on the table.

Then Rindol was flung aside, to crash against the table and send precious Waters of Kiev trickling down cracks in the floor. Vandien's dark eyes did not change as Ki bent over him.

Ki pulled the stopper from her flask, held it to his mouth, only to discover that the muscles of his jaw were no longer his to control. Madness came into her green eyes as she pressed the hinge of his jaw between her thumbs. Squeezing forced his mouth to open. She shoved gloved fingers between his teeth to hold it and dumped the contents of the flask down his throat. Vandien swallowed convulsively, choked, and swallowed again. Ki released him and stood up.

"That's all I can do, friend. Now we wait." With a venomous look at Rindol, she seated herself and took Vandien's swollen hand in hers.

Sigurd shook his head until his gray mane flew. Even staid Sigmund snorted restlessly. Ki glared impatiently at the inn door. Vandien emerged. The bruises on his jaw were fading, but his limp was still pronounced. He swung up onto the wagon seat next to Ki, grunting as he settled his stiff leg.

"It takes you that long to get a jug?" Ki asked acidly. She shook the reins and the grays stepped out.

"I paused to hear the sage words of a holy man," Vandien explained innocently. Ki glanced across at his wryly pursed mouth.

"What caught your religious fancy?"

"Certain villagers are disturbed. Their homes grow noisome with the dead. Dulath has been lax in his grave digging. They ask the holy man what they must do with their dead."

"And?" prodded Ki.

"He bids them take their dead as gifts and go to seek their god in the pass. He fears they may have displeased him. They plan to seek out his last pit and track him from there, bearing their fragrant offerings."

Ki shook the reins and the grays stepped up their pace. "I

fear this village may not be a healthful place for us when Dulath is found, my friend."

"You could be right." For a moment they traveled in silence. Then Vandien rose slightly on the seat, to gesture at a horse trader leading his string of weary wares into the village.

"You do owe me a horse, Ki," he reminded her, nodding appreciatively at a bay.

"Go to hell, Vandien," Ki replied affably.

NORTHERN CHESS

Tanith Lee

A week's worth of submissions had left me a tad bid discouraged, when along came something with imagery, humor, and suspense which provided a genuine feast for my imagination. A relatively new writer, Tanith Lee is already a superstar, establishing herself in the top ranks of the field right from the start with her 1975 novel Birthgrave. *Other titles have included:* Companions on the Road, East of Midnight, Quest of the White Witch, Night's Master, Storm Lord, *and a great many others.*

"Northern Chess" has a moral—but it is a moral incidental to, or rather, in addition to *a superior story. I received many manuscripts packed with "messages" that completely gobbled up the plots and characters; and I avoided these with a passion, even when I wholeheartedly agreed with the points made. My feeling has been (and it is subject to revision) that the depiction of strong women in heroic fantasy (or any other art) is, in and of itself, so innately political to our male-dominant society that any additional polemic is redundant—and not nearly as effective. Tanith Lee proves the difference between a good rhetorician and a genuine storyteller— the latter is always the greater moralizer.*

Of her story, Ms. Lee says, "Rather than Barbaric, its influences are medieval and Carolingian France, with a touch of Shakespeare and Agincourt irrepressibly chucked in." It's beautifully told.

Sky and land had the same sallow bluish tinge, soaked in cold light from a vague white sun. It was late summer, but summer might never have come here. The few trees were

171

bare of leaves and birds. The cindery grassless hills rolled up
and down monotonously. Their peaks gleamed dully, their
dips were full of mist. It was a land for sad songs and dismal
rememberings. and, when the night came, for nightmares and
hallucinations.

Fifteen miles back, Jaisel's horse had died. Not for any apparent cause. It had been healthy and active when she rode
from the south on it, the best the dealer had offered her,
though he had tried to cheat her in the beginning. She was
aiming to reach a city in the far north, on the sea coast there,
but not for any particular reason. She had fallen into the
casual habit of the wandering adventurer. Destination was an
excuse, never a goal. And when she saw the women at their
looms or in their greasy kitchens, or tangled with babies, or
broken with field work, or leering out of painted masks from
shadowy town doorways, Jaisel's urge to travel, to ride, to fly,
to run away, increased. Generally she was running from
something in fact as well as in the metaphysical. The last city
she had vacated abruptly, having killed two footpads who
had jumped her in the street. One had turned out to be a
lordling, who had taken up robbery and rape as a hobby. In
those parts, to kill a lord, with whatever justice, meant hanging and quartering. So Jaisel departed on her new horse, aiming for a city in the north. And in between had come this
bleak northern empty land where her mount collapsed slowly
under her and died without warning. Where the streams
tasted bitter and the weather looked as if it wished to snow in
summer.

She had seen only ruins. Only a flock of grayish wild sheep
materialized from mist on one hand and plunged away into
mist on the other. Once she heard a raven cawing. She was
footsore and growing angry, with the country, with herself,
and with God. While her saddle and pack gained weight on
her shoulders with every mile.

Then she reached the top of one of the endless slopes,
looked over and saw something new.

Down in a pool of the yellowish-bluish mist lay a village.
Primitive and melancholy it was, but alive, for smokes spi-
raled from roof-holes, drifting into the cloudless sky. Mourn-
ful and faint, too, there came the lowing of cattle. Beyond
the warren of cots, a sinister unleafed spider web of trees. Beyond them, barely seen, transparent in mist, something some

distance away, a mile perhaps—a tall piled hill, or maybe a
stony building of bizarre and crooked shape. . . .

Jaisel started and her eyes refocused on the closer vantage
of the village and the slope below.

The fresh sound was unmistakable: jingle-jangle of bells on
the bridles of war horses. The sight was exotic, also, unexpected here. Two riders on steel-blue mounts, the scarlet ca-
parisons flaming up through the quarter-tone atmosphere like
bloody blades. And the shine of mail, the blink of gems.

"Render your name!" one of the two knights shouted.

She half smiled, visualizing what they would see, what they
would assume, the surprise in store.

"My name is Jaisel," she shouted back.

And heard them curse.

"What sort of a name is that, boy?"

Boy. Yes, and not the only time.

She started to walk down the slope toward them.

And what they had supposed to be a boy from the top of
the incline, gradually resolved itself into the surprise. Her fine
flaxen hair was certainly short as a boy's, somewhat shorter.
A great deal shorter than the curled manes of knights. Slender in her tarnished chain mail, with slender strong hands
dripping with frayed frosty lace at the wrists. The white lace
collar lying out over the mail with dangling drawstrings each
ornamented by a black pearl. The left ear-lobe pierced and a
gold sickle moon flickering sparks from it under the palely
electric hair. The sword belt was gray leather, worn and
stained. Dagger on right hip with a fancy gilt handle, thin
sword on left hip, pommel burnished by much use. A girl
knight with intimations of the reaver, the showman, and, (for
what it was worth), the prince.

When she was close enough for the surprise to have com-
menced, she stopped and regarded the two mounted knights.
She appeared gravely amused, but really the joke had palled
by now. She had had twelve years to get bored with it. And
she was tired, and still angry with God.

"Well," one of the knights said at last, "it takes all kinds to
fill the world. But I think you've mistaken your road, lady."

He might mean an actual direction .He might mean her
mode of living.

Jaisel kept quiet, and waited. Presently the second knight
said chillily: "Do you know of this place? Understand where
you are?"

"No," she said. "It would be a courteous kindness if you told me."

The first knight frowned. "It would be a courteous kindness to send you home to your father, your husband and your children."

Jaisel fixed her eyes on him. One eye was a little narrower than the other. This gave her face a mocking, witty slant.

"Then, sir," she said, "send me. Come. I invite you."

The first knight gesticulated theatrically.

"I am Renier of Towers," he said. "I don't fight women."

"You do," she said. "You are doing it now. Not successfully."

The second knight grinned; she had not anticipated that.

"She has you, Renier. Let her be. No girl travels alone like this one, and dressed as she is, without skills to back it. Listen, Jaisel. This land is cursed. You've seen, the life's sucked out of it. The village here. Women and beasts birth monsters. The people fall sick without cause. Or with some cause. There was an alchemist who claimed possession of this region. Maudras. A necromancer, a worshipper of old unholy gods. Three castles of his scabbed the countryside between here and Towers in the west. Those three are no more—taken and razed. The final castle is here, a mile off to the northeast. If the mist would lift, you might see it. The Prince of Towers means to expunge all trace of Maudras from the earth. We are the prince's knights, sent here to deal with the fourth castle as with the rest."

"And the castle remains untaken," said Renier. "Months we've sat here in this unwholesome plague-ridden wilderness."

"Who defends the castle?" Jaisel asked. "Maudras himself?"

"Maudras was burned in Towers a year ago," the second knight said. "His familiar, or his curse, holds the castle against God's knights." His face was pale and grim. Both knights indeed were alike in that. But Renier stretched his mouth and said to her sweetly: "Not a spot for a maid. A camp of men. A haunted castle in a blighted country. Better get home."

"I have no horse," said Jaisel levelly. "But coins to buy one."

"We've horses and to spare," said the other knight. "Dead men don't require mounts. I am called Cassant. Vault up behind me and I'll bring you to the camp."

She swung up lightly, despite the saddle and pack on her shoulders.

Renier watched her, sneering, fascinated.

As they turned the horses' heads into the lake of mist, he rode near and murmured: "Beware, lady. The women in the village are sickly and revolting. A knight's honor may be forgotten. But probably you have been raped frequently."

"Once," she said, "ten years back. I was his last pleasure. I dug his grave myself, being respectful of the dead." She met Renier's eyes again and added gently, "and when I am in the district I visit his grave and spit on it."

The mist was denser below than Jaisel had judged from the slope. In the village a lot was hidden, which was maybe as well. At a turning among the cots she thought she spied a forlorn hunched-over woman, leading by a tether a shadowy animal, which seemed to be a cow with two heads.

They rode between the trees and out the other side, and piecemeal the war camp of Towers evolved through the mist. Blood-blotch red banners hung lankly; the ghosts of tents clawed with bright heraldics that penetrated the obscurity. Horses puffed breath like dragon-smoke at their pickets. A couple of Javelot-cannon emplacements, the bronze tubes sweating on their wheels, the javelins stacked by, the powder casks wrapped in sharkskin but probably damp.

At this juncture, suddenly the mist unravelled. A vista opened away from the camp for two hundred yards northeast, revealing the castle of the necromancer-alchemist, Maudras.

It reared up, stark and peculiar against a tin-colored sky.

The lower portion was carved from the native rock-base of a conical hill. This rose into a plethora of walls and craning. squinnying towers, that seemed somehow like the petrification of a thing once unnaturally growing. A causeway flung itself up the hill and under an arched doormouth, barricaded by iron.

No movements were discernible on battlements or roofs. No pennant flew. The castle had an aura of the tomb. Yet not necessarily a tomb of the dead.

It was the camp which had more of the feel of a mortuary about it. From an oblique quarter emanated groanings. Where men were to be found outside the tents, they crouched listlessly over fires. Cook-pots and heaps of accoutrements plainly went unattended. By a scarlet pavilion two knights sat at chess. The game was sporadic and violent and seemed likely to end in blows.

Cassant drew rein a space to the side of the scarlet pavilion, whose cloth was blazoned with three gold turrets—the insignia of Towers. A boy ran to take charge of the horse as its two riders dismounted. But Renier remained astride his horse, staring at Jaisel. Soon he announced generally, in a herald's carrying tone: "Come, gentlemen, welcome a new recruit. A peerless knight. A damsel in breeches."

All around, heads lifted. A sullen interest bloomed over the apathy of the camp: the slurred spiteful humor of men who were ill, or else under sentence of execution. They began to get up from the pallid fires and shamble closer. The fierce knights paused and gazed arrogantly across with extravagant oaths.

"Mistress, you're in for trouble," said Cassant ruefully. "But be fair, he warned you of it."

Jaisel shrugged. She glanced at Renier, nonchalantly posed on the steel-blue horse, right leg loose of the stirrup now and hooked across the saddlebow. At ease, malevolently, he beamed at her. Jaisel slipped the gaudy dagger from her belt, let him catch the flash of the gilt, then tossed it at him. The little blade, with its wasp-sting point, sang through the air, singeing the hairs on his right cheek. It buried itself, where she had aimed it, in the picket post behind him. But Renier, reacting to the feint as she had intended, lunged desperately aside for the sake of his pretty face, took all his own weight on the yet-stirruped leg and off the free one, unbalanced royally, and plunged crashing to the ground. At the same instant, fully startled, the horse tried to rear. Still left-leggedly trapped in the stirrup, Renier of Towers went slithering through the hot ashes of a fire.

A hubbub resulted—delighted unfriendly mirth. The soldiers were as prepared to make sport of a boastful lord on his ears in the ash as of a helpless girl.

And the helpless girl was not quite finished. Renier was fumbling for his sword. Jaisel leaped over him like a lion, kicking his hands away as she passed. Landing, she wrenched his foot out of the stirrup and, having liberated him, jumped to the picket to retrieve her dagger. As Renier gained his knees, he beheld her waiting for him, quiet as a statue, her pack slung on the ground, the thin sword, slick with light, ready as a sixth long murderous finger to her hand.

A second he faltered, while the camp, ferociously animated, buzzed. Then his ringed hand went to the hilt of his own sword. It was two to three thirds its length from the scabbard when a voice bellowed from the doorway of the scarlet and gold pavilion: "Dare to draw upon a woman, Renier, and I'll flay you myself."

Gasping, Renier let the sword grate home again. Jaisel turned and saw a man incarnadine with anger as the tent he had stepped from. Her own dormant anger woke and filled her, white anger not red, bored anger, cold anger.

"Don't fear him slain, sir," she said. "I will give him only a slight cut, and afterward spare him."

The incarnadine captain of the camp of Towers bent a baleful shaggy lour on her.

"Strumpet, or witch?" he thundered.

"Tell me first," said Jaisel coolly, "your title. Is it coward or imbecile?"

Silence was settling like flies on honey.

The captain shook himself.

"I never yet struck a wench—" he said.

"Nor will you now, by God's wounds."

His mouth dropped ajar. He disciplined it and asked firmly: "Why coward and why imbecile?"

"Humoring me, are you?" she inquired. She strolled toward him and let the sword tip weave a delicate pattern about his nose. To his credit, having calmed himself, he retained the calm. "Coward or imbecile," she said, drawing lines of glinting fire an inch from his nostrils, "because you cannot take a castle that offers no defenders."

A response then. A beefy paw thrust up to flick the sword away from him and out of her hand. But the sword was too quick. Now it rested horizontally on the air, tip twitching a moment at his throat. And now it was gone back into its scabbard, and merely a smiling strange-eyed girl was before him.

"I already know enough of you," the captain said, "that you are a trial to men and an affront to heaven is evident. Despite that, I will answer your abuse. Maudras' last castle is defended by some sorcery he conjured to guard it. Three assaults were attempted. The result you shall witness. Follow, she-wolf."

And he strode off through the thick of the men who parted to let him by, and to let the she-wolf by in his wake. No one touched her but one fool, who had observed, but learned nothing. The pommel of her dagger in his ribs, bruising through mail and shirt, put pain to his flirtation.

"Here," the captain barked.

He drew aside the flap of a dark tent, and she saw twenty men lying on rusty mattresses and the two surgeons going up and down. The casualties of some savage combat. She beheld things she had beheld often, those things which sickened less but appalled more with repetition. Near to the entrance a boy younger than herself, dreaming horribly in a fever, called out. Jaisel slipped into the tent. She set her icy palm on the boy's forehead and felt his raging heat burn through it. But her touch seemed to alleviate his dream at least. He grew quieter.

"Again," she said softly, "coward, or imbecile. And these are the sacrificial victims on the altar of cowardice or imbecility."

Probably, the captain had never met such merciless eyes. Or, perhaps not so inexplicably, from between the smooth lids of a young girl.

"Enchantment," he said gruffly. "And sorcery. We were powerless against it. Do you drink wine, you virago? Yes, no doubt. Come and drink it with me then in my pavilion and you shall have the full story. Not that you deserve it. But you are the last thrown stone that kills a man. Injustice atop all the rest, and from a *woman*."

Abruptly she laughed at him, her anger spent.

Red wine and red meat were served in the red pavilion. All the seven knights of the Towers camp were present, Cassant and Renier among the rest. Outside, their men went on sitting around the fires. A dreary song had been struck up, and was repeated, over and over, as iron snow-light radiated from the northern summer sky.

The captain of the knights had told again the story Cassant had recounted to Jaisel on the slope: The three castles razed, the final castle which proved unassailable. Gruff and bellicose, the captain found it hard to speak of supernatural items and growled the matter into his wine.

"Three assaults were offered the walls of the castle. Montaube led the first of these. He died, and fifty men with him. Of what? We saw no swordsmen on the battlements, no javelots were fired, no arrows. Yet men sprinkled the ground, bloody and dying, as if an army twice our numbers had come to grips with them unseen. The second assault, I led. I escaped by a miracle. I saw a man, his mail split as if by a bolt shot from a great distance. He dropped with a cry and blood bursting from a terrible wound. Not a soul was near but I, his captain. No weapon or shot was visible. The third assault—was planned, but never carried through. We reached the escarpment, and my soldiers began falling like scythed grain. No shame in our retreat. Another thing. Last month, three brave fools, men of dead Montaube's, decided secretly to effect entry by night over the walls. A sentry perceived them vanish within. They were not attacked. Nor did they return."

There was a long quiet in the pavilion. Jaisel glanced up and encountered the wrathful glare of the captain.

"Ride home to Towers, then," she said. "What else is there to do?"

"And what other council would you predict from a woman?" broke in Renier. "We are *men*, madam. We'll take that rock, or die. Honor, lady. Did you never hear of it in the whorehouse where you were whelped?"

"You have had too much wine, sir," said Jaisel. "But by all means have some more." She poured her cup, measured and deliberate, over his curling hair. Two or three guffawed, enjoying this novelty. Renier leapt up. The captain bellowed familiarly, and Renier again relapsed.

Wine ran in rosy streams across his handsome brow.

"Truly, you do right to reprove me, and the she-wolf is right to annoint me with her scorn. We sit here like cowards, as she mentioned. There's one way to take the castle. A challenge. Single combat between God and Satan. Can the haunting of Maudras refuse that?" Renier got to his feet with precision now.

"You are drunk, Renier," the captain snapped.

"Not to drunk to fight." Renier was at the entrance. The captain roared. Renier only bowed. "I am a knight. Only so far can you command me."

"You fool—" said Cassant.

"I am, however, my own fool," said Renier.

The knights stood, witnesses to his departure. Respect, sorrow and dread showed in their eyes, their nervous fingers fiddling with jewels, wine cups, chess figures.

Outside, the dreary song had broken off. Renier was shouting for his horse and battle gear.

The knights crowded to the flap to watch him armed. Their captain elect joined them. No further protest was attempted, as if a divine ordinance were being obeyed.

Jaisel walked out of the pavilion. The light was thickening as if to hem them in. Red fires, red banners, no other color able to pierce the gloom. Renier sat his horse like a carved chess figure himself, an immaculate knight moving against a castle on a misty board.

The horse fidgeted, trembled. Jaisel ran her hand peacefully down its nose amid the litter of straps and buckles. She did not look at Renier, swaggering above her. She sensed too well his panic under the pride.

"Don't" she said to him softly, "ride into the arms of death because you think I shamed your manhood. It's too large a purge for so small an ill."

"Go away, girl," he jeered at her. "Go and have babies as God fashioned you to do."

"God did not fashion you to die, Renier of Towers."

"Maybe you're wrong in that," he said wildly, and jerked the horse around and away from her.

He was galloping from the camp across the plain toward the rock. A herald dashed out and followed, but prudently hanging some yards behind, and when he sounded the brass, the notes cracked, and his horse shied at the noise. But Renier's horse threw itself on as if in preparation for a massive jump at the end of its running.

"He's mad; will die," Cassant mumbled.

"And my fault," Jaisel answered.

A low horrified moan went through the ranks of the watchers. The iron barricades of the huge castle's mouth were sluggishly folding aside. Nothing rode forth. It was, on the contrary, patently an invitation.

One man yelled to Renier across a hundred yards of gray ground. Several swelled the cry. Suddenly, three quarters of the camp of Towers was howling. To make sport of a noble was one thing. To see him seek annihilation was another. They screamed themselves hoarse, begging him to choose reason above honor.

Jaisel, not uttering a word, turned from the spectacle. When she heard Cassant swearing, she knew Renier had galloped straight in the iron portal. The commotion of shouting

crumbled into breathings, oaths. And then came the shock
and clangor of two iron leaves meeting together again across
the mouth of hell.

Impossible to imagine what he might be confronting now.
Perhaps he would triumph, re-emerge in glory. Perhaps the
evil in Maudras' castle had faded, or had never existed. Was
an illusion. Or a lie.

They waited. The soldiers, the knights. The woman. A cold
wind blew up, raking plumes, pennants, the long curled hair,
plucking bridle bells, the gold sickle moon in Jaisel's left ear,
the fragile lace at her wrists, and the foaming lace at the
wrists of others.

The white sun westered, muddied, disappeared. Clouds like
curds forming in milk formed in the sky.

Darkness slunk in on all fours. Mist boiled over, hiding the
view of the castle. The fires burned, the horses coughed at
their pickets.

There was the smell of a wet rottenness, like marshland—
the mist—or rotting hope.

A young knight whose name Jaisel had forgotten was at
her elbow. He thrust in her face a chess piece of red amber.

"The white queen possessed the red knight," he hissed at
her. "put him in the box then. Slam the lid. Fine chess game
here in the north. Castles unbreachable and bitches for
queens. Corpses for God's knights."

Jaisel stared him down till he went away. From the corner
of her eye, she noticed Cassant was weeping tears, frugally,
one at a time.

It was too easy to get by the sentries in the mist and dark.
Of course, they were alert against the outer environs, not the
camp itself. But, still too easy. Discipline was lax. Honor had
become everything, and honor was not enough.

Yet it was her own honor that drove her, she was not immune. Nor immune to this sad region. She was full of guilt
she had no need to feel, and full of regret for a man with
whom she had shared only a mutual dislike, distrust, and
some quick verbal cuts and quicker deeds of wrath. Renier
had given himself to the castle, to show himself valiant, to
shame her. She was duly shamed. Accordingly, she was
goaded to breach the castle also, to plumb its vile secret. To
save his life if she could, avenge him if not. And die if the
castle should outwit her? No. Here was the strangest fancy of

all. Somewhere in her bones she did not believe Maudras'
castle could do that. After all, her entire life had been a suc-
cession of persons, things, fate itself, trying to vanquish her
and her aims. From the first drop of menstrual blood, the
first husband chosen for her at the age of twelve, the first
(and last) rape, the first swordmaster who had mocked her
demand to learn and ended setting wagers on her—there had
been so many lions in her way. And she had systematically
overcome each of them. Because she did not, *would* not, accept that destiny was unchangeable. Or that what was merely
named unconquerable could not be conquered.

Maudras' castle then, just another symbol to be thrown
down. And the sick-sweet twang of fear in her vitals was no
more than before any battle, like an old scar throbbing,
simple to ignore.

She padded across the plain noiselessly in the smoky mist.
Sword on left hip, dagger on the right. Saddle and pack had
been left behind beneath her blanket. Some would-be goat
might suffer astonishment if he ventured to her sleeping
place. Otherwise they would not detect her absence till sunrise.

The mist ceased thirty feet from the causeway.

She paused a moment, and considered the eccentric edifice
pouring aloft into overcast black sky. Now the castle had a
choice. It could gape invitingly as it had before Renier the
challenger. Or leave her to climb the wall seventy feet high
above the doormouth.

The iron barricades stayed shut.

She went along the causeway.

Gazing up, the cranky towers seemed to reel, sway. Certainly it had an aura of wickedness, of impenetrable lingering
hate. . . .

White queen against bishop of darkness.

Queen takes castle, a rare twist to an ancient game.

The wall.

Masonry jutted, stonework creviced, protruded. Even
weeds had rooted there. It was a gift, this wall, to any who
would climb it. Which implied a maleficent joke, similar to
the opening doors. *Enter. Come, I welcome you. Enter me
and be damned within me.*

She jumped, caught hold, began to ascend. Loose-limbed
and agile from a hundred trees, some other less lordly walls,

one cliff-face five years ago—Jaisel could skim up vertical buildings like a cat. She did not really require all the solicitous help Maúdras' wall pressed on her.

She gained the outer battlements in minutes and was looking in. Beyond this barrier, the curtain, a courtyard with its central guard—but all pitch black, difficult to assess. Only that configuration of turrets and crooked bastions breaking clear against the sky. As before, she thought of a growth, petrified.

The sound was of ripped cloth. But it was actually ripped atmosphere. Jaisel threw her body flat on the broad parapet and something kissed the nape of her neck as it rushed by into the night. Reminiscent of a javelot bolt. Or the thicker swan-flighted arrows of the north. Without sentience, yet meant for the heart, and capable of stilling it.

She tilted herself swiftly over the parapet, hung by her fingers, and dropped seven feet to a platform below. As she landed, the tearing sound was reiterated. A violent hand tugged her arm. She glanced and beheld shredded lace barely to be seen in the blackness. The mail above her wrist was heated.

Some power which could make her out when she was nearly blind, but which seemed to attack randomly, inaccurately. She cast herself flat again and crawled on her belly to the head of a stair.

Here, descending, she became the perfect target. No matter. Her second swordsmaster had been something of an acrobat—

Jaisel launched herself into air and judging where the rims of the steps should be, executed three bold erratic somersaults, arriving ultimately in a hedgehog-like roll in the court.

As she straightened from this roll, she was aware of a suddn dim glow. She spun to meet it, sword and dagger to hand, then checked, heart and gorge passing each other as they traveled in the wrong directions.

The glow was worse than sorcery. It was caused by a decaying corpse half propped in a ruined cubby under the stairs. Putrescent, the remnants gave off a phosphorescent shine, matched by an intolerable stench that seemed to intensify with recognition. And next, something else. Lit by the witch-light of dead flesh, an inscription apparently chiselled in the stone beside it. Against her wits, Jaisel could not resist studying it. In pure clerical calligraphy it read:

MAUDRAS SLEW ME

One of Montaube's men.

Only the fighter's seventh sense warned Jaisel. It sent her ducking, darting, her sword arm sweeping up—and a great blow smashed against the blade, singing through her arm into her breast and shoulder. A great invisible blow.

The thought boiled in her—*How can I fight what I cannot see?* And the second inevitable thought: *I have always fought that way, combat with abstracts.* And in that extraordinary instant, wheeling to avoid the slashing lethal blows of a murderous nonentity, Jaisel realized that though she could not *see*, yet she could *sense*.

Perhaps twenty further hackings hailed against her sword, chipped the stones around. Her arm was almost numbed, but organized and obedient as a war machine, kept up its parries, feints, deflectings, thrusts. And then, eyes nearly closed, seeing better through her instinct with a hair's-breadth, dancing-with-death accuracy, she paid out her blade the length of her arm, her body hurtling behind it, and *felt* tissue part on either side of the steel. And immediately there followed a brain-slicing shriek, more like breath forced from a bladder than the protest of a dying throat.

The way was open. She sensed this too, and shot forward, doubled over, blade swirling its precaution. A fresh doorway, the gate into the guard, yawning unbarred, and across this gate, to be leaped, a glow, a reeking skeleton, the elegant chiselling in the stone floor on this occasion:

MAUDRAS SLEW ME.

"Maudras" Jaisel shouted as she leaped.

She was in the wide hollow of the castle guard. In the huge black, which tingled and burned and flashed with colors thrown by her own racing blood against the discs of her eyes.

Then the darkness screamed, an awful shattering of notes, which brought on an avalanche, a cacophany, as if the roof fell. It took her an extra heart-beat to understand, to fling herself from the path of a charging destruction no less potent for being natural. As the guard wall met her spine, the screaming nightmare, Renier's horse, exploded by her and out into the court beyond the door.

She lay quiet, taking air, and something stirred against her arm. She wrenched away and raised her sword, but Montaube's ultimate glowing soldier was there, draped on the base of what looked to be a pillar trunk. A lamp, he shone for her as the circulatory flashes died from the interior of her eyes. So she saw Renier of Towers sprawled not a foot from her.

She kneeled, and tested the quality of the tension about her. And she interpreted from it a savoring, a cat's-paw willingness to play, to let out the leash before dragging it tight once more.

The corpse (MAUDRAS SLEW ME inscribed on the pillar) appeared to glow brighter to enable her to see the mark on Renier's forehead, like the bruise caused by some glancing bolt. A trickle of blood where formerly wine had trickled. The lids shivering, the chest rising and falling shallowly.

She leaned to him and whispered: "You live then. Your luck's kinder than I reckoned. To be stunned rather than slaughtered. And Maudras' magic waiting for you to get up again. Not liking to kill when you would not know it. Preferring to make a meal of killing you, unfair and unsquare."

Then, without preface, terror swamped the hollow pillared guard of Maudras' castle.

A hundred, ten hundred, whirling slivers of steel carved the nothingness. From the blind vault, blades swooped, seared, wailed. Jaisel was netted in a sea of death. Waves of death broke over her, gushed aside, were negated by vaster waves. She sprang from one edge and reached another. The slashing was like the beaks of birds, scoring hands, cheeks; scratches as yet, but pecking, diligent. While, in its turn, her sword sank miles deep in substances like mud, like powder. Subhuman voices squalled. Unseen shapes tottered. But the rain of bites of pecks, of scratches, whirled her this way, that way, against pillars, broken stones, downward, upward. And she was in terror. Fought in terror. Terror lent her miraculous skills, feats, and a crazy flailing will to survive, and a high wild cry which again and again she smote the darkness with, along with dagger and sword.

Till abruptly she could no longer fight. Her limbs melted and terror melted with them into a worse state of abject exhaustion, acceptance, resignation. Her spirit sank, she sank, the sword sank from one hand, the dagger from the other. Drowning, she thought stubbornly: Die fighting, at least. But she did not have the strength left her.

Not until that moment did she grow aware of the cessation of blows, the silence.

She had stumbled against, was partly leaning on, some upright block of stone that had been in her way when she
dropped. Dully, her mind struggled with a paradox that
would not quite resolve. She had been battling shadows,
which had slain others instantly, but had not slain Jaisel.
Surely what she supposed was a game had gone on too long
for a game. While in earnest, now she was finished, the mech-
anism for butchery in this castle might slay her, yet did not.
And swimming wonder surfaced scornfully: Am I charmed?

There was a light. Not the phosphorus of Montaube's soldiers. It was a light the color the wretched country had been
by day, a sallow snow-blue glaze, dirty silver on the columns,
coming up like a Sabbat moon from out of nowhere.

Jaisel stared into the light, and perceived a face floating in
it. No doubt. It must be the countenance of burned Maudras,
the last malicious dregs of his spirit on holiday from hell to
effect menace. More skull than man. Eye sockets faintly
gleaming, mouth taut as if in agony.

With loathing and aversion, and with horror, the skull regarded her. It seemed, perversely, to instruct her to shift her
gaze downward, to the stone block where she leaned power-
lessly.

And something in the face ridiculously amused her, made
her shake with laughter, shudder with it, so that she knew before she looked.

The light was snuffed a second later.

Then the castle began, in rumbling stages , to collapse on
every side. Matter of factly, she went to Renier and lay over
his unconscious body to protect him from the cascading
granite.

He was not grateful as she bathed his forehead at the chill
pool equidistant between the ruin and the camp of Towers.

Nearby, the horse licked the grudging turf. The mist had
fled, and a rose-crimson sun was blooming on the horizon. A
hundred yards off, the camp gave evidence of enormous turmoil. Renier swore at her.

"Am I to credit that a strumpet nullified the sorcery of
Maudras? Don't feed me that stew."

"You suffer it too hardly. As ever," said Jaisel, honed to
patience by the events of the night. "Any woman might have
achieved this thing. But women warriors are uncommon."

"There is one too many, indeed."

Jaisel stood. She started to walk away. Renier called after her huskily:

"Wait. Say to me again what was written in the stone."

Her back to him, she halted. Concisely, wryly smiling, she said: "'I, Maudras, to this castle do allot my everlasting bane, that no man shall ever approach its walls without hurt, nor enter it and live long. Nor, to the world's ending, shall it be taken by any *man*.'"

Renier snarled.

She did not respond to that, but walked on.

Presently he caught up to her, and striding at her side, said: "How many other prophecies could be undone, do you judge, lady Insolence, that dismiss women in such fashion?"

"As many as there are stars in heaven," she said.

Brooding, but no longer arguing, he escorted her into the camp.

THE WOMAN WHO LOVED THE MOON

Elizabeth A. Lynn

If only two stories in this book prove long-standing classics of fantasy, "The Woman Who Loved the Moon" will be one. Its theme is bold, its imagery astounding. The mythic quality is the stuff of the oldest folktales and legends. I hazard that it was born as much of a deep-rooted, highly refined philosophy as from immeasurable writing talent and a genuine love of the characters and of women.

A faintly Oriental flavor, the tale is reminiscent of the historic Trung sisters of Southeast Asia, who liberated their people after a thousand years of occupation. Today a street in Hanoi bares the name of the Trungs, and the word "trung" has become the equivalent of "amazon" and indicative of valor and victory—much as Lizzy's central character comes to be known as "mirror ghost" and is well-remembered by her people.

Elizabeth A. Lynn is the author of A Different Light, Sardonic Net, *and a fantasy trilogy especially recommended to all who seek strong female characters, beginning with* The Northern Girl *from Berkley. I've placed Lizzy's story last because I think it will leave every reader with a feeling of strength and hope for our individual lives and for all of humanity. "The Woman Who Loved the Moon" particularly reminds us that this is a collection of more than fiction—these are stories in honor of every woman's heroic measure!*

They tell this story in the Middle Counties of Ryoka, and especially in the county of Issho, the home of the Talvela family. In Issho they know that the name of the woman who loved the Moon was Kai Talvela, one of the three warrior sisters of Issho. Though the trees round the Talvela house grow taller now than they did in Kai Talvela's time, her people have not forgotten her. But outside of Issho and in the cities they know her only as the Mirror Ghost.

Kai Talvela was the daughter of Roko Talvela, at a time when the domain of the Talvelai was smaller than it is now. Certainly it was smaller than Roko Talvela liked. He rode out often to skirmish at the borders of his land, and the men of the Talvelai went with him. The hills of Issho county resounded to their shouts. While he was gone the folk of the household went about their business, for the Talvela lands were famous then as they are now for their fine orchards and the fine dappled horses they breed. They were well protected, despite the dearth of soldiery, for Lia Talvela was a sorcerer, and Kai and her sisters Tei and Alin guarded the house. The sisters were a formidable enemy, for they had learned to ride and to fight. The Talvela armorer had fashioned for them fine light mail that glittered as if carved from gems. At dawn and dusk the three sisters rode across the estate. Alin wore a blue-dyed plume on her peaked helmet, and Tei wore a gold one on hers. Kai wore a feather dyed red as blood. In the dusk their armor gleamed, and when it caught the starlight it glittered like the rising Moon.

Kai was the oldest of the sisters; Alin the youngest. In looks and in affection the three were very close. They were—as Talvela women are even in our day—tall and slim, with coal-black hair. Tei was the proudest of the three, and Alin was the most laughing and gay. Kai, the oldest, was quietest, and while Tei frowned often and Alin laughed, Kai's look was grave, direct, and serene. They were all of an age to be wed, and Roko Talvela had tried to find husbands for them. But Kai, Tei, and Alin had agreed that they would take no lover and wed no man who could not match their skills in combat. Few men wished to meet the warrior sisters. Even the bravest found themselves oddly unnerved when they faced Tei's long barbed spear and grim smile, or Alin's laughing eyes as she spun her oaken horn-tipped cudgel. It whirled like a live thing in her palms. And none desired to meet Kai's great curved blade. It sang when she swung it, a thin clear

sound, purer than the note of the winter thrush. Because of
that sound Kai named her blade *Song*. She kept it sharp,
sharp as a shadow in the full Moon's light. She had a jeweled
scabbard made to hold it, and to honor it, she caused a great
ruby to be fixed in the hilt of the sword.

One day in the late afternoon the sisters rode, as was their
custom, to inspect the fences and guardposts of the estate,
making sure that the men Roko Talvela had left under their
command were vigilant in their job. Their page went with
them. He was a boy from Nakasé county, and like many of
the folk of Nakasé he was a musician. He carried a horn
which, when sounded, would summon the small company of
guards, and his stringed lute from Ujo. He also carried a
long-necked pipe, which he was just learning how to play. It
was autumn. The leaves were rusty on the trees. In the dry
sad air they rattled in the breeze as if they had been made of
brass. A red sun sat on the horizon, and overhead swung the
great silver face of the full Moon.

The page had been playing a children's song on the pipe.
He took his lips from it and spoke. The storytellers of Ujo, in
Nakasé county, when they tell this tale, insist that he was in
love with one of the sisters, or perhaps with all three. There
is no way to know, of course, if that is true. Certainly they
had all, even proud Tei, been very kind to him. But he gazed
upon the sisters in the rising moonlight, and his eyes wor-
shipped. Stammering, he said, "O my ladies, each of you is
beautiful, and together you rival even the Moon!"

Alin laughed, and swung her hair. Like water against dia-
mond it brushed her armor. Even Tei smiled. But Kai was
troubled. "Don't say that," she said gently. "It's not lucky,
and it isn't true."

"But everyone says it, Lady, said the page.

Suddenly Tei exclaimed. "Look!" Kai and Alin wheeled
their horses. A warrior was riding slowly toward them, across
the blue hills. His steed was black, black as obsidian, black as
a starless night, and the feather on his helmet was blacker
than a raven's wing. His bridle and saddle and reins and his
armor were silver as the mail of the Talvela women. He bore
across his lap a blackthorn cudgel, tipped with ivory, and
beside it lay a great barbed spear. At his side bobbed a
black sheath and the protruding hilt of a silver sword. Silently he rode up the hill, and the darkness thickened at his

back. The hooves of the black horse made no sound on the pebbly road.

As the rider came closer, he lifted his head and gazed at the Talvelai, and they could all see that the person they had thought a man was in fact a woman. Her hair was white as snow, and her eyes gray as ash. The page lifted the horn to his lips to sound a warning. But Alin caught his wrist with her warm strong fingers. "Wait," she said. "I think she is alone. let us see what she wants." Behind the oncoming rider darkness thickened. A night bird called *Whooo?*

Tei said, "I did not know there was another woman warrior in the Middle Counties."

The warrior halted below the summit of the hill. Her voice was clear and cold as the winter wind blowing off the northern moors. "It is as they sing; you are indeed fair. Yet not so fair, I think, as the shining Moon."

Uneasily the women of Issho gazed at this enigmatic stranger. Finally Kai said, "you seem to know who we are. But we do not know you. Who are you, and from where do you come? Your armor bears no device. Are you from the Middle Counties?"

"No," said the stranger, "my home is far away." A smile like light flickered on her lips. "My name is—Sedi."

Kai's dark brows drew together, and Tei frowned, for Sedi's armor was unmarred by dirt or stain, and her horse looked fresh and unwearied. Kai thought, what if she is an illusion, sent by Roko Talvela's enemies? She said, "You are chary of your answers."

But Alin laughed. "O my sister, you are too suspicious," she said. She pointed to the staff across the stranger's knees. "Can you use that pretty stick?"

"In my land," Sedi said, "I am matchless." She ran her hand down the black cudgel's grain.

"Then I challenge you!" said Alin promptly. She smiled at her sisters. "Do not look so sour. It has been so long since there has been anyone who could fight with me!" Faced with her teasing smile, even Tei smiled in return, for neither of the two older sisters could refuse Alin anything.

"I accept," said Sedi sweetly. Kai thought, *An illusion can not fight. Surely this woman is real.* Alin and Sedi dismounted their steeds. Sedi wore silks with silver and black markings beneath her shining mail. Kai looked at them and thought, I have seen those marks before. Yet as she stared at them she

saw no discernible pattern. Under her armor Alin wore blue
silk. She had woven it herself, and it was the color of a summer sky at dawn when the crickets are singing. She took her
white cudgel in her hands, and made it spin in two great
circles, so swiftly that it blurred in the air. Then she walked
to the top of the hill, where the red sunlight and the pale
moonlight lingered.

"Let us begin," she said.

Sedi moved opposite her. Her boots were black kid, and
they made no sound as she stepped through the stubby grass.
Kai felt a flower of fear wake in her heart. She almost turned
to tell the page to wind his horn. But Alin set her staff to
whirling, and it was too late. It spun and then with dizzying
speed thrust toward Sedi's belly. Sedi parried the thrust, moving with flowing grace. Back and forth they struck and
circled on the rise. Alin was laughing.

"This one is indeed a master, O my sisters," she called. "I
have not been so tested in months!"

Suddenly the hard horn tip of Sedi's staff thrust toward
Alin's face. She lifted her staff to deflect the blow. Quick as
light, the black staff struck at her belly. Kai cried out. The
head blow had been a feint. Alin gasped and fell, her arms
folding over her stomach. Her lovely face was twisted with
pain and white as moonlight on a lake. Blood bubbled from
the corner of her mouth. Daintily, Sedi stepped away from
her. Kai and Tei leaped from their horses. Kai unlaced her
breastplate and lifted her helmet from her face.

"O," said Alin softly. "It hurts."

Tei whirled, reaching for her spear.

But Alin caught her arm with surprising strength. "No!"
she said. "It was a fair fight, and I am fairly beaten."

Lightly Sedi mounted her horse. "Thy beauty is less than it
was, women of Issho," she said. Noiselessly she guided her
steed into the white mist coiling up the hill, and disappeared
in its thick folds.

"Ride to the house," Kai said to the frightened page.
"Bring aid and a litter. Hurry." She laid a palm on Alin's
cheek. It was icy. Gently she began to chafe her sister's
hands. The page raced away. Soon the men came from the
house. They carried Alin Talvela to her bed, where her
mother the sorcerer and healer waited to tend her.

But despite her mother's skills, Alin grew slowly more
weak and wan. Lia Talvela said, "She bleeds within. I cannot

stanch the wound." As Kai and Tei sat by the bed, Alin sank into a chill silence from which nothing, not even their loving touch, roused her. She died with the dawn. The folk of the household covered her with azure silk and laid her oaken staff at her hand. They coaxed Kai and Tei to their beds and gave them each a poppy potion, that they might sleep a dreamless sleep, undisturbed even by grief.

Word went to Roko Talvela to tell him of his daughter's death. Calling truce to his wars, he returned at once to Issho. All Issho county, and lords from the neighboring counties of Chuyo, Ippa, and Nakasé, came to the funeral. Kai and Tei Talvela rode at the head of the sad procession that brought the body of their sister to burial. The folk who lined the road pointed them out to each other, marveling at their beauty. But the more discerning saw that their faces were cold as if they had been frost-touched, like flowers in spring caught by a sudden wayward chill.

Autumn passed to winter. Snow fell, covering the hills and valleys of Issho. Issho households put away their silks and linens and wrapped themselves in wool. Fires blazed in the manor of the Talvelai. The warrior sisters of Issho put aside their armor and busied themselves in women's work. And it seemed to all who knew them that Kai had grown more silent and serious, and that proud Tei had grown more grim. The page tried to cheer them with his music. He played war songs, and drinking songs, and bawdy songs. But none of these tunes pleased the sisters. One day in desperation he said, "O my ladies, what would you hear?"

Frowning, Tei shook her head. "Nothing," she said.

But Kai said, "Do you know 'The Riddle Song?' " naming a children's tune. The page nodded. "Play it." He played it. After it he played "Dancing Bear" and "The Happy Hunter" and all the songs of childhood he could think of. And it seemed to him that Tei's hard mouth softened as she listened.

In spring Roko Talvela returned to his wars. Kai and Tei re-donned their armor. At dawn and at dusk they rode the perimeter of the domain, keeping up their custom, accompanied by the page. Spring gave way to summer, and summer to autumn. The farmers burned leaves in the dusk, covering the hills with a blue haze.

And one soft afternoon a figure in silver on a coal-black horse came out of the haze.

The pale face of the full Moon gleamed at her back. "It's she!" cried the page. He reached for his horn.

Tei said, "Wait." Her voice was harsh with pain. She touched the long spear across her knees, and her eyes glittered.

"O my sister, let us not wait," said Kai softly. But Tei seemed not to hear. Sedi approached in silence. Kai lifted her voice. "Stay, traveler. There is no welcome for you in Issho."

The white-haired woman smiled a crooked smile. "I did not come for welcome, O daughters of the Talvelai."

"What brought you here, then?" said Kai.

The warrior woman made no answer. But her gray eyes beneath her pale brows looked at Kai with startling eloquence. They seemed to say, patience. You will see.

Tei said, "She comes to gloat, O my sister, that we are two, and lonely, who once were three."

"I do not think—" Kai began.

Tei interrupted her. "Evil woman," she said, with passion. "Alin was all that is trusting and fair, and you struck her without warning." Dismounting from her dappled mare, she took in hand her long barbed spear ."Come, Sedi. Come and fight *me*."

"As you will," said Sedi. She leaped from her horse, spear in hand, and strode to the spot where Tei waited for her, spear ready. They fought. They thrust and parried and lunged. Slowly the autumn chill settled over the countryside. The spears flashed in the moonlight. Kai sat her horse, fingering the worked setting of the ruby on her sword. Sometimes it seemed to her that Sedi was stronger than Tei, and at other times Tei seemed stronger than Sedi. The polish on their silver armor shone like flame in the darkness.

At last Tei tired. She breathed heavily, and her feet slipped in the nubby grass.

Kai had been waiting for this moment. She drew *Song* from the sheath and made ready to step between them. "Cease this!" she called. Sedi glanced at her.

"No!" cried Tei. She lunged. The tip of her spear sliced Sedi's arm. "I shall win!" she said.

Sedi grimaced. A cloud passed across the Moon. In the dimness, Sedi lunged forward. Her thrust slid under Tei's guard. the black-haired woman crumpled into the grass. Kai sprang to her sister's side. Blood poured from Tei's breast. "Tei!" Kai cried. Tei's eyes closed. Kai groaned. She knew death when she saw it. Raging, she called to the page, "Sound the horn!"

The sweet sound echoed over the valley. In the distance came the answering calls from the Talvela men. Kai looked at Sedi, seated on her black steed. "Do you hear those horns, O murderous stranger? The Talvela soldiers come. You will not escape."

Sedi smiled. "I am not caught so easily," she said. At that moment Tei shook in Kai's arms, and life passed from her. The ground thrummed with the passage of horses. "Do you wish me caught, you must come seek me, Kai Talvela." Light flashed on her armor. Then the night rang with voices shouting.

The captain of the guard bent over Kai. "O my lady, who has done this thing?"

Kai started to point to the white-haired warrior. But among the dappled horses there was no black steed, and no sign of Sedi.

In vain the men of the Talvelai searched for her. In great sadness they brought the body of Tei Talvela home, and readied her for burial. Once more a procession rode the highway to the burial ground of the Talvelai. All Issho mourned.

But Kai Talvela did not weep. After the burial she went to her mother's chambers, and knelt at the sorcerer's knee. "O my mother, listen to me." And she told her mother everything she could remember of her sisters' meetings with the warrior who called herself Sedi.

Lia Talvela stroked her daughter's fine black hair. She listened, and her face grew pale. At last Kai ended. She waited for her mother to speak. "O my daughter," Lia Talvela said sadly, "I wish you had come to me when this Sedi first appeared. I could have told you then that she was no ordinary warrior. *Sedi* in the enchanter's tongue means Moon, and the woman you describe is one of the shades of that Lady. Her armor is impervious as the moonlight, and her steed is not a horse at all but Night itself taking animal shape. I fear that she heard the songs men sang praising the beauty of the women warriros of the Talvelai, and they made her angry. She came to earth to punish you."

"It was cruel," said Kai. "Are we responsible for what fools say and sing?"

"The elementals are often cruel," said Lia Talvela.

That night, Kai Talvela lay in her bed, unable to rest. Her

bed seemed cold and strange to her. She reached to the left and then to the right, feeling the depressions in the great quilts where Alin and Tei had been used to sleep. She pictured herself growing older and older until she was old, the warrior woman of Issho, alone and lonely until the day she died and they buried her beside her sisters. The Talvelai are a long-lived folk. And it seemed to her that she would have preferred her sisters' fate.

The following spring travelers on the highways of Ryoka were treated to a strange apparition—a black-haired woman on a dappled horse riding slowly east.

She wore silver armor and carried a great curved sword, fashioned in the manner of the smiths of the Middle Counties. she moved from town to town. At the inns she would ask, "Where is the home of the nearest witch or wizard?" And when shown the way to the appropriate cottage or house or hollow or cave, she would go that way.

Of the wisefolk she asked always the same thing: "I look for the Lady who is sometimes known as Sedi." And the great among them gravely shook their heads, while the small grew frightened, and shrank away without response. Courteously she thanked them and returned to the road. When she came to the border of the Middle Counties, she did not hesitate, but continued into the Eastern Counties, where folk carry straight, double-edged blades, and the language they speak is strange.

At last she came to the hills that rise on the eastern edge of Ryoka. She was very weary. Her armor was encrusted with the grime of her journey. She drew her horse up the slope of a hill. It was twilight. The darkness out of the east seemed to sap the dappled stallion's strength, so that it plodded like a plowhorse. She was discouraged as well as weary, for in all her months of traveling she had heard no word of Sedi. I shall go home, she thought, and live in the Talvela manor, and wither. She gained the summit of the hill. There she halted. She looked down across the land, bones and heart aching. Beyond the dark shadows lay a line of silver like a silken ribbon in the dusk. And she knew that she could go no farther. That silver line marked the edge of the world. She lifted her head and smelled the heavy salt scent of the open sea.

The silver sea grew brighter. Kai Talvela watched. Slowly the full Moon rose dripping out of the water.

So this is where the Moon lives, thought the woman warrior. She leaned on her horse. She was no fish, to chase the Moon into the ocean. But the thought of returning to Issho made her shiver. She raised her arms to the violet night. "O Moon, see me," she cried. "My armor is filth covered. My horse is worn to a skeleton. I am no longer beautiful. O jealous one, cease your anger. Out of your pity, let me join my sisters. Release me!"

She waited for an answer. None came. Suddenly she grew very sleepy. She turned the horse about and led it back down the slope to a hollow where she had seen the feathery shape of a willow silhouetted against the dusk, and heard the music of a stream. Taking off her armor, she wrapped herself in her red woolen cloak. Then she curled into the long soft grass and fell instantly asleep.

She woke to warmth and the smell of food. Rubbing her eyes, she lifted on an elbow. It was dawn. White-haired, cloaked in black, Sedi knelt beside a fire, turning a spit on which broiled three small fish. She looked across the wispy flames and smiled, eyes gray as ash. Her voice was clear and soft as the summer wind. "Come and eat."

It was chilly by the sea. Kai stretched her hands to the fire, rubbing her fingers. Sedi gave her the spit. She nibbled the fish. They were real, no shadow or illusion. Little bones crunched beneath her teeth. She sat up and ate all three fish. Sedi watched her and did not speak.

When she had done, Kai Talvela laid the spit in the fire. Kneeling by the stream, she drank and washed her face. She returned to the place where she had slept, and lifted from the sheath her great curved blade. she saluted Sedi. "O Moon," she said, "or shade of the Moon, or whatever you may be, long have I searched for you, by whose hand perished the two people most dear to me. Without them I no longer wish to live. Yet I am a daughter of the Talvelai, and a warrior, and I would die in battle. O Sedi, will you fight?"

"I will," said the white-haired woman. She drew her own sword from its sheath.

They circled and cut and parried and cut again, while light deepened in the eastern sky. Neither was wearing armor, and so each stroke was double-deadly. Sedi's face was serene as the lambent Moon as she cut and thrust, weaving the tip of her blade in a deadly tapestry. *I have only to drop my guard,* Kai Talvela thought, *and she will kill me.* Yet something held her back. Sweat rolled down her sides. The blood pounded in her temples. The salty wind kissed her cheeks. In the swaying willow a bird was singing. She heard the song over the clash of the meeting blades. It came to her that life was sweet. *I do not want to die,* she thought. *I am Kai Talvela, the warrior woman of Issho. I am strong. I will live.*

Aloud she panted, "Sedi, I will kill you." The white-haired woman's face did not change, but the speed of her attack increased. *She is strong,* Kai Talvela thought, *but I am stronger.* Her palms grew slippery with sweat. Her lungs ached. Still she did not weaken. It was Sedi who slowed, tiring. Kai Talvela shouted with triumph. She swept Sedi's blade to one side and thrust in.

Song's sharp tip came to rest a finger's breadth from Sedi's naked throat. Kai Talvela said, "Now, sister-killer, I have you."

Across the shining sword, Sedi smiled. Kai waited for her to beg for life. She said nothing, only smiled like flickering moonlight. Her hair shone like pearl, and her eyes seemed depthless as the sea. Kai's hands trembled. She let her sword fall. "You are too beautiful, O Sedi."

With cool, white fingers Sedi took *Song* from Kai's hands. She brought her to the fire, and gave her water to drink in her cupped palms. She stroked Kai's black hair and laid her cool lips on Kai's flushed cheek. Then she took Kai's hand in her own, and pointed at the hillside. The skin of the earth shivered, like a horse shaking off a fly. A great rent appeared in the hill. Straight as a shaft of moonlight, a path cut through earth to the water's smooth edge. Sedi said, "Come with me."

And so Kai Talvela followed the Moon to her cave beneath the ocean. Time is different there than it is beneath the light of the sun, and it seemed to her that no time passed at all. She slept by day, and rose at night to ride with the Moon across the dark sky's face, to race the wolves across the plains and watch the dolphins playing in the burnished sea. She drank cool water from beneath the earth. She did not seem to need to eat. Whenever she grew sad or thoughtful Sedi would laugh and shake her long bright hair, and say, "O my love, why so somber?" And the touch of her fingers drove all complaint from Kai's mind and lips.

But one sleep she dreamed of an old woman standing by a window, calling her name. There was something familiar and beloved in the crone's wrinkled face. Three times she dreamed that dream. The old voice woke in her a longing to see sunlight and shadow, green grass and the flowers on the trees. The longing grew strong. She thought, Something has happened to me.

Returning to the cave at dawn, she said to Sedi, "O my friend and lover, let us sit awhile on land. I would watch the sunrise." Sedi consented. They sat at the foot of an immense willow beside a broad stream. A bird sang in the willow. Kai watched the grass color with the sunrise, turning from gray to rose, and from rose to green. And her memories awoke.

She said, "O my love, dear to me is the time I have spent with you beneath the sea. Yet I yearn for the country of my birth, for the sound of familiar voices, for the taste of wine and the smell of bread and meat. Sedi, let me go to my place."

Sedi rose from the grass. She stretched out both hands. "Truly, do you wish to leave me?" she said. There were tears in her gray eyes. Kai trembled. She almost stepped forward to take the white-haired woman in her arms and kiss the tears away.

"I do."

The form of Sedi shuddered, and changed. It grew until it towered in silver majesty above Kai's head, terrible, draped in light, eyes dark as night, a blazing giantess. Soft and awful as death, the Moon said, "Dare you say so, child of earth?"

Kai swallowed. Her voice remained steady. "I do."

The giantess dissolved into the form of Sedi. She regarded Kai. Her eyes were both sad and amused. "I cannot keep you. For in compelling you to love me I have learned to love you. I can no more coerce you than I can myself. But you must know, Kai Talvela, that much human time has passed since you entered the cave of the Moon. Roko Talvela is dead. Your cousin, Edan, is chief of the Talvelai. Your mother is alive but very old. The very steed that brought you here has long since turned to dust."

"I will walk home," said Kai. And she knew that the old woman of her dream had been her mother, the sorcerer Lia.

Sedi sighed. "You do not have to do that. I love you so well that I will even help you leave me. Clothes I will give you, and armor, and a sword." She gestured. Silk and steel rose up from the earth and wrapped themselves about Kai's waist. The weight of a sword dragged at her belt. A horse trotted to her. It was black, and its eyes were pale. "This steed will bring you to Issho in less than a day."

Kai fingered the hilt of the sword, feeling there the faceted lump of a gem. She pulled it upward to look at it and saw a ruby embedded within it. She lifted off her helmet. A red plume nodded in the wind. She lifted her hands to the smooth skin of her face.

"You have not aged," said Sedi. "Do you wish to see?" A silver mirror appeared in her hands. Kai stared at the image of the warrior woman. She looked the same as the day she left Issho.

She looked at the Moon, feeling within her heart for the compulsion that had made her follow Sedi under the sea. She could not feel it. She held out her hands. "Sedi, I love you," she said. They embraced. Kai felt the Moon's cold tears on her cheek.

Sedi pressed the mirror into Kai's hands. "Take this. And on the nights when the Moon is full, do this." She whispered in Kai's ear.

Kai put the mirror between her breasts and mounted the black horse. "Farewell," she called. Sedi waved. The black horse bugled, and shook its ebony mane, and leaped. When Kai looked back she could not see the willow. She bowed her head. Her hair whipped her face. Beneath the silent hooves of Night the earth unrolled like a great brown mat. Kai sighed, remembering the laughter and the loving, and the nightly rides. Never would she race the wolves across the plains, or watch the dolphins playing in the moonlit sea.

The black horse traveled so fast that Kai had no chance to observe the ways in which the world beneath her had changed. But when it halted she stared in puzzlement at the place it had brought her. Surely this was not her home. The trees were different. The house was too big. Yet the token of the Talvelai family gleamed on the tall front gate.

Seeing this lone warrior, the talvela guards came from the gatehouse. "Who are you?" they demanded. "What is your business here?"

"I am Kai Talvela," she said.

They scowled at her. "That is impossible. Kai Talvela disappeared fifty years ago!" And they barred her way to the house.

But she laughed at them; she who had fought and loved the Moon. She ripped her sword from its sheath, and it sang in the air with a deadly note. "I am Kai Talvela, and I want to see my mother. I would not suggest that any of you try to stop me." She dismounted. Patting the horse, she said, "Thank you, o swift one. Now return to Sedi." The horse blew in her ear and vanished like smoke. The soldiers of the Talvelai froze in fear.

Kai Talvela found her mother in her bedroom, sitting by the window. She was ancient, tiny, a white-haired wrinkled woman dressed in lavender silk. Kai crossed the room and knelt by her mother's chair. "Mother," she said.

An elderly man, standing at the foot of the bed, opened his mouth to gape. He held a polished wooden flute. "Lady!"

Lia Talvela caressed her daughter's unaged cheek. "I have missed you," she said. "I called and called. Strong was the spell that held you. Where have you been?"

"In the cave of the Moon," Kai Talvela said. She put off her helmet, sword, and mail. Curled like a child against her mother's knee, she told the sorcerer everything. The old flute player started to leave the room. A gesture of Lia Talvela's stopped him. When she finished, Kai Talvela lifted her mother's hands to her lips. "I will never leave Issho again," she said.

Lia Talvela stroked her child's hair and said no more. Her hands stilled. When Kai looked up, her mother's eyes had closed. She was dead.

It took a little time before the Talvelai believed that this strange woman was truly Kai Talvela, returned from her journey, no older than the day she left Issho. Edan Talvela was especially loth to believe it. Truthfully, he was somewhat nervous of this fierce young woman. He could not understand why she would not tell them all where she had been for fifty years. "Who is to say she is not enchanted?" he said. But the flute master, who had been the sisters' page, recognized her, and said so steadfastly. Edan Talvela grew less nervous when Kai told him that she had no quarrel with his lordship of the Talvelai. She wished merely to live at peace on the Issho estate. He had a house built for her behind the orchard, near the place of her sisters' and her mother's graves. During the day she sewed and spun, and walked through the orchard. It gave her great pleasure to be able to walk beneath the sun and smell the growing things of earth. In the evening she sat beside her doorway, watching night descend. Sometimes the old musician came to visit with her. He alone knew where she had been for fifty years. His knowledge did not trouble her, for she knew that her mother had trusted him. He played the songs that once she had asked him to play; "The Riddle Song" and other songs of childhood. He had grown to be both courtly and wise, and she liked to talk with him. She grew to be quite fond of him, and she blessed her mother's wisdom.

In the autumn after her return the old musician caught a cold, and died. The night after his funeral Kai Talvela wept into her pillow. She loved Issho. But now there was no one to talk to, no one who knew her. The other Talvelai avoided her, and their children scurried from her path as if she were a ghost. Her proper life had been taken away.

For the first time she thought, *I should not have come home. I should have stayed with Sedi.* The full Moon shining through her window seemed to mock her pain.

Suddenly she recalled Sedi's hands cupped around a mirror, and her whispered instructions. Kai ran to her chest and dug beneath the silks. The mirror was still there. Holding it carefully, she took it to the window and positioned it till the moonlight filled its silver face. She said the words Sedi had told her to say. The mirror grew. The moon swelled within it. It grew till it was tall as Kai. Then it trembled, like still water when a pebble strikes it. Out from the ripples of light stepped Sedi. The Moon smiled, and held out her arms. "Have you missed me?" she said. They embraced.

That night Kai's bed was warm. But at dawn Sedi left. "Will you come back?" Kai said.

"I will come when you call me," promised the elemental. Every month on the night of the full Moon Kai held the mirror to the light, and said the words. And every month Sedi returned.

But elementals are fickle, and they are not human, though they may take human shape. One night Sedi did not come. Kai Talvela waited long hours by the window. Years had passed since her return to Issho. She was no longer the woman of twenty who had emerged like a butterfly from the Moon's cave. Yet she was still beautiful, and her spirit was strong as it had ever been. When at last the sunlight came, she rose from her chair. Picking up the mirror from its place, she broke it over her knee.

It seemed to the Talvelai then that she grew old swiftly, aging a year in the space of a day. But her back did not bend, nor did her hair whiten. It remained as black as it had been in her youth. The storytellers say that she never spoke to anyone of her journey. But she must have broken silence one time, or else we would not know this story. Perhaps she spoke as she lay dying. She died on the night of the full Moon, in spring. At dawn some of her vigor returned, and she insisted that her attendants carry her to the window, and dress her in red silk, and lay her sword across her lap. She wore around her neck a piece of broken mirror on a silver chain. And the tale goes on to say that as she died her face brightened to near youthful beauty, and she lifted her arms to the light and cried, "Sedi!"

They buried Kai Talvela beside her mother and her sisters, and then forgot her. Fickleness is also a human trait. But some years later there was war in Issho county. The soldiers of the Talvelai were outnumbered. Doggedly they struggled, as the orchards burned around them. Their enemies backed them as far as the manor gate. It was dusk. They were losing. Suddenly a horn blew, and a woman in bright armor rode from out of nowhere, her mount a black stallion. She swung a shining sword in one fist. "Talvela soldiers, follow me!" she called. At her indomitable manner, the enemy was struck with terror. They dropped their swords and fled into the night. Those soldiers who were closest to the apparition swore that the woman was tall and raven-haired, as the women of the Talvelai are still. They swore also that the sword, as it cut the air, hummed a note so pure that you could almost say it sang.

That was the first appearance of Kai Talvela's shade. Sometimes she comes unarmored, dressed in red silk, gliding through the halls of the Issho estate. When she comes in this guise, she wears a pendant: a broken mirror on a silver chain. When she appears she brings courage to the Talvelai, and fear to their enemies. In the farms and the cities they call her the Mirror Ghost, because of the mirror pendant and because of her brilliant armor. But the folk of the estate know her by name. She is Kai Talvela, the warrior woman of Issho, who loved and fought the Moon, and was loved by her in return.

The daughters of the Talvelai never tire of the story. They ask for it again and again.

ADDITIONAL READING

compiled with Susan Wood

I. *NON FICTION RESOURCES*

Boulding, Elise: *The Underside of History. A View of Women through* Time. Westview Press, 1976.

Diner, Helen: *Mothers and Amazons* (1930). Doubleday/Anchor Books, 1973.

Hickok, Jane Cannary: *Calamity Jane's Letters to her Daughter.* Shameless Hussy Press, 1976.

Myron, Nancy and Charlotte Bunch: *Women Remembered.* Diana Press, 1974.

O'Faolain, Julia and Lauro Martines (eds): *Not in God's Image. Women in History from the Greeks to the Victorians.* Harper and Row, 1973.

Pomeray, Sarah: *Goddesses, Whores, Wives and Slaves. Women in Classical Antiquity.* Shocken, 1975.

Reiter, Rayna R.: *Toward an Anthropology of Women.* Monthly Review Press, 1975.

Rosaldo, Michelle Zimbalist and Louise Lamphere: *Woman, Culture, and Society.* Stanford University Press, 1974.

Russ, Joanna: "What Can a Heroine Do?" and "The Image of Women in Science Fiction." In Cornillon, Susan Koppelman (ed): *Images of Women in Fiction. Feminist Perspectives.* Ohio University Press, 1972.

Russ, Joanna: "Amor Vincit Feminam. The Battle of the Sexes in Science Fiction." In *Science Fiction Studies.* Indiana University Press, 1978.

Salmonson, Jessica: "The Golden Age of Sexism." In *Windhaven* #6. Atalanta Press, 1979.

Seltman, Charles: *Women in Antiquity*. Thames and Hudson, 1956.

Sobol, Donald: *The Amazons of Greek Mythology*. A. S. Barnes, 1972.

Stone, Merlin: *When God Was a Woman*. Dial Press, 1978.

II. AMAZON HEROIC FANTASY

Bradley, Marion Zimmer: *The Shattered Chain*. DAW, 1975.

Chapman, Vera: *The King's Damosel* (1976). Avon, 1978.

Charnas, Suzy McKee: *Motherlines*. Berkley, 1978.

Cherryh, C.J.: *Gave of Ivrel*. DAW, 1976. *Well of Shiuan*. DAW, 1978. See also introduction to "Dreamstone" in this anthology for other titles.

Clayton, Jo: The Diadem series from DAW Books, Inc.

Dibell, Ansen: *Pursuit of the Screamer*. DAW, 1978.

Duane, Diane: *The Door Into Fire*. Dell, 1979.

Fearn, John Russell: *Conquest of the Amazon* (1949). Futura, 1976.

Frank, Janrae: *The Ruined Tower*. Chapbook illustrated by Mary Bohdanowicz. Atalanta Press, 1979.

Gearhart, Sally: *The Wanderground*. Persephone, 1978.

Howard, Robert E.: *The Sword Woman*. Zebra, 1977.

Karr, Phyllis Ann: *Thorn and Frostflower*. Jove, 1979.

Lee, Tanith: *The Birthgrave*. DAW, 1975. *Night's Master*. DAW, 1978. See also introduction to "Northern Chess" in this anthology for other titles.

Lupoff, Richard A.: *Sword of the Demon*. Harper & Row, 1977.

Lynn, Elizabeth A.: *The Northern Girl*. Berkley, 1979. *Watchtower*. Berkley, 1979. *The Dancers of Arun*. Berkley, in press. See also introduction to "The Woman Who Loved the Moon" for other titles.

Moore, C.L.: *Black God's Shadow*. The collected Jirel of Joiry stories from the 1930s, illustrated in this edition by Alica Austin. Donald A. Grant, 1977.

Morgan, T.J.: *Dark Tide*. Chapbook illustrated by Theresa Troise-Heidel. Atalanta Press, 1979.

Norton, Andre: Especially the Witch World series; see introduction to "Falcon Blood" in this anthology for a selected list of titles.

Piserchia, Doris: *Star Rider*. Bantam, 1974. *Earthchild*. DAW, 1977. *Spaceling*. DAW, 1979.

Russ, Joanna: *Alyx*. Gregg Press, 1977. *Kittitiny, A Tale of Magic*. Daughters, 1978. See also the introduction to "The Death of Augusta" in this anthology for other titles.

Sargent, Pamela (Ed): *The New Women of Wonder*, especially stories by Emshwiller, Reed, and Russ. Vintage, 1978.

Varley, John: *Titan*. Berkley, 1979.

Vinge, Joan: *Snow Queen*. Dell, 1979.

Weinbaum, Stanley G.: *The Red Peri*. Fantasy Press, 1952.

Wittig, Monique: *Les Guérillières* (1969). Avon, 1973.

A good ongoing resource is the small press magazine *Windhaven*, which features essays, news, reviews and letters regarding fantasy and s-f from a feminist point of view, and includes amazon fantasy stories regularly. It is available from Atalanta Press, Box 5688, University Station, Seattle, Washington 98105. Comments regarding the anthology *Amazons* can be directed to Jessica Amanda Salmonson, c/o DAW books, or Atalanta Press.